D0947787

THE IRRESISTIBLE INTRUDER

Honora Dillon was brave enough to live outside fashionable society's rules. She earned her own living with her pen as a romantic novelist. She raised a daughter on her own, without the help of any man.

Then one day a man did enter her life, knocking on her cottage door. And not just any man. He was the Viscount Marcus Vane, handsome, brilliant, charming, kindly, and single. The kind of lord every lady dreamed of. The kind Honora most feared.

For Honora knew she could not risk letting the Viscount into her heart. For then she would have to let him into her past—and that she could never do . . . .

MARJORIE FARRELL was born in New York City and currently resides outside of Boston, Massachusetts, where she is an assistant professor teaching psychology, writing, and literature to adult students.

SIGNET REGENCY ROMANCE
COMING IN FEBRUARY 1991

Charlotte Louise Dolan
The Substitute Bridegroom

Mary Balogh
A Certain Magic

Dorothy Mack
The Unlikely Chaperone

AUTUMN ROSE

Marjorie Farrell

A SIGNET BOOK

SIGNET
Published by the Penguin Group
Penguin Books USA Inc., 375 Hudson Street,
New York, New York, 10014, U.S.A.
Penguin Books Ltd, 27 Wrights Lane, London W8 5TZ, England
Penguin Books Australia Ltd, Ringwood, Victoria, Australia
Penguin Books Canada Ltd, 2801 John Street,
Markham, Ontario, Canada L3R 1B4
Penguin Books (N.Z.) Ltd, 182-190 Wairau Road,
Auckland 10, New Zealand

Penguin Books Ltd, Registered Offices:
Harmondsworth, Middlesex, England

First published by Signet, an imprint of New American Library, a division of Penguin
Books USA Inc.

First Printing, January, 1991

10 9 8 7 6 5 4 3 2 1

Copyright© Marjorie Farrell, 1991
All rights reserved

 REGISTERED TRADEMARK—MARCA REGISTRADA

PRINTED IN THE UNITED STATES OF AMERICA

Without limiting the rights under copyright reserved above, no part of this
publication may be reproduced, stored in or introduced into a retrieval
system, or transmitted, in any form, or by any means (electronic, mechanical,
photocopying, recording, or otherwise), without the prior written permission of both the copyright owner and the above publisher of this book.

BOOKS ARE AVAILABLE AT QUANTITY DISCOUNTS WHEN USED TO PROMOTE
PRODUCTS OR SERVICES. FOR INFORMATION PLEASE WRITE TO PREMIUM
MARKETING DIVISION, PENGUIN BOOKS USA INC., 375 HUDSON STREET,
NEW YORK, NEW YORK 10014.

For 'ma ain dearie''—with such young women
we may well have a "brave new world.''

AUTHOR'S NOTE

Although the friendship between Joanna and Nora is fictional, Joanna Baillie herself is not.

Born in 1762, Baillie lived in Hampstead from 1806 until her death in 1851. She wrote and published verse, and then the tragedies which brought her fame. "If you wish to speak of a real poet," said Sir Walter Scott, "Joanna Baillie is now the highest genius of our country." Byron himself declared she was the only woman who could write tragedy.

She was described by contemporaries as a lovable, sincere and trustworthy woman, one who might well have been Nora's friend. Her longtime residence, Bolton House, still stands on Holly Bush Hill, Hampstead.

Prologue

1798

The rain fell all of April, washing away the gravel from the drive, plastering the daffodils on the grass and running down the windows of Moorview in rivers, making it almost impossible for Margaret to see anything, were she really looking. She had been staring out the library windows, watching the rain, for days now. Her father had been locked away in his bedroom, drinking brandy steadily, and staring at the pattern of his Aubusson carpet as blankly as his daughter stared out the window.

It had been over a month since her mother's funeral, and Margaret thought that it must be raining so to make up for her inability to weep one tear for her mother. Instead of crying, she was eating. Her dresses got tighter and tighter, although at sixteen and a half she was well past the age of puppy fat. But her need, beyond appetite, was to fill herself out, to cover with flesh the emptiness that was always there, waiting.

After the funeral, when all the neighbors had come back to the house, Margaret could think of nothing but the food. She swallowed blancmange and cakes and said "Thank you for coming" automatically to each one who came up to console her.

"Now you will have to take care of your father," almost every neighbor murmured to her. She had been imagining the same. She saw long evenings of father and daughter together, playing cards or reading after dinner, and her father coming to her for advice on estate business just as he had done with her mother.

Only he does not want my comfort, she thought as she watched the spring rain pour down. He sits and drinks and admits no one. But he will have to come out soon, she said to herself, as she reached for another comfit, and then he will realize he needs me.

The marquess did eventually emerge, although it took another

9

month. He stopped drinking, at least during the day. But he did not seem to need Margaret. At the breakfast table he would ask her plans for the day, and warn her that she was growing a little plump and did she really want that second muffin? He would tell her his plans for the day, which usually included a long ride over the moors in the afternoon, ending at the squire's house, where he would begin the drinking which ended at home late at night. He never asked her for advice, he never invited her to ride with him, and he seemed to have nothing to say to her. She had always felt loved by both her parents, but had never realized what a large part her mother had played in conveying to her the inarticulate caring of her father. Her mother had been the heart of the household, mediating disagreements and explaining her father to Margaret and Margaret to her father. Now there was no one to do this. The marquess was so lost in his own grief he could not see hers. So Margaret packed it down with an extra muffin or second serving of trifle, and tried to pretend no great loss had occurred.

The spring and summer went by and Margaret rode and walked and socialized within the prescribed limits. She began to consult with Mrs. Tabor, the housekeeper, and made some decisions of her own, since her father seemed willing to leave it all in her hands.

By late September Margaret could see that her father was beginning to come back to life. The summer had lulled both of them, but the autumn winds seemed to make him restless and she hoped he would at last turn to her for companionship. What he did, instead, was to leave abruptly for London. He had hardly looked at her when he told her of his plans. "Now that the harvesting is done, Meg, I have little to do and am a bit restless. I will stay with your great-aunt, and renew some old acquaintances. Of course, since I am in mourning," he added almost as an afterthought, "I will not really take part in the Little Season, but a few days at Brooks's will do me good." And so he was gone the next morning, leaving her behind to face who knew how many weeks even more alone than she had been.

But when he returned, she wished for isolation again, for he came back with the news that he was engaged to be married. "And you will love her, Meg, just as I do," he said, looking more alive than he had in months. "We will wait the full year, of course, and you will not be able to meet her until the spring. She is Lady Evelyn Lovell, and a widow, so she knows what it is to have lost someone."

All Margaret could say to him was a stunned, "I wish you happy, Father." And for the next month she went around saying to herself: But my mother's wish was to have him happy. She would not want him to be alone. But he's *not* alone, he has *me*. And she would pull down her battered copy of Shakespeare and turn to *Hamlet* and read his soliloquy, screaming inside her head: "Oh bloody, bawdy villain; remorseless treacherous lecherous *villain*! . . . oh, vengeance." There was nowhere else to turn besides that young man who had also lost a parent, and to dramatic words which alone seemed to mirror her feelings. Squire Hawkes and his lady, indeed all their neighbors, seemed relieved, if not exactly pleased at the news. They knew the marquess would not have survived long at the rate he had been drinking, and hoped his new lady would serve as a mother for his daughter.

The winter passed slowly. The marquess was drinking less, and gave more of his attention to the estate. He made one trip down to London, remaining longer than he had planned because of the weather. Margaret rode and walked whenever she could. A great restlessness seemed to have taken over from the lethargy of the summer. Her appetite diminished, and by the spring she had lost her excess weight, and her clothes were fitting her again.

The wedding was private, attended only by Margaret and Lady Lovell's father and mother. Lady Evelyn was originally from Hampshire, so Margaret and her father traveled down in April.

Margaret had hoped her father's bride would not be a "wicked" stepmother, and wished she would turn out to be a motherly woman who would treat Margaret as the daughter she had never had.

Lady Lovell was neither. She was almost too young to fit the category of stepmother, and not matronly in the least. She was only twelve years older than Margaret, and completely infatuated with the still-young-looking marquess, and he with her. If Margaret had imagined this marriage would help settle her father and enable him to turn some of his affection and attention on his daughter, she could not have been more wrong. He had eyes only for his fiancée.

She stood dazed at the wedding, and watched her father passionately kiss his new wife after the ceremony. At the small wedding breakfast, the marquess, unwilling to let Lady Evelyn look at anyone but himself, did not talk to the rest of the guests. Margaret sat near them, embarrassed and lost, pulling rolls apart with her fingers and leaving rolled lumps of dough on her plate.

She was returned to Northumberland in her father's coach, the newlyweds having decided to spend a part of the Season in town as their honeymoon. By the time the marquess and his new wife returned to Northumberland, Margaret had had several new dresses made up and attended the first assembly since her mother's death. Her father was pleased that she seemed to have at last put her mourning aside. "She was quite close to her mother, you know," he told Evelyn, "and one of the reasons I married again was to provide her with another woman for companionship and guidance."

"And what were the other reasons?" teased his new wife.

The marquess bent down to kiss the nape of her neck. "To be able to do this . . . and this . . . and this. And to keep myself from going mad with grief," he added, and the marchioness pulled his head down to her lips.

It was unfortunate that Margaret had not overheard their conversation as she passed by the morning room that day, but only saw another intimte scene, with her besotted father making a fool of himself with a woman as unlike her mother as he could have found. The marquess was not the strong man Margaret had fantasied him to be throughout her childhood. She had never seen how much her mother had encouraged and supported him. So her feelings of being abandoned were all the stronger, since it seemed to her that in the space of a year she had lost both parents and was herself becoming more and more peripheral to her old life.

"You are coming to the Whitmarkes' dinner dance?" queried Penelope, Margaret's close friend.

"Yes, I think we are all attending," replied Margaret, with little interest in her voice.

"I hear that Julia's second cousin will be there. He is from the Irish side of the family, you know. I have heard he is quite charming, and mean to have him dance with me. Even his name is romantic. Dillon Breen."

Mr. Dillon Breen lived up to Penelope's expectations. Although he was not much above medium height and rather slender, there was a certain way he had with women that made them feel small and protected. His blond hair and blue eyes were set off wonderfully by his impeccably tailored dark blue coat. Not one lady noticed that his cuffs were a bit shiny and his pumps worn when at the receiving end of his wit and charm. He had every woman in the room eager to dance with him except one.

"Who is that sitting in the corner?" he asked Mrs. Whitmarke, piqued that the young lady with the curly chestnut hair had not tried to get his eye or fluttered around him like the others.

"That is the Lady Margaret Ashton."

"And is the Lady Margaret always so dull?"

"Margaret is usually great fun, but her mother died last year and her father recently remarried, so she has only started socializing again this spring. I daresay she is a bit dazed by the changes in her life."

Breen felt a thrill of sympathy, for he had lost his own mother at an early age, and he guided his cousin so that when their dance ended they were next to Margaret and Mrs. Whitmarke had to introduce them.

"May I have a dance later this evening, Miss Ashton?" asked Breen. "Or is your card already filled?"

"No. I mean, no, my card is not filled," replied Margaret, flustered that the most-sought-after gentleman at the dance was gazing at her quite intently.

"Then I may have a dance later?" Breen smiled.

"Why, yes, I suppose so." And Margaret watched as he walked off without further conversation, seemingly intent on whatever confidence Mrs. Whitmarke was conveying. He did return, however, and Margaret blushed as he claimed her hand.

"You are from Ireland, I believe?"

"The family is, as you can tell by the name, but my grand-father left years ago. I was born in Scotland."

"So you are a Scotsman?"

"Ah, just because a man is born in a stable, that doesn't make him a horse," replied Breen in an exaggerated brogue. Margaret laughed.

"There, now I know why I wished to dance with you. When you laugh, you are quite the prettiest girl here."

Margaret, having lifted her face up in amusement, lowered it immediately. She could not, for anything, face those blue eyes looking so hard into her own.

Breen moved his hand from her back and lightly caressed the back of her head so quickly that no one could have seen it, and Margaret wondered if she had imagined it. But she wasn't imagining the feelings that flooded her. She could have melted away at his feet at that moment, so starved had she been for any affection.

They finished their dance in silence, and were stiffly polite to one another in saying their thank-yous. But Breen had felt that brief moment of surrender and decided that his visit to his English cousins might be more rewarding than he had anticipated.

For the next few weeks Margaret was in a state she had never experienced before. It was as though she had been struck down with a palsy, for whenever she thought of Breen, she trembled. And whenever she saw him, at Penelope's picnic, or on the varied excursions Julia arranged, she quite literally found herself shaking. The sight of the back of his golden head made her heart lift. All her energy, all her attention, was concentrated upon him: would he be at the squire's for dinner; would she see him riding tomorrow?

She knew she loved him after that first night. How could she not? He was so bright, so warm, so utterly charming, and he had, with that one brush of his hand, touched something in her that no one else had.

Breen knew also. He was well aware of his ability to wreak havoc in a young woman's breast, but his charm was not cultivated; it was a natural part of him. He could no more turn it off than stop breathing. And he was genuinely interested in Margaret. He had felt protective of her from the first, because of her situation. She was not precisely neglected by her father, but certainly left alone to her own devices. When Breen met the new marchioness, he could understand why. And he could sympathize with a man's reaction to the loss of a beloved wife. When his mother had died, he had gone a bit crazy himself, and he found himself, at eighteen, involved with another man's wife, without even knowing how it had come about.

The more he saw of Margaret, the more he was attracted to her. The fact that she was in love with him played no small part in his growing interest. Nor the fact that she was the daughter of a marquess. He was not sure he was ready to settle down yet, but if he ever was . . . why not with Margaret? And so there was never a time when they were together that he didn't pay her some special attention: smiling intimately into her eyes, causing her to blush when he stood a bit closer than was allowed and their hands brushed, and holding her a little longer than was necessary when he helped her down from her horse.

Margaret was only more convinced that she loved him as the days went on. She *had* to love him, for she wanted to kiss him so much it could only be love. She wanted him to touch her, as if by accident, she wanted his eyes to meet hers in that special way, she wanted him to . . . She didn't know quite what, but she knew she wanted something else from him too.

One morning, on one of her early rides across the moors, she spied the bay gelding that Breen rode grazing aimlessly, and feared his rider had been thrown. As she kicked her mare into a gallop, she realized she would literally die if anything had happened to him. As she drew closer, she saw a blond head lifting up, and threw herself recklessly off her horse and started running.

"Don't move, Dillon," she cried, and knelt down beside him, placing his head gently in her lap. "Oh, my dear, where are you hurt?"

Breen did look disoriented, his eyes unfocused. But this was understandable, for he had fallen asleep in the warm sun and had just been awakened by the sound of Margaret's horse. It took him a few lovely moments in her lap before he realized what must have happened. Here he was, with Margaret dropping little kisses on his forehead and murmuring incoherent endearments. He could feel laughter rising, but knew how cruel it would be to release it. So he lay still with great difficulty, trying not to smile at the lovely absurdity of the scene.

"Margaret . . ." he finally said, rising on one elbow.

"You can speak?"

"Yes, my dear," he said gently, and pulled himself up to face her. "I am afraid," he continued, smiling affectionately, "you came upon me not after a fall, but in the middle of a nap!"

Margaret sat stock-still, a blush rising to the top of her head from her very core. She was appalled at how completely she had revealed herself.

"My dear, don't look like that. I felt I had awakened in paradise."

"Don't laugh at me, sir. I might have made myself ridiculous, but I am fully aware of it myself, and don't need taunts from you."

Breen took her by the shoulders and pushed her chin up so that she was looking at him—yet not, since her long black eyelashes were brushing her cheeks. He bent his head and lightly kissed her lips. Her eyes flew open in wonderment, and then closed again, as he gave her another kiss, this one longer and deeper. The combination of innocence and her unconscious passion acted on him like no coquetry could ever have done. He pulled her down on the rough grass and traced her eyebrows and the planes of her face tenderly, and when he reached her mouth, it was half-open, waiting for his tongue.

Margaret uttered one low moan, and both were lost. Neither heard the horses' teeth crunching the moor grass, nor the cries of the rooks sailing above them. It was only a few minutes later, as Margaret lay back against his arm, still fully clothed (although she hardly knew how she could be, since she had been shamelessly ready for anything he may have wanted from her), that full awareness returned. A fat bumblebee, seeking clover, buzzed by them. The clouds were high and wispy, scudding across the sky like dandelion clocks. And she was lying on her beloved's arm and could lie like this forever.

"Sweetheart, we can't be alone like this again, or I do not trust myself," whispered Breen in her ear.

Margaret nodded. "But when we are married, then this can

go on forever,'' she replied dreamily, not really aware that she
had spoken a private thought aloud. Breen hesitated only a
moment. After all, why not? She was lovely, hot, the daughter
of a marquess, and probably he did love her. Certainly he had
never felt quite this tender and protective toward any woman,
so it must be love.

"I must speak to your father immediately,'' he said, breaking
the spell.

"Oh, I didn't mean to . . . I just spoke without thinking . . .
you mustn't if you don't want to,'' Margaret stammered. "Now
you must think me one of those women who compromise
themselves only to trap some man into marrying them.''

"You don't have a devious bone in your body. That is why
I love you. No, it is something I have been thinking of myself.
Will you be my wife, Margaret?''

Margaret could only nod her head yes. She knew this moment
would stay with her forever: the sun, the smell of the earth,
Breen's fingers pushing her hair back from her face, the feeling
of being wanted and cherished. She had not felt appreciated for
so long.

Breen got up suddenly. "Come, my dear, we must go.'' He
pulled her to her feet and started brushing the grass from her
habit. "I will ride over this afternoon. Will your father be in?
Should you prepare him, do you think?''

"Why would I need to? Surely he could have no objections.
He has never played tyrant with me, and he has so little time
for me lately that I would think he would be happy to have me
out of the way.''

Breen was not as certain as Margaret. The marquess might
have been neglectful lately, but he was a father, and would want
to know that his daughter was well-provided-for. How he would
view an untitled Irishman with little to offer but his affection
was another question. I *am*, after all, a gentleman, Breen
reassured himself. And with her portion, which should be
generous, and one of the smaller family estates, we would do
very well, so I will have to convince him.

They pulled their horses together as they came in sight of
Moorview for one last embrace, and Margaret felt like she was
saying good-bye to her very life.

"I will be there at three o'clock sharp,'' promised Breen as he finally pulled himself away and rode off. Margaret rode slowly, unwilling to lose that languorous, floating feeling. All of her had turned into a slow river that moved in the sunlight like poured honey.

Unfortunately for the lovers, the marquess had a been a bit more attentive to Margaret's state of mind than they thought. Admittedly, it had taken Lady Evelyn's prompting to wake him to it, but he respected her opinion, for women knew about these things. He had made a few discreet inquiries of Whitmarke, and found nothing particular to object to in Breen. Neither did he find much that would make him desirable as a match for his daughter. Breen sounded innocuous, but not very serious. He was from a good family, but so removed by circumstances of birth from any fortune that he would have to make his way through the law or the military. The fact that he had not yet chosen any path was the only negative thing one could say about his character. But it said enough to the marquess. At three-and-twenty, the young man should have had some sense of direction. Had Breen chosen a career for himself, perhaps he might have looked more appealing. But the young man seemed to have found no direction, so when Breen arrived promptly at three, he faced the not particularly friendly marquess and had some of the most uncomfortable minutes of his life as Margaret's father grilled him about his background and his prospects.

Breen had not assumed an easy acceptance of his suit, so he was prepared to attempt a convincing response.

"I admit that I have concentrated too much on my 'expectations.' When I was twenty, I had no focus nor motive save my own support. But my feelings for your daughter have made me realize it is time to settle down."

"I am happy for you if Margaret has had that effect," the marquess said. "But it is not clear to me where you will concentrate these efforts."

"I had thought . . . perhaps . . . that is . . ." Even Breen could not easily say. " . . . that there must be a small estate in Margaret's family that we could settle on. I do have some talent and experience in managing the land." As he finally got this out, Breen had the grace to blush.

"Tell me, Mr. Breen, if you were a father, would you give

your daughter to someone who might only be after her inheritance?''

Breen looked up and said, with some dignity, ''No, I would not.''

''Why, then, should I?''

''Because you value your daughter's happiness and because that happiness depends on me.''

''You rate yourself very highly, young man!''

''Forgive me, sir, but my feelings for your daughter are strong enough that I needed to say that, however immodest it may sound.''

''I have no real reason to doubt your sincerity,'' the marquess answered, ''but neither have I reason, as yet, to trust your commitment. I would reconsider your suit in a few years if Margaret is still unattached. But until you have made your way in the world, I cannot permit an engagement.''

Breen could feel the implacability behind this statement, and decided to waste no time pleading. He thanked the marquess for his time and bowed himself out of the room. Margaret was waiting for him by the door and he could tell from her eager expression that she had no inkling of her father's disapproval. When she saw his set face, however, she became concerned.

''He said yes, didn't he?''

Breen took her hands in his. ''I am afraid not. In a way, I cannot blame him, for I am not what the world would consider an ideal suitor.''

''What do I care what the world thinks! *Why* did he refuse?''

''Because we would have nothing to live on.''

''But we could live at Grantwood.''

''Even as I mentioned that, I realized that makes me sound a fortune-hunter.''

''How could he think that, when we love each other? What difference does it make whose money we live on, if there is some money there?''

''To a concerned father, it makes a difference.''

''Concerned!'' All of Margaret's anger and hurt from the last year surfaced. ''He hasn't looked at me or at anyone but his new wife for almost a year. He left me to myself from the minute my mother died. And now that there is someone who does care about me, he would separate us . . .''

"Margaret, we cannot stand here like this. Your father may be out in a minute. I must go. Let us meet tomorrow. . . . He did not rule out an engagement forever. He said that if, in a few years, I prove myself—"

"A few years. That is forever," she groaned.

"It may seem that way now—"

Margaret interrupted. "Do you know where the old graveyard is?"

"Yes. By the church."

"Well, I often go there to tend my mother's grave. Can you meet me there tomorrow morning?"

Breen was willing to agree to anything to calm her down and give himself some time to think. He was torn between his desire for her and his own inability to think beyond the present. He had no great hopes his situation would change in the next few years. And he could not begin to imagine himself as soberly industrious as . . . as what? A secretary to some nobleman? No, what he was good at, what he needed, was the opportunity to work the land. He had no other way but marriage to gain the opportunity. Marriage or cards, he thought, and I promised my aunt I would give up the cards, so it must be marriage. He kissed Margaret gently on the cheek and whispered: "Until tomorrow, love."

Had her mother still been alive, Margaret would have gone to her to plead with the marquess, or even confronted her father herself. But she had felt so abandoned by him that even her anger would not carry her in. When he came down from the library and asked her if she had seen Breen on the way out, she answered quite coolly:

"Yes, Father, and he tells me that you have denied his suit."

"I had to, my dear. He seems a pleasant-enough young man, but with little substance. He has nothing to offer you right now?"

Nothing? thought Margaret. Only the fact that he loves me.

"I hope," continued the marquess a little stiffly, for he was uncomfortable dealing with emotion and had left that work to his wife, "your affections were not deeply involved. I have not forbidden him your company, and, indeed, I told him he could return if his situation changed. Though I must say, Margaret, I do not think he is the sort of man who has much depth. I would not count on him to work that faithfully toward a goal, even if the goal be you.''

"Do not worry about me, Father. I will not go into a decline over this,'' replied Margaret. Because I will elope with him before I will let him go, she thought wildly.

The marquess was relieved that she shed no heartbroken tears and made no pleas. He would have hated to make her suffer, and was inarticulate and helpless in such situations. He had no inkling as to the true state of her heart, for having no gift for intimacy with anyone other than his wife, he had let his daughter slip further away from him, and though he loved her, he did not know her.

"I am glad to find you so sensible,'' said the marquess, and watched Margaret as she smiled and walked upstairs to her own room. Breen had exaggerated her feeling for him, of course, he thought, and dismissed all his uncomfortable musings. He went up to meet his wife for tea, a ritual she had initiated so that he had a break from estate business.

Breen found Margaret in the little churchyard the next morning. She was kneeling in front of her mother's grave. At first he thought she was praying, and then he saw that she was clearing weeds from around the stone. He came up behind her and read " 'Lady Honora Margaret Ashton, beloved wife and mother . . .' That is a lovely name.''

"She was a lovely woman. It is my name too.'' Margaret smiled. "Neither of us used 'Honora.' ''

"Sure, and it is a formidable name,'' crooned Breen in his assumed brogue. "But in Ireland it is shortened to 'Nora.' ''

Margaret got up off her knees and brushed her dress off. There was a small bench in the graveyard under an ancient oak which spread to shelter almost the whole yard. Breen led her over to it and they sat down, silent for a moment. Margaret's hands were in her lap, and Breen took one and examined it as though he found the combination of dirt and slender fingers fascinating.

"Margaret . . .'' he began. She turned to him, and her trusting look, her vulnerability, affected him more than any woman's coquetry had ever done. He bent down to kiss her, and once again Margaret was carried away from all of her former life.

There was no Lady Honora Margaret Ashton, virtuous and careful of her reputation. There was only her self, a self she had not known existed before this man had awakened it.

"We cannot do this," Breen groaned, as he pulled back. "Someone might see us."

"No one ever comes here," Margaret whispered, reluctant to talk, wanting only to feel his lips against hers.

"But there is also the fact we are not engaged. Your father would have every right to call me out, did he hear about this."

"But we *are* engaged," replied Margaret. "Oh, not in his eyes, but I love you and consider myself promised to you."

"As I to you. But it can never come to anything."

"Why not?" she protested. "Why should we let him keep us apart? What if we went away and came back married? What could he do but give in then?"

Breen had, in fact, already thought of an elopement. He was sure the marquess would not be vindictive, and if presented with a *fait accompli,* would not deprive them of Margaret's portion. But he had been hesitant to approach the subject. He was not sure he wanted to take even that small a risk. He loved her, but not enough to take her with nothing. After all, love didn't last long in poverty. He knew that well enough. But if she herself thought it would work . . . ? She knew her father better than he did. He looked down at her. "You would risk that?"

"I would risk anything to be with you."

"Well, it might do. We could drive north, marry at Gretna, and continue east to Edinburgh. We could stay with my uncle and his wife until the scandal died down and then come back, the settled married couple."

"We must do it immediately," responded Margaret, her determination and recklessness burning in her eyes. "Tonight!"

Breen smiled at her. "Your eagerness gives me courage, sweetheart. But we need at least a day's preparation. I must hire a chaise, you must pack . . . but I agree, the sooner the better. Tomorrow night the moon will be almost full, so we could start at night and avoid notice. Could you get out after ten?"

"Yes. My father and Lady Evelyn have usually retired by then, and the servants will also be in bed. I can slip out the kitchen door."

"All right. I will come for you tomorrow night. Are you sure you want to do this?"

"Surer than I've ever been of anything in my life."

The marquess and his new wife retired early every night they were not socializing. "Besotted" was how Margaret had characterized this behavior of her father, but she was grateful for it after all, for she had no trouble slipping out. She had packed only the necessary things: toiletries, a walking dress, nightgown and slippers, and her blue silk. She would change into that for the wedding, she thought, picturing Breen and herself clasping hands over an anvil. She shivered as she walked down the drive, and looked back at her home. She would not see it for a while, and when she returned, she would be a married woman.

Breen was waiting at the gate with the hired chaise. He kissed Margaret quickly and lifted her in. His horse was tied behind, for he had not wanted to risk a hired groom who might spread gossip afterward. The border was not much more than fifty miles as the crow flies, but it would take all night and part of the next day for them to reach Scotland, since they had first to go south to Hayden Bridge in order to continue northeast to Gretna.

"You will find a rug in there, Margaret. Why don't you try to get some sleep?"

Margaret protested she couldn't possibly sleep, but once they were out of Bellingham, she found herself nodding, and settled into a corner with the rug pulled over her shoulders. She awoke a few hours later, thinking they must have arrived, only to hear Breen cursing softly under his breath. The moon was still high and the countryside looked unfamiliar, so she guessed that they must have passed Hayden Bridge and were on their way west. She peered out and saw Breen kneeling in a pool of light from the carriage lamp, examining the front-left hoof of the horse.

"What is it?"

"The damned horse has thrown a shoe, Margaret. I beg your pardon for my language, but I should have known that he was too cheap to be sound. I don't know how we will make the border by morning. We will have to stop."

"Here?" Margaret asked, groggily.

"No, I think we are not far from a town, if I remember the

map correctly. We will have to find an inn for what is left of the evening."

"All right."

Both were too tired to consider the implications, much less discuss them. When they finally pulled into the inn at Halfwhistle and awakened the innkeeper, Margaret hardly heard Breen's request for a room for himself and his wife.

"I will sleep on the floor," Breen said, after they had stumbled to the small chamber.

"No, no," Margaret said. "I will lie under the covers and you on top with the rug over you, and we will be fine." She smiled. "You must be exhausted."

"I confess I would not mind a mattress," he replied, and, arranged as she suggested, they were both asleep within minutes.

Margaret awoke once, to the sound of a rooster. The early-morning sun was pouring in, and Breen's head lay on the pillow, golden in a pool of light. She smiled, ran her hand gently over his hair, and went back to sleep. When she next awoke a few hours later, it was to see him looking down at her with a hungry look in his eyes.

"Good morning," she said softly, and stretched reflexively, like a cat. He captured one of her hands as it returned to her side and stroked it.

"How did you sleep, Margaret?"

"Wonderfully well. I awoke for a short while to the rooster. What time is it now?"

Breen reached for his pocket watch. "After ten o'clock." He turned back to her, and Margaret, as though pulled by a magnet, turned to meet him. Their kiss was long and deep.

"We should get up immediately. Were anyone to find out we'd spent the night together, you would be ruined."

"I am ruined already, is that not so?" Margaret smiled. "Just by going away with you, even if we had not been delayed."

"I suppose that is true," Breen agreed.

"I love you, Dillon," Margaret whispered as she slipped out of the covers. Her hands seemed to have a life of their own, for she could not resist feeling his mouth with her thumb or stroking the hair on his arms.

"Margaret, you will be my undoing," he murmured as he

kissed her behind her ear, sending shivers down her spine. "I want you too much."

"I want you too," she replied, her head bent, for she could not look at him and reveal the extent of her desire to save her life. She nuzzled against his shirt, reveling in the smell of clean linen combined with his own scent. She wanted to get more of him, and she started unbuttoning his shirt and sliding it off of him. His chest was smooth and white, his arms well-muscled and the hair under them red and cumin-scented. Margaret was aware of only one thought: I love him and we are to be married today, so why must we wait? He gently lifted her nightgown over her head, and she lay there, blushing, as he unbuttoned his breeches. Breen had no thoughts of love or marriage. He was only alive to the moment, and he wanted to awaken her to her own womanhood as he delighted himself in it. The women he had had before had taught him well; unlike many men, he was accomplished in pleasuring a woman, and so he moved slowly, only moving on top of her after his fingers had made her wet, warm, and ready for him. He entered her as gently as he could, but it was painful, and she lay underneath him, brought back to normal awareness by the strangeness of it all. After all that pleasure, is this all it is? Well, it is enough, she thought as he collapsed beside her and held her close. They both slept again, curled up against one another, only to awaken in about an hour, aroused again. "This time it will not hurt," Breen said, "and this time I will pleasure you." And Margaret realized that before had not been enough, that nothing would ever be enough, for how would it be possible to have him any deeper inside her, while she came shuddering down from those heights to which he had brought her.

They spent the day in bed, and only in the late afternoon did Breen get up and go down to the stables to inquire about the horse. It seemed ironic to him that on a trip to Gretna they should require the more usual services of a blacksmith. He found the horse had been shod and they could make a new start in the morning. As he stood outside the stall, absentmindedly cupping the horse's muzzle, Breen thought more about their situation. There was no need now to rush to Gretna. Instead of going west and then back to Bellingham, perhaps it would be wiser to continue on to Edinburgh. We could marry there and send the marquess a letter. Wait a few weeks for his anger to dissipate. And I could pick up a little money on the tables. What difference does it make now if we marry tomorrow or next week, after all?

Margaret was so dazed that she agreed immediately. She had been in another world all day, a world of undreamed-of pleasure, and did not want to think of anything practical. And to her, they were as good as married already. Her feelings for her father had undergone such changes over the last few months that she no longer cared what his response to her was. She now had someone in her life who saw her, who loved her, and who wanted to take care of her.

And so the next day they started out, retracing their route, past Hayden Bridge to Corbridge, and finally north to Edinburgh. It was a long journey, tedious at times during the day, but remembered by Margaret only for the passionate evenings they spent in inns along the way. The trip took more than two weeks and almost all their money to accomplish. They were both exhausted by the time they reached Breen's uncle's house in Edinburgh, and Margaret, having grown used to it, hardly noticed that Breen introduced her as his wife. She felt so married that the ceremony might well have happened.

They were able to find only cheap rooms off the Canongate in the old city, and Margaret spent her days bargaining with shopkeepers, cleaning, and cooking. She also spent hours sleeping, but dismissed her tiredness as the aftereffects of their journey. Breen was out many nights "making their fortune," as he laughingly put it. In reality, the money he was able to bring in from gambling was all they had to live on, since the Edinburgh branch of the family was clearly the poor one. The Whitmarkes had most certainly not known that Breen's uncle managed a pub, having married the owner's daughter years ago.

Margaret was taken aback by Breen's willingness to earn their bread by the roll of the dice or the fall of a card. He promised her they would marry as soon as he made enough at the tables to find more appropriate lodgings. "Tonight for sure, ma dear," he would say, rolling his R's like a Scotsman.

And Margaret found that she was able to shut the door on

that nagging little voice that kept asking questions that brought her down to earth: How could she respect a man who lived the way Dillon seemed to? Why wait to marry? Shouldn't they wed and return to Moorview to make peace with her father and settle down at last to the proper life of husband and wife? The voice was silenced in bed, however, for in bed she believed in him. How could she not, when he felt like a part of her soul and body that had been missing all her life, at last to be found and refound every night.

After a month in Scotland, however, she realized her tiredness was not fatigue from her journey, nor from the changes in her situation, but the lassitude of early pregnancy. She was ecstatic, and at the same time terrified. She could think of no better proof of their love than a child, but she delayed her announcement to Breen. She told herself it was because she wanted to be sure, but knew deep down that she wondered if he would despise her for conceiving out of wedlock.

It was finally Breen himself who delicately queried about the absence of her monthly flow. When she nodded a yes to his quiet questions, he pulled her to him.

"Ah, Honora Margaret, we will have to make an honest woman of you this very week." He laughed, and she relaxed in his arms. He did love her and they would be married.

Breen put his head on her belly and said softly, "If it is a boy, we will name him after your father."

"And what if he is a she?" Margaret teased.

"Then we will call her Miranda."

1

1818

The Countess of Alverstone to see you, my lord."

Marcus Samuel Vane, known to his intimates as Sam, looked up from his desk. "Damn and blast! What does the woman want this time?" he muttered, and immediately felt ashamed of his irritated response. After all, the countess was the widow of his best friend, and had been, many years ago, his own first love. But over the years, and especially since Charles's death, those characteristics which had drawn both of them to her, her air of fragility and helplessness, had become more than occasional sources of annoyance. What was most attractive in an eighteen-year-old girl was less so in a twenty-five-year-old and positively irritating in the thirty-nine-year-old woman she was now. And Sam, in the last four years, had had plenty of exposure to Lavinia's worst side, since he had been named guardian of the late earl's son and heir.

The young earl was no wilder than any young man his age, and, in fact, seemed to be growing into as fine a man as his father. Lavinia, however, became hysterical at his occasional high-spirited escapades, and on those occasions Sam had endeavored to explain to Lavinia that too tight a rein would only cause rebellion.

"Both his father and I turned into responsible men, after all, my dear, and we both got into as many scrapes as Jeremy."

"I cannot believe that of Charles."

"Oh, but you can of me?" replied Sam with a glint in his eye.

"You know what I mean, Sam," Lavinia replied hastily. "You always seemed less serious to me. Charles was . . . well, someone to lean on. That is why I married him. I needed his strength."

And an earl is, after all, a better catch than a viscount, thought Sam. The knowledge that Charles had been the better catch no longer rankled, as it had done in the early days of the Whitford marriage. A marriage, he had to admit, that was certainly grounded in mutual affection. Lavinia's love for her husband had been genuine and she had clearly not recovered from his death. Which was why, Sam knew, she often felt so inadequate to the task of raising Jeremy on her own. As the boy matured and settled into his studies, however, Lavinia recognized that her son was growing into a fine, steady man. And although, like an ivy whose oak has been cut down, she tended to twine around whatever was available, usually Sam, he had not had such a visit in months. When Lavinia walked in, still wearing one glove and not as impeccably dressed as she usually was, he knew something serious, to her at least, had occurred.

"Come, sit down, my dear. Now, tell me, what is the problem?" he queried.

Lavinia sat down and then stood up again, and began to pace back and forth across the library. She pulled at the fingers of her kid glove, which had stuck on her engagement ring, a large emerald she had not taken off since Charles had placed it on her finger. Sam watched her pace, knowing that she would eventually wear down, but he hoped she would come to the point quickly this time, since he was in the middle of researching a speech on Catholic emancipation.

Lavinia's pacing slowed and then stopped and she sank into a chair gracefully, twisting her glove in her hand until it resembled a short piece of rope. Wells knocked softly at the door and entered on the viscount's signal. He set down a tray with sherry and two glasses, and Sam dismissed him with a grateful nod.

"May I pour you some sherry, Lavinia?"

Lavinia finally looked at him with those cornflower-blue eyes which had faded only a little over the years. They filled as quickly as they ever had, and she smiled tremulously as she said:

"Thank you, Sam. I know I have burdened you often over the years with my small problems. You have been a good friend to me . . . more than a friend, almost a member of the family . . ."

Sam bent to pour the sherry. Lavinia had made such subtle and not-so-subtle hints over the past two years. He knew her grief over Charles was genuine and deep, but he also suspected he would be a welcome suitor. As it was, his infatuation, although not his affection, had died years ago, and he had no intention of becoming her second husband. So he tactfully ignored any flirting or helpless glances which he was sure were meant to inspire warmer feelings. He had to admit she did it well, and were he younger, or less well-acquainted with her, he would have been in a fair way to being caught. But he did feel like a member of the family, and he loved her son as though he were his own. So he put up with her foibles, and thought of his friendship with Charles and of his determination that Jeremy not be smothered by her neediness.

After a few sips of sherry the countess stopped torturing her glove with her free hand and let it rest in her lap, relaxing slightly as the amontillado hit her stomach. She took a deep breath.

"It must be something rather serious to put you in such a state."

"It is worse than anything," she replied. "I know if dear Charles were here this would never have happened. I must be a terrible mother, or Jeremy could never have done this to me."

"Nonsense. You are an excellent mother, and have raised a fine young man. Charles would be very proud of you."

"Do you really think so, Sam?" Lavinia, who was, under her affectation of helplessness, truly insecure and in need of constant reassurance, looked up gratefully at Sam.

"I do. Now, tell me. What has Jeremy done to upset you so? Lost this quarter's allowance at the tables? Boxed the watch? Taken up with an opera dancer?" Sam knew Jeremy was unlikely to have done any of these things. On the other hand, he couldn't think of anything Jeremy *could* have done to upset his mother so.

"It is far worse than that. Oh, I know you think me inclined to be foolish over him, but this time, Sam, I know you will be in complete agreement. He has fallen in love."

At this anticlimactic statement, Sam was dumbstruck. Of all the feather-witted women, he thought, Lavinia was the worst. He tried hard to mask his anger as he said:

"Lavinia, I know Jeremy has been a great support and comfort to you since Charles's death, but you cannot depend on him too much, or expect him—"

"Oh, I know what you are thinking, that I am a pitiful, jealous old woman—"

"Never old." Sam smiled.

"Thirty-nine. Old woman. Who wants to keep her son in leading strings. Of course I know he will fall in love someday. It is all I hope for him that he is lucky enough to make a marriage of mutual affection, like Charles's and mine."

"Then what is the problem?"

"The problem is, he thinks that he has fallen in love with the daughter of . . ."

"A cit?" Sam could think of nothing else that would cause Lavinia to look so horrified.

"Worse. I don't even know what you would call her. An . . . authoress. An Irish authoress to boot! For what kind of name is Dillon if not Irish?" Lavinia spat out the word "Irish" as though it had been "leper."

The viscount was torn between amusement and genuine concern. He was not the snob the countess was, but on the other hand, had no romantic illusions that unequal matches led to anything but unhappiness for both partners and their families. A daughter of an authoress, Irish or not, was certainly not the wife Charles would expect him to sanction as Jeremy's guardian.

"Lavinia, you say he thinks he has fallen in love. Is it not early days to worry? Surely he is due his experience of first love? He will tire of such an inappropriate young woman once he gets to know her better, surely? How did he meet her?"

Lavinia shuddered. "It could not have happened more 'romantically.' He was riding home from visiting the Worthingtons and passed through Hampstead. He stopped for an ale and was looking out the tavern window when he heard an awful commotion and saw a young child swooped up from under the wheels of a curricle racing through. The rescuer was, he says, the loveliest girl he has ever met. She was shaken, of course, so he walked her home. She lives there in some rustic cottage. He has been calling on her since March."

"And what of her mother? Surely she does not encourage this?"

"Of course she does. You men are sometimes so naive. What more could a mother ask than to have her daughter married to an earl? I am sure she has trapped Jeremy in some way."

"Do you not think his interest will die a natural death, Lavinia? After all, we are not speaking of marriage."

"But that is precisely the point, Sam. He *is* speaking of marriage. He tells me he and this girl have some sort of informal agreement. She says she will not agree to anything public, however, until he is sure his family approves."

"Does her mother know of this?"

"Jeremy tells me no, but I am convinced the mother has been behind this all along, feeding her daughter lines from some Minerva novel, lines to convince my son that she may be poor but has a sense of honor."

The viscount had to admit he was unpleasantly surprised that Jeremy had informally betrothed himself to an unknown. If the mother and daughter were smart enough, they could very well institute a breach-of-promise suit. Which could be what this is all about, Sam thought, unwilling to be so cynical, but having seen precedents in several noble families. At the very least, Jeremy would have to pay a considerable sum to release himself. At the worst, the mother could create a real scandal that could take the young man several years to recover from.

"What do you want me to do, Lavinia?" Sam asked quietly.

"Oh, my good friend, I knew you would see it my way this time. I am afraid for Jeremy. He is only twenty, and I can't bear to have him used or ruined by this harpy and fake blue-stocking. Couldn't you see her and frighten her off in some way? Buy her off, if need be. I authorize you to do anything to get her claws out of my son."

Lavinia was quite impressive in her outrage, Sam thought. Underneath her superficial airs and blond beauty, there was some real feeling. Her love for Charles had been real and her love for Jeremy was too, the viscount knew even though he teased her about her overreactions. At times like these, when she revealed a bit of herself, Sam felt a little less cynical about himself and his youthful passion. There had been something, after all, to be passionate about.

He sat down next to Lavinia and took her hands in his. "My dear, I will go tomorrow to visit this Mrs. Dillon and her daughter and try to discover exactly what the situation is. Now, what is her full name?"

"You *will* go tomorrow? Early in the morning, before Jeremy

has a chance to visit? And I do not want him to know I have
been to see you, Sam. He will hold it against me, I know.''

"Well, I can hardly say I just happened to stop in by chance.
But I am willing to play down your concern and exaggerate
mine as his guardian. Now, what is the woman's name?''

"Honora Dillon. Mrs. Honora Dillon.''

2

The viscount was usually up early, so his appearance at eight in the breakfast room surprised none of his staff. As he ate, he found his concern of the day before increasing. After Lavinia left, he had gone back to his writing, being the sort of person who rarely suffered anxiety about future problems, but instead, took them as they presented themselves. He had even enjoyed himself at Lady Sedgewick's dinner dance, to which he had gone in the hopes of seeing Jeremy and trying to discern for himself any sign of lovesickness. Jeremy had been there, but aside from a short conversation at the punch bowl, the viscount had had little contact with him. His godson had looked perfectly happy to be dancing and flirting with the young ladies. He even danced with the Honorable Susan Burrows twice. Sam did not want to appear to be watching over Jeremy, so he busied himself by doing his duty with several young ladies and exerting his charm with one widow on whom he had had his eye all Season.

The viscount had been the despair of the matchmaking mamas for years. When Charles married Lavinia, he had thought his heart was broken. He had thrown himself into government affairs, and over the years, won a place in Whig circles. By the time he realized his heart was still intact, several crops of young ladies had been presented and married off and he had developed a reputation for being distant and somewhat cynical. This never stopped being a challenge for some young women, but his air of cynicism was real, although, could they have known it, as much directed at himself as at them. Over the years, he had had several long-term mistresses, but had never shown any interest in marriage. In fact, hostesses were beginning to invite him as a confirmed, if not old, bachelor who could be trusted not to seduce the prettiest, and to dance with the plainest young ladies, to converse wittily at the supper table, and to join his excellent baritone to a soprano in duets after dinner. It was a great waste, they all agreed, for the viscount was quite attractive and very eligible.

Lady Sedgewick had given him her usual scold last night as he left, asking him when, if ever, he would really *look* at a young woman. "If you are not careful, Sam, Jeremy will be married and a father and you will be bouncing someone else's babies on your knee!"

The viscount had taken her teasing words more seriously than usual, and this morning, recalling them, set his mind to the problem at hand. It was hard to imagine this Mrs. Dillon as anything but the harpy Lavinia described. Although his natural inclination would have been to speak with Jeremy first, elicit his confidence, and then advise him against such a connection, he had to agree with Lavinia that scaring or buying off the mother and daughter would be the quickest and, in the long run, least painful way. Jeremy would be disillusioned and hurt, but not lastingly so. And he would be less naive in the future, more aware of the attraction his title and position would have for certain types of women.

The ride from London to Hampstead took almost an hour. Sam was quite familiar with the little village fast becoming a full-fledged town, for he had, like many Londoners, enjoyed the occasional afternoon ride or tramp on the Heath, happy to be breathing the fresh air of Parliament Hill after the fogs and miasmas of the city. He had also been several times to dinner at Heath House, where Samuel Hoare gathered like-minded politicians and writers to discuss the abolition of slavery or the plight of the poor.

It was a beautiful early-June morning, and the further he got from London, the more relaxed he became. He was confident he could settle this affair with only a little unpleasantness and by next year see Jeremy happily married to someone like Susan Burrows. And by then, perhaps he himself would have found the right widow—the right widow being a woman who valued her independence and at the same time would welcome a long-term affectionate liaison with himself.

He was rudely shaken out of his daydreaming by his horse's shying away from several of the notorious black pigs which overran the village. One of them, a large sow, just stood in the middle of the High Street as though daring Sam's chestnut mare to come any further. It took all his skill to coax her and convince her that while, yes, this snorting creature *was* a bit scary, she was much smaller than a horse and it was all right to move on. As he passed the animal, he shook his crop and grinned to see her move off slowly, sauntering away as though it was her own idea. His mental picture of Mrs. Honora Dillon, which had become more and more detailed, was complete. She would, of course, be a heavy, vulgar, and stubborn woman with a pink-and-white daughter like a porcelain pig.

The viscount had no direction for her, so he decided to stop at the Bird in Hand and make inquiries. In such a small town, he was sure someone would recognize the name. He tethered his horse and inquired of the innkeeper, a rotund, cheery-looking man, who was busy drying glasses at the bar.

"Pardon me, but I am looking for the house of a Mrs. Dillon. I believe that she lives in Hampstead with her daughter."

"Eh . . . and what would you be wanting with Mrs. Dillon, if I did know her? Which I am not sure if I do or I don't, if you understand?"

"I am a friend of Lord Jeremy Whitford's, and having heard him speak of her daughter, I wished to meet them both."

The landlord's face lit up at Jeremy's name, and he put down the last glass and came out from behind the bar, wiping his hands on his apron.

"Well, then, that does mean something. John Barker here," he said with a smile, and reached out his hand.

"Marcus Vane," replied the viscount. "Pleased to meet you. You know my young friend, then?"

"Yes. He stops in for the occasional ale on his way back to London, and a finer young gent I have yet to meet. He and Miss Dillon make a lovely couple."

Sam nodded and said, "Speaking of the Dillons, I do need to get on. Can you direct me?"

"Continue on up the High Street, past Windmill Hill and you will come to three cottages on your right. Go past the first two, then turn right down the path, and you'll be in front of Mrs. Dillon's. She calls it Heathside, though it is not as close to the Heath as all that."

"Thank you, Mr. Barker."

"John. Call me John. Any friend of Nora Dillon's is a friend of mine. Come back for an ale, if you have the time."

"I will," replied the viscount. The landlord had surprised him. Nora! She must indeed be Irish, and Lavinia would be furious.

It was a short ride from the tavern, and the landlord's directions were excellent. Heathside, identified by a weather-beaten sign on the gate, was a respectable little house with only a small yard to the right separating it from its neighbor, but with a well-tended flower garden to the left, two apple trees, and then a small open field. Sam dismounted in front and opened the gate. He was about to continue up the walk and knock on the door when he became aware of movement behind the flowers. There appeared to be a vegetable garden next to the flowers, in which, from what he could see, a young woman in a laborer's green smock was on her knees, weeding.

"Young woman," he called.

The woman rose and looked behind her and then over at Sam. "Are you calling to me, sir?"

"Yes, I am. I am looking for a Mrs. Dillon. Do you work for her?"

"Yes," the woman replied after the slightest hesitation.

"Is she at home this morning?"

"Yes."

"Well, could you announce me?" Sam asked patiently.

"I could, if you will tell me who you are."

"Yes. Please tell her that Marcus Samuel Vane, Viscount Acland, is here to speak with her."

A puzzled look flitted across the woman's face, but she curtsied quite gracefully, albeit rather exaggeratedly, Sam thought, for one in such a smock and with hands caked with soil.

"Please go right into the parlor, m'lord. The door is open. I must go around the back," she said as she gestured at her clothes. "I'll send Mrs. Dillon in."

"Thank you." The viscount retraced his steps and opened the door, expecting to find himself in some overdone setting, and was surprised to find the parlor a tastefully done room, comfortable rather than fashionable. The furniture was not new, but seemed to have been collected, piece by piece, with little regard for era, so in one corner was a Queen Anne table and

in another a Sheraton chair. The floorboards were wide, but
well-polished and covered with some small Turkey rugs in
shades of red and blue. Sam sat down in a comfortable chair
of no particular "period" and gazed around the room. There
were fresh-cut roses in a vase, and hanging on the wall was
a small portrait of a child of about three. The style seemed
familiar, and Sam got up to view it more closely. The little girl
had wavy blond hair and blue eyes. She was dressed in a simple
blue smock, and looked like a country child. The delicacy and
loving attention to the details of complexion and hair reminded
the viscount of Romney's portraits of Emma, Lady Hamilton,
and then he realized that he was indeed looking at a Romney.

"I see you admiring my daughter," said a voice behind him,
and he turned quickly, embarrassed to be caught out in his
curiosity. The woman in the garden stood before him, and he
saw that she was not young, as he had thought. But he was not
surprised that he had taken her for a younger woman, for her
face was free of paint and tinged with a healthy glow from
working outside, and she had kept her figure, he could tell.

"I was waiting for Mrs. Dillon, and was drawn to this
portrait. It is a Romney, if I am not mistaken."

"Yes. Miranda caught his eye and there was nothing for it
but he *would* paint her. She sat very nicely, for a three-year-
old, if I do say so myself."

"Miranda?"

"Miranda Dillon. My daughter."

Of all the pictures Sam had conjured up, none bore any
relation to the reality of the small woman before him. Instead
of an overbearing vulgarity, there stood before him an
unassuming woman dressed in a faded blue muslin dress, with
newly washed face and hands (though he could still see dirt
under her nails), who extended her hand to him gracefully and
finally introduced herself.

"I am Honora Dillon, my lord. And I already know your
name. That 'young woman' I employ in the garden told me,"
she said with a mischievous smile.

"Now I *am* embarrassed."

"Why so? I haven't been called a young woman in years.
I am pleased, not insulted. Come, sit down. What are you here

to see me about? I must confess I did not recognize your name. Should I have?''

The viscount decided to come straight to the point. ''I am the Earl of Alverstone's godfather.''

''You are *Sam*! I am pleased to meet you. Although I wish that Jeremy had told me you were coming. I would have been dressed to meet you and had tea ready. Speaking of which, let me put a kettle on to boil.''

Before Sam could stop her, she was gone. He sat there feeling more and more uncomfortable. She was so different from what he had imagined. And clearly on a very familiar footing with his godson. He would have to proceed differently.

When Mrs. Dillon returned, she brought in a tray with two cups of tea and a plateful of sliced brown bread and fresh curls of butter.

''I am afraid that today is not a baking day,'' she said apologetically, ''so I have nothing fresh to offer you. But the bread was baked only yesterday.''

Eager to do anything but begin what he had come for, Sam dug in. He was hungry and the bread was delicious.

''This is like the brown loaf they serve in Ireland,'' he said.

''Why, yes. How unusual that you would have been there and tasted something so homely.''

''I spent some time there on government business, but I did get to know the countryside and its people.''

''My husband was Irish, and I got this recipe from his aunt.''

''You are a widow?''

''My husband died many years ago.'' There seemed to be a difference in tone as she answered, but Sam put that down to embarrassment or a lingering sadness.

''But you are not Irish yourself, I think?''

''No. I am originally from the north.''

''And you write novels, according to Jeremy.'' Sam was trying to sound natural, but at this last, Mrs. Dillon looked up at him questioningly.

''Forgive me if I am wrong, my lord, but your questioning and this sudden visit lead me to believe that you are not here on just a friendly mission.''

Sam had hoped to continue his ''subtle'' probing for a while longer. It was quite unlike a lady to bring the conversation to a point so quickly, but then, of course, Mrs. Dillon was not a lady.

"You are correct," he replied quietly.

Mrs. Dillon's face flushed, whether from anger or embarrassment, Sam was not sure. It was unusual to see a grown woman blush, and such openness of feeling surprised him.

"I think I begin to see the purpose of your visit, but if I am right, I would be so disappointed in Jeremy's 'Sam' that I would rather you not go on."

"Jeremy does not know I have come here."

"That is becoming clear to me."

"In fact, I hope you will not tell him."

"That depends."

"On what?"

"On what else you have to say."

"Lady Whitford, Jeremy's mother, told me of his involvement with your daughter."

"His involvement? They are fast friends, if that is what you mean. But perhaps his mother objects to that friendship for some reason?"

"I am not sure it is only a friendship they have found, and yes, Lavinia does have some objections."

"Which are . . . ?"

The viscount was having a hard time of it. He could hardly say to this woman that Lavinia did not want her son associated with the daughter of a scheming Irish lady-writer, since she was neither vulgar nor, it seemed, Irish. Whether she was scheming remained to be determined.

"The earl's mother naturally wishes him to make a connection with a young lady of his own rank. She does not believe, nor do I, that unequal matches lead to anything but unhappiness for both parties." Sam thought he had phrased the objections in a most diplomatic way. He had said nothing personal, nor anything shocking. Therefore he was a bit taken aback to see the surprise on Mrs. Dillon's face.

"As another mother, I would have to agree with the countess. But we are speaking only of friendship, after all. I suppose that it may seem unconventional to someone in society. Perhaps I have a more lenient view, but I find no cause for concern in the companionship that Jeremy and Miranda have found.''

"I see your daughter has not been as open with you as my godson has been with his mother. The earl told her that he and Miss Dillon have an informal agreement.''

Mrs. Dillon's eyes widened at this, and Sam could have sworn the expression in them was one of genuine surprise and concern.

"If this is so—and Jeremy . . . the earl has always seemed to me to be an open and honest young man—then I begin to understand the purpose of your visit.'' She placed a heavy emphasis on ''earl'' as if to say indirectly: I see what you are trying to say by using his title and not his name. "It was not merely to meet me or to discourage their friendship, was it? It was to warn me off. You are quite correct, the daughter of a Mrs. Dillon, novelist, could never be right for the Earl of Alverstone.''

"I am sorry to surprise you with this, Mrs. Dillon. Of course, we thought you knew.''

"Of course, you thought me behind it all,'' she replied in a low voice shaking with anger. "You thought me some scheming woman who would try to entrap a young man for her daughter's advancement. Or even worse,'' and she looked up at Sam, her eyes flashing, "who would use her daughter to blackmail the earl's mother. How much would you have been prepared to pay, had I been that sort of woman?''

"It is not like that at all,'' the viscount protested. Not *now*, anyway, he thought to himself. "The countess and I merely wished to make sure that you knew we could not, in good conscience, agree to such a match. We were hoping, in fact, you would ask your daughter not to see the earl again.''

"The earl? Jeremy, you mean. It makes it quite easy, doesn't it, not to think about his feelings or Miranda's when you use his title. Then he sounds so above her that the reality of their feelings for one another is diminished. And if I refuse to ask her?''

"Then we would take it up with the earl . . . I mean, Jeremy. I am his guardian until he comes of age next year, and I would forbid him to continue his acquaintance with her.''

"Do you think he would obey you?''

"He has always respected my wishes and those of his mother in the past, Mrs. Dillon,'' Sam said firmly.

"I will tell you something that may come as a surprise to you, Lord Acland. I did not know Jeremy and Miranda's friendship was anything more that just that. I was happy to see them together. Jeremy is a fine, intelligent young man, and my daughter has been rather isolated from young people of her own caliber, if not class. They met by chance, you know, and seemed immediately to recognize a kindred spirit in each other. I see nothing to object to in their friendship, although society would not agree with me."

"No do I," Sam reflected, "although I fear the countess would not agree with either of us."

"But, while I have no objection to their friendship," Nora Dillon continued, "I do have my own objections to anything more intimate. Miranda is barely eighteen and Jeremy only twenty. If they believe it to be love, then it is clearly a first love, for her at least. I do not think one's first love is ever one's last. And the difference in position is as much a concern to me as to the countess, I assure you, although for different reasons."

Sam did not know how to proceed. Having come prepared to bully or bribe a very different sort of woman, having realized, almost immediately, that he would instead have to make a reasoned argument, having begun to marshal rational statements in his head, he now felt like a soldier standing fully armed and ready to charge at an enemy who had already left the field. Mrs. Dillon was not a schemer, nor was she a romantic, whatever sort of novels she wrote. There was no need to do anything, it seemed, but to agree upon tactics.

"So you will tell your daughter that she must not see Jeremy again?"

"I did not precisely say that, my lord," Mrs. Dillon looked amused at the viscount's obvious consternation. "Let us look at the situation in the way a dramatist might," she said lightly. "We have here two young people, a Montague and a Capulet, as it were. Both families are against the match. Both families keep them away from one another, going on about the unsuitableness of the match. What better way to fan the fires of a first love than to forbid it? If you will forgive both my literary allusions and alliteration."

"You don't think your daughter would obey you?"

"I think in matters of the heart—and if Miranda agreed to

even an informal betrothal, her heart is given—even the most obedient and conforming children cannot help but disobey. I know this from experience.'' This last was spoken so low that Sam almost didn't hear it. ''And,'' she continued, ''I suspect Jeremy would not take an arbitrary dismissal easily. He would pursue her, don't you see?''

''I am beginning to. But if we are both agreed the connection will not do, then what *do* you suggest? That they continue to see one another?''

''Yes. They are both intelligent, and are of course aware already of the conventional reasons against the match, hence the secret betrothal. They no doubt expect an argument . . . although I doubt Jeremy would have expected the countess to go quite this far . . .''

The viscount had the grace to blush. ''You think if we accept their betrothal, they will eventually call it off?''

''I think if we surprise them by not objecting, and if we support each other in acting as though this were agreeable to both families, by the end of the summer they will realize themselves that it is impossible. If they are treated with respect, perhaps they will be able to hold on to the friendship and let go of the romance.''

''Are you sure they will come to see their situations are too different to make for a happy marriage?''

''Up until now, they have been together only here, away from the eye of society and their families. Jeremy is quite unspoiled, and Miranda has never been exposed to the superficialities of the *ton*. She is an unusually lovely and intelligent young woman—even if I say it, who shouldn't—but she would not be comfortable at balls and routs. I think if we bring Jeremy's family and friends more into our world and you invite Miranda and me into yours, they will come to share their elders' opinion. At any rate, while I can't be absolutely certain this will happen, I *know* forbidding them each other's company will only make them long for one another more.''

''I am convinced,'' Sam replied after some minutes of silence. ''My task will be to convince the countess!''

''I don't envy you that. But you can assure her I want this match even less than she does.''

''I must confess, and I don't wish to be offensive, your attitude

surprises me, Mrs. Dillon. Most mothers would be eager to
see their daughters move up in the world, and to go from being
Miss Dillon to the Countess of Alverstone is not something to
be taken lightly.''

"I quite agree," Mrs. Dillon said coolly. "It is not something
to be taken lightly. And now," she continued, "we must decide
how best to begin our strategy."

It was clear to the viscount that Mrs. Dillon was not about
to reveal to him the grounds of her objection, which apparently
were strong. And so, for the moment, he put aside his curiosity
and listened to her plans.

"You must have the countess speak to Jeremy further about
this. Perhaps she could convince him that a secret betrothal is
insulting to Miranda and that she is in favor of an announcement, so long as he can convince you. We could plan an outing
on the Heath, and then you could invite us to whatever seems
appropriate. But we have to have them in company enough so
that Miranda's unsuitability is made clear."

"I begin to feel diabolically interfering," Sam confessed.

"How so?" Mrs. Dillon lifted her eyebrows and looked
straight at him. "You were quite prepared to buy or bully me
off."

"Yes," he admitted. "But that was before I had made your
acquaintance. Now that we have met, I worry we will cause
pain both to your daughter and to my godson. If we forbade
the connection, it would be a severe but at least a swift and direct
blow."

"Yes, but I want them to come to the decision themselves."

"You are so sure they will?"

"I am certain that when Miranda and Jeremy become more
aware of the differences between their backgrounds, they will
no longer wish to rush into marriage."

"Well, let us hope you are right," Sam said as he rose
to go. "I must take my leave. Thank you for the tea
and the advice. We will, no doubt, be seeing more of one
another."

Mrs. Dillon stood in the door as Sam rode off, and when
he looked back, he saw her move into the garden, her back
to him as though she had forgotten his existence. Had he

watched longer, he would have seen the self-possessed Mrs. Dillon sink down on the lawn against one of the apple tees and lean back as though she were seeking support from an old friend.

3

The viscount decided to stop at Mount Street on his way home, in order to forestall a visit from Lavinia. He had no doubt he could convince her that her suspicions of Mrs. Dillon were mistaken, but decided to claim their plan as his own, since the scheme could sound as though it were a way for that imagined harpy to worm her way into the family.

Sam could not have put into words the reasons *he* trusted Mrs. Dillon. The most obvious, of course, were her appearance and demeanor. She was not vulgar. In fact, he was convinced that she must have come from a good family, for she had refinement, natural dignity, and had spoken to him as an equal. Perhaps she herself had made a bad marriage, he thought. She had been very careful not to enumerate her objections to the match. But he believed they were there, and intended to convince Lavinia.

He was lucky Lavinia was in when he reached Mayfair. Her days were usually filled with shopping and visiting. The butler admitted him with a smile, took his hat and gloves, and said that the countess, who had a mild headache, was recovering and would be happy to receive him. He sent the viscount up to the morning room, where he found Lavinia lying on a sofa, a scented handkerchief on her forehead.

He cleared his throat and she turned slowly, popping up immediately when she saw who it was, and realized, from his buckskins and boots, where he must have been.

"Tell me you *have* seen her this morning and have come to tell me you succeeded," she begged.

"You are correct on both counts." The viscount smiled.

"Oh, Sam, I knew you could handle that harpy. How much did you have to give her?"

"Nothing."

"Nothing?"

"She is quite different from what we had imagined, Lavinia," Sam replied. "And indeed, now that I think of it, we should have guessed. After all, we know Jeremy. We should have trusted he could never have fallen in love with the daughter of the Mrs. Dillon we imagined."

"Of course he could have. Young men do it all the time," the countess said, restored to worldly wisdom by the good news. "But why would she agree to give up her scheme so easily?"

"Because there was no scheme, my dear Lavinia. Mrs. Dillon does not want the betrothal any more than we do."

"You mean she *said* she did not."

"Hear me out."

The countess sat back on the sofa and motioned Sam over to a chair. "You look hot and tired, Sam. Do you want me to ring for some lemonade?"

"Yes," he said gratefully. "Now, let me finish before you get agitated all over again."

Having rung for Matthew and ordered the drinks, the countess was ready to listen. "Go on, tell me about her. Does she live in a wretched set of hired rooms? What is the daughter like?"

"One question at a time. No, she lives in a comfortable cottage near the Heath, which includes a small piece of land, so she is certainly not poverty-struck."

"And her daughter?"

"I did not meet her. Although I did see a small portrait of her as a child. If she kept her looks, she must be quite lovely, all blond curls and rosy cheeks. It was a Romney, you know."

"What was a Romney?" asked Lavinia with some impatience in her voice.

"Oh . . . the portrait . . . I suppose it is not surprising that a novelist would come into contact with artists," Sam mused.

Lavinia dismissed Sam's observations on the way of life of such oddities as painters and writers and demanded a description of what had occurred.

"Mrs. Dillon did not know of the betrothal. She thought their friendship to be just that—a bit unconventional, she was willing to admit—but she seemed disturbed by the thought of anything more serious. We both agreed the match would be undesirable. She understood your objections, but did not elaborate on her own, except to say her daughter was too young and the disparity in background would eventually doom the relationship.''

"It was as easy as that," Lavinia marveled, "to get her to agree to forbid her daughter Jeremy's company?"

Sam cleared his throat and took a sip of lemonade before continuing with his story. He knew the hardest part was coming.

"I'm afraid we decided that would not be the way to discourage the attachment, but, in fact, would help to keep it alive.''

"Whatever do you mean?" Lavinia asked.

"I suggested that keeping them apart would be a tactical error. They are so young, and in the throes of a first love. The more obstacles put in their way, the more they will try to overcome them."

"And what did you suggest, then? That we honor the betrothal and begin to socialize with our in-laws-to-be?" Lavinia asked sarcastically.

"As a matter of fact, that is what we agreed upon," Sam replied carefully.

"I cannot believe you let the woman manipulate you like that, Sam."

"Lavinia, just think a minute. Right now, neither Jeremy nor Miss Dillon has had to think much about the outside world. They are friends, then fall in love, all in a sort of vacuum. But do we begin to intrude upon that dream world, visit Hampstead and invite the Dillons here, they will begin to see what a gap there is between them. Instead of firing up their resistance, we let them continue with an informal, unannounced betrothal for the summer. By the fall, they will see for themselves that it will not do."

When the viscount emphasized "unannounced," Lavinia could begin to hear him. Perhaps the plan was not so absurd. After all, how could a little miss from Hampstead ever begin to fit in with Jeremy's friends and contemporaries? And the mother? Well, whatever Sam said about her, she was most likely pushy and grasping at heart.

"What do you think, Lavinia?"

"I think it is worth trying. After all, we can always forbid it in the end."

"I hope it will not come to that. Now, the question is, how do we begin?"

"Since Jeremy has told me, I think that I shall suggest we meet the Dillons. Should our first skirmish be here or in Hampstead, do you think?"

"Why don't we leave it up to Jeremy and Miss Dillon, Lavinia? Let them begin to cope straight off."

"Good. I am actually beginning to look forward to this, Sam. It will be amusing to see this Mrs. Dillon humiliated, for I still cannot believe but that she is a good actress and has taken you in."

Sam only smiled and bowed his way out. A few hours spent with Mrs. Dillon would convince Lavinia more than any protests he could make. He had only to await a visit from Jeremy and an invitation to a prospective family gathering.

4

After the viscount left, Nora was unable to pick up the pieces of her day. She had intended to finish weeding the cabbages, have a light luncheon, and spend the rest of her afternoon writing. But now . . . she was not sure what upset her more: the news of the betrothal or the fact that Miranda had kept it a secret.

She and her daughter were very close, and up until now, openness and honesty had been the hallmark of their relationship. And she was not, she hoped, one of those mothers who used their children for companionship. She knew Miranda would one day leave her. In fact, she wished for nothing more than that her daughter would find a loving husband. Although they lived out of the city, Nora's range of acquaintances was wide, and she had hoped Miranda would eventually form an attachment to some young writer or publisher's assistant. Hampstead was home to enough artists and writers that her hopes were certainly not unrealistic. But eighteen was far too young. And dearly as she loved Jeremy herself, it was impossible for her daughter to marry him.

I must have been blind not to see this, she thought. Perhaps I just didn't want to. But they seemed just good friends and I counted on their social distance for safety.

She could not settle in to weeding or writing, so she grabbed an old bonnet to shade her face and set out for a walk on the Heath, her time-proven way of coping with everything from a temporary inability to write to heartache. Today it would need to be vigorous and long, for she was suffering from both. It wasn't often these days she spent time regretting her past, but this morning's news had shaken her.

The two-hour tramp calmed her and cleared her mind, so

when she returned and found Miranda at home, she decided no time need be wasted in opening up the subject. Her daughter was sitting in the old wicker swing which hung from the larger apple tree. They had never raised it, so that the eighteen-year-old Miranda's feet dragged as she swung slowly, aware only of the book of poetry she was reading and not the little scuffs of dust which were rising and falling and clinging to her gown, so that it was scalloped brown in front. Nora could not help but smile at the picture. There were ways in which they were alike, and a love of words was one of them. Certainly in appearance they were quite different. Miranda was two inches taller than her mother, and slender, while Nora's figure was fuller and more solid. Both were pale, but Miranda's skin had the tone of milk after it has been skimmed, a blue-white, where veins were close to the surface. Her eyes were blue, rather than gray, and her hair, although it had darkened since the Romney portrait, was still blond. It was straighter, much to her despair, and she wore it unfashionably long. She looked delicate and helpless. In fact, she was as athletic as her mother, able to walk for hours, always ready to help in the garden, and loving to dance all night on those rare occasions that they took part in the social life of the village.

As Nora looked at her, she thought: Of course Jeremy has fallen in love with her. How could he not? She stood in front of the swing so she could catch the ropes, and brought her daughter to a halt.

"Mother! I wondered where you were. I thought you had planned to write this afternoon. Here I was keeping myself quiet and occupied so you could work," she teased.

Nora smiled at her sally. It was amusing now, that negotiation of a balance between mothering and writing, but it had been difficult for both of them in the early years before Miranda could understand why her mother scribbled away and needed to be left alone. Nora could remember saying to the eight-year-old: "I just need one hour, but you must not interrupt." And then the call, fifteen minutes later, "Mama, Mama, look what I found!" And the immediate "I'm sorry, I forgot." Nora, at those moments, would be torn between fury at the interruption and awful guilt that she was imposing such restrictions on her daughter. But had she not continued, they would have had nothing . . . and all in all, Miranda seemed to have survived.

"I had been planning to, but I received a surprise visitor this morning who gave me some news which . . ."

Miranda looked immediately concerned. "Nothing wrong, I hope, Mother? Who was it?"

"It was Jeremy's godfather, the Viscount Acland."

"Oh?" Miranda looked a bit apprehensive.

"He told me that you and the earl have contracted a secret engagement."

Miranda lowered her eyes and her face flamed. "Yes, we have."

"And why secret?" Nora asked quietly. "This is the first time you have ever lied to me. Were you afraid?"

"Oh, no, Mama, it wasn't a lie," her daughter gasped.

"An act of deception is the same as one in words, my dear."

"I suppose you are right. I never thought of it that way. I am sorry. But we only wished to keep it a secret a little while for ourselves. To enjoy our happiness, just the two of us. Before . . ."

"Before you met your families' objections?"

"I suppose we were a little worried that Jeremy's mother would object. But you do not. I know you love Jeremy." Miranda smiled.

Nora answered slowly and carefully. "You are right. The earl is a lovable young man. But I am concerned about two things: your age and the disparity in your situations."

"Is that why you keep calling him the earl, which you have never done since the first day we met him? You have raised me to believe we are all equal, Mama. Why should that not work upward, as it were? And as for age, well, you were just as young when you married my father, so you could hardly object to that."

"I have raised you in those beliefs, my young radical, but I doubt very much that Lady Lavinia feels the same. Jeremy's mother expects him to marry some young woman whose birth and fortune are equal to his own. I cannot see her welcoming as a daughter-in-law an obscure young girl from Hampstead."

Miranda's eyes began to shine with the righteous anger of

idealistic youth, and Nora knew she was right in her advice to the viscount. "Did the countess send the viscount here to warn me off?"

"No, nothing like that. But you can't imagine she wouldn't want to know something about her son's fiancée."

"Then she won't forbid the match!" The battle light faded as Miranda's eyes grew soft with happiness.

"Neither of us would forbid a marriage if the young people concerned are sincerely attached to one another. But both of us would like to wait for a formal announcement until our families become better acquainted."

"Why, that is just what we were hoping, Mother. Jeremy said he was going to tell his mama soon so that before the Season was over we could meet her. And how could she fail to approve of you, Mother? You are a lovely, intelligent woman and the match for any countess!"

"Thank you, my dear. Your objectivity does you credit," Nora said ironically, and they both laughed.

"No, seriously, Mother, I believe once we all get to know one another, there will be no doubts is anyone's mind. How did you like the viscount, by the way? He sounds splendid, from the way Jeremy talks about him."

"I didn't spend much time with him, but he seems nice enough. I assume we will see more of him this summer, for he seems quite a confidant of the countess's."

"Jeremy says he was one of her old suitors, but she fell in love with his father, and that was that. He thinks his mother would be happy to reattach the viscount, but his godfather seems content to remain just that."

Nora was aware of a fleeting sense of disappointment. Despite her anger this morning, she had not gotten the feeling that the viscount was as much of a snob as Jeremy's mother would seem to be. To be sure, she had only her own picture in her mind, which, writer-fashion, she was making more and more detailed, of a vain, frivolous woman whose only concern for her son was material and superficial. The man she had met did not seem like the sort to be attracted to her imaginary countess . . . but what business was it of hers, after all? After this summer, they would never see one another again.

"We will, no doubt, hear from her soon. Should we invite them here first, do you think?"

"Oh, yes. Jeremy says his mother hardly ever gets out of town during the Season. What about a short walk and a picnic on the Heath?"

"I think that would do very well," Nora responded, feeling more and more like a hypocrite. It would do very well, she was sure, to show the two young people that their families' ideas of entertainment and enjoyment were quite opposite. And here she was, berating her daughter for deception, while she was embarked upon a much more serious one, which could eventually cause pain to someone who was dearer to her than her self. But the heartache will soon pass, she thought. And she *cannot* marry Jeremy, or much greater heartache will follow.

5

The day following his visit to Hampstead, the viscount was again interrupted, this time by Jeremy himself. The earl apologized for the disturbance, but said he had something of the greatest importance to speak to his godfather about. Sam invited Jeremy to take a seat and looked over at him expectantly. The young man stopped nervously smoothing his trousers and began.

"I have some news, Sam, which I know you have received unofficially from my mother."

"Yes?"

"The truth is, I am engaged to be married."

"So I understand," Sam replied. "I was surprised it was not the Burrows chit."

Jeremy was more flustered by this calm response than he would have been by the expected protest.

"No, no. Why ever would you think of her? She is a charming girl, but not my sort at all."

"You have been quite attentive to her lately."

"Why, yes, but out of nothing more than friendship. She cannot compare with Miranda."

"Ah, yes. This Miss Dillon. However did you meet her?"

"I always stop for an ale when I am coming back into town from the north. I did a few months ago, and saw a most heroic act: Miss Dillon pushing a little boy out of the path of a racing curricle. She risked her own life. As it was, she was brushed by the wheels and quite shaken by the whole thing. I ran out and supported her back to the inn, where I made sure she was all right before I walked her home. Her mother was most grateful and invited me back for tea. I liked her so much, Miranda, that is . . . well, I like her mother too . . ." Jeremy, who had started out calmly, was, as he approached the climax of his story, beginning to be nervous. "Well, I have been visiting regularly, we became great friends, and then, in one moment, it seemed, we realized we loved one another."

"And Miss Dillon agreed to this secret betrothal?"

"I know it sounds improper, Sam, but neither of us wanted the world to intrude upon such new feelings. Yet, since we knew they were lasting, we wished to make a commitment to one another."

"And what of your mother? Your position as earl? Who *is* Miss Dillon, aside from her bravery?"

"Her mother is an authoress. She supports them both by writing novels. Popular ones, I'm afraid," Jeremy said with a smile. "Miss Dillon has been educated by her mother. They are both widely read and I am sure you will love their conversations as much as I do."

"And when you told your mother?"

"She was quite shocked, of course, since she expected me to play the field for a few years and then settle down with some society miss. But I know when she meets Miranda she will love her. And I know I can count on you, Sam, to help her over her disappointment."

The viscount was touched by this evidence of Jeremy's trust in him, and surprised the boy thought he was so unconventional as to countenance a bad match. He was even a bit ashamed of himself, for he and his godson had spent many an evening discussing the issues of the day, and Sam had only himself to blame if Jeremy had developed a libertarian perspective. But that he expected it to extend to domestic matters surprised the viscount. No matter what one's political leanings, one followed society's dictates. As a matter of the nobility, it was expected that one marry within one's class.

"Jeremy, do you think your mother unreasonable to be disappointed and upset?" queried the viscount.

Jeremy stood and started pacing in front of the window. He turned to Sam and said earnestly: "Had I not met Miranda, I believe I would understand, Sam. I expected to wait a few years, to marry the usual way, and do my duty to the family. Not because I am at heart convinced of the rightness of that course; merely because it is what one *does*. Having met Miranda, however, and having fallen deeply in love with her, I feel like someone who has been saved from hurling himself over a cliff along with all the other sheep headed in the same direction."

Jeremy turned to face the viscount, and Sam looked at him closely for the first time since he had arrived. The boy combined the best of his mother and father, in appearance and character. He had the striking blondness of Lavinia, made even more striking because he had his father's brown eyes and the strength and intelligence of the late earl. His face had lost its adolescent downiness, and for a twenty-year-old, was surpisingly mature. But the passion was a young man's passion, thought Sam. The belief that because one *wanted* so much, everyone must also see the rightness of it and want the same for him. He remembered how he had thought Lavinia must love him, if only because he loved her. And as his passion for Lavinia had died, so too would Jeremy's love for this unknown girl.

"Well, it certainly sounds as though a meeting were in order."

"Then you do understand! I knew you would."

"Better than you would think, for a gentleman of my advanced years."

"Pah. You are in better shape than many of my friends, who spend their time drinking and gambling. You don't look a day over thirty-five!"

"Thank you, Jeremy," Sam replied dryly. "Now I must ask you one thing, which is not, I think, unreasonable."

"Yes?"

"I think it best to keep the engagement informal for a few months." As Jeremy started to protest, Sam held up his hand. "Hear me out. This will allow your mother and me time to become aquainted with the Dillons. You will have a sanctioned, if private betrothal, and should any change of heart take place on either side, neither you nor Miss Dillon will suffer in the eyes of society. And, to be quite truthful, I cannot, at this point, imagine getting your mother to agree to anything else."

Jeremy sighed, and gave in. "You are probably right. And since there will be no change of heart, we can make our announcement at the beginning of the Little Season and introduce Miranda to society then."

"Now, how do we arrange our first meeting?"

"I think I will ride out to Hampstead this afternoon," Jeremy said. "I will speak with Miranda's mother, and we will decide who should call on whom first."

"You hadn't spoken with Mrs. Dillon either, I understood from her."

Jeremy had the grace to blush. "No, we kept it secret from her also. I can see now it was a thoughtless thing to do. How did you like her?"

"She seems an independent sort."

"Yes, Nora has supported them both on her own," Jeremy said. "And, Sam, one of the wonderful things about this is that I can offer her some help after all her years of poverty."

"You are generous, Jeremy."

"But I have so much," Jeremy replied, with that openness he had had even as a small boy, when he was forever giving toys and puppies away.

And I mean to see you are not taken advantage of, thought Sam, who could not help but have lingering doubts about a woman who seemed honest enough, but who was, after all, a mother. And what mother would not want to advance her daughter and herself?

6

It was not until more than a week later that the first meeting took place. By the time Jeremy and his mother spoke again and he and the Dillons met, having the most formal conversation since they had been acquainted, with Jeremy taking the responsibility for the deception, the earliest convenient time for both the families was the second Tuesday in June. The meeting was to be in Hampstead: a picnic on the Heath with tea later back at the cottage.

Jeremy and Sam dressed comfortably for a day in the country, but had not been able to convince Lavinia that half-boots would be more appropriate than kid slippers and that an everyday round gown was more appropriate than the muslin walking dress she chose to wear.

"I am meeting my son's fiancée for the first time, and no matter that she is beneath him, I intend to dress according to the occasion. And surely I have dressed like this for other picnics. It is quite the thing," said Lavinia at the door when Sam had remarked upon the formality of her attire. Jeremy grimaced behind her and said: "I tried to convince my mama that a picnic at Richmond is a bit different than one on the Heath, but with no great success."

"No matter," Sam said, thinking things were going according to plan. Lavinia had always been at her best in the city, and aside from riding, enjoyed no physical activity. It was the one discordant note in her marriage to Charlies, for he would have spent most of his time in Sussex, had he not been such a doting husband. Lavinia, if he and Mrs. Dillon were lucky, would no doubt ruin the day and the two young lovers were bound to wake up to the difficulties inherent in trying to join two such different families. "Let us go or we will be late," Sam urged.

"Late," moaned Lavinia, as she settled back into the chaise. "This is the earliest I have been out in an age."

Jeremy had chosen to ride inside with his mother, a choice he regretted after the first ten minutes, since she hated traveling and suffered from quite genuine motion sickness. She held her vinaigrette in one hand and the strap in the other and looked paler and paler as the chaise proceeded at a snail's pace. They had chosen a busy market day, so the pig population, as well as sheep and cattle, was out, and the journey to the High Street, and, indeed, part way up, was slow and smelly. Jeremy, although he would never have admitted it, was almost ready to give up and turn back. He loved his mother, but her weaknesses, which often amused him, were at the moment annoying. He was torn between sympathy for her real distress and the disloyal wish that she was more like Miranda's mother.

The air and the road cleared as they approached the Dillons', however, and Lavinia revived. She was not about to disgrace Jeremy, especially in front of this upstart female and her daughter. So there was a hint of battle in her eyes when they pulled up in front of the cottage.

Miranda and Nora were sitting in the parlor. Or rather, Nora was sitting calmly, reading, and Miranda was up and down at the slightest noise. "Jeremy is more than half an hour past the time he promised," she said to her mother, "and he is never late. Do you suppose they are not coming after all?"

"Jeremy is with two other people, dear. Perhaps his mother is delayed," replied her mother calmly.

When the chaise at last pulled up, Miranda was up and out before Nora could stop her. She stopped suddenly on the walk and smoothed her dress and hair unconsciously as she watched Jeremy hand his mother down.

Sam could see a resemblance to the child Romney had painted in her flushed cheeks and startlingly blue eyes. But she is no child, he thought as he watched her control her agitation. She is quite a beautiful young woman. Had she remained inside, in imitation of a polite society miss, or rushed up to Jeremy gushing in a possessive way, Sam would have felt more optimistic. But she walked quietly down the path to meet them, saying, "You must be Jeremy's mama. I am Miranda Dillon.

You are as elegant as he promised," she continued easily, "but you look worn-out from your drive. We must get you into the house and settled with a glass of water or lemonade."

Jeremy threw a grateful look at Miranda, and Sam felt a twinge of jealousy as their eyes met in what was obviously perfect understanding. They were not gazing soulfully at each other, like calf-lovers, all intent upon themselves, but were, instead, working like partners to handle an awkward situation. He dismounted, and watched Miranda murmuring sympathetically to the countess as they proceeded up the walk. He grinned to himself as he realized that Lavinia had lost the first round immediately. There had been no chance for her to come over the proud countess, and it would be hard to pull off now, with such an attentive young lady.

Nora met them at the door and let them past her as she turned to meet the viscount. She felt like a conspirator as he smiled and took her extended hand.

"My lord. Please come and join us in the parlor. You look like you had a dry and dusty journey."

Sam brushed himself off. "There did seem to be an over-abundance of livestock as we came into town," he replied.

"Oh, I am sorry," Nora said. "We are so used to market day that I never thought that Tuesday would not be ideal. Although the weather is perfect for our picnic," she said as she looked up at the almost-clear blue sky. "This dry spell might have raised the dust, but it has also dried out the Heath, so our walk will not be muddy and our rugs will not get damp. Please come in."

Lavinia had been settled and Miranda was in the kitchen getting lemonade and glasses. The color was returning to the countess's face and she was trying to take in the room without looking vulgarly curious. She had to admit that while it was not a richly or fashionably furnished room, it was quite comfortable and not at all vulgar.

Jeremy got up immediately as Nora entered the room, and introduced her to his mother. She walked over to shake hands, and Lavinia looked up into calm gray eyes. Surely this could not be the encroaching Mrs. Dillon, this soft-spoken, attractive woman?

"We are honored to have you with us, Lady Whitford," Nora said. "Jeremy has told us so much about you, we feel we know you already."

Lavinia replied frostily: "I can't say he has told us anything about you."

Nora colored, and with a naturalness that bespoke an easy intimacy, placed a hand on Jeremy's arm. "I know, and I have scolded him for it."

Jeremy looked down and smiled ruefully. "I know this is a surprise for all of us," Nora continued, "and I am sure not the match you might have chosen. But I feel it is important to respect the feelings of our children, do you not?"

Lavinia looked up into the studiously bland face of Mrs. Dillon and remembered what the "plan" was. "You are quite correct on both counts, Mrs. Dillon," she answered coolly.

Miranda came in with the lemonade, and Nora turned to Jeremy again. "My dear, there is a crock of ale in the larder. Would you pour out a glass for the viscount and yourself, if you want something stronger."

Nora, finally realizing that the viscount was waiting for her to sit down, sat and poured the lemonade for the three ladies.

"You must be quite eager to stretch your legs after your long ride," she said to the countess.

Lavinia was taken aback, for the last thing she had been thinking about was exercise. What she was eager to do was stretch out on her own sofa and nap. But Sam had said they must be agreeable, so she murmured something about a stroll being welcome.

"We only planned a short walk for you for this first time," said Miranda. "There is a path right up from the cottage, which will take us to the Heath for our picnic, and then it circles back. We need to walk only twenty minutes or so to get there."

Bless the girl, Nora thought, as she looked at Lavinia's face struggling not to frown at the thought of more exercise off horseback than she had had in years. They had originally planned an hour's walk out, but Miranda had taken the countess's measure in a glance and realized she would never make it. Indeed, should she walk half the distance in those slippers, it would be a miracle. Whatever was she thinking of, dressing like that?

Mrs. Dillon's face was so open that Sam almost laughed out loud as he saw her look down with consternation at Lavinia's shoes. She herself was comfortably dressed, as was Miranda, in a gown suitable for walking, as most "walking dresses" weren't, thought Sam. And he guessed, quite correctly, that mother and daughter would exchange their slippers for some sort of footwear worn by hours of walking.

Conversation could not be said to be sprightly. After a few polite inquiries, Lavinia gave up. It would not have done to get personal, and no one was relaxed enough to utter more than stilted comments on the weather, and the inevitable remarks upon the ubiquitous black pigs. The only sincere words were Sam's and Jeremy's praises for the ale.

Miranda and Jeremy had not imagined it would be so difficult. They, after all, could talk for hours and had no more in common than their respective parents. But they had forgotten that in addition to the sweet inanities of young lovers, their conversations ranged over everything from literature to politics, Miranda being better read than most of Jeremy's friends who had come down from Oxford. But Lady Lavinia had little conversation aside from the *ton* gossip. After a few aborted attempted to relate the latest *on-dit,* she realized that the Dillons not only did not know the Duchess of Handley or the Earl of Staveley, but were only being polite when they expressed their interest. So Lavinia sipped her lemonade slowly, and the others watched her, as though it were the most original act in the world.

Nora realized the first meeting was going almost too well, from the parental point of view. She could not stand the increasing discomfort, and suggested they set off for their picnic. Even Lavinia seemed to welcome the suggestion.

"Would you like to borrow a pair of boots, Lady Whitford?" asked Nora. "We look of a size, and I promise you would be more comfortable."

The countess looked with distaste at the brogues Nora was holding out to her.

"No, thank you. My slippers are sufficiently comfortable."

"You are sure, Mother?"

Lavinia was not about to ruin her appearance for anything. So she refused again, and once they had distributed the rugs and picnic baskets, they set off.

7

The day was unusually warm for June, and it took only ten minutes for them to realize the countess was not going to make even the shorter walk. At first, she was bothered only by the fact that the bottom of her gown was getting dusty. But then she began to feel the pebbles and ruts in the path through her slippers. To give her credit, she did try to keep up, and made only one despairing cry when, after limping alone in the rear, she was slapped in the face by a rebounding twig. Miranda, who had moved back to give Lavinia her arm, hurried up to the front of their small procession to speak with her mother and Jeremy.

Nora walked back with her daughter and said, with genuine sympathy: "Lady Whitford, we had forgotten how used we are to walking. Perhaps we can picnic a little closer to the cottage. Do you think you can walk just five more minutes? There is a spot ahead, not as ideal as what we had planned, but adequately shaded."

Lavinia was so grateful to be spared ten minutes of torture that she offered Nora a genuine smile and admitted that perhaps she was not properly dressed for this kind of exercise.

"Jeremy," called Nora, "come and take your mother's arm."

Jeremy, who had wanted his mother and Miranda to become better acquainted, had been walking ahead with Sam and was quite oblivious to Lavinia's discomfort. He came back immediately and took his mother's arm. Miranda fell in front of them, and Nora strode quickly to catch up with the viscount.

"My lord, I think we will have to cut short our walk. The countess is quite obviously miserable, and even though it would suit our purpose well, I cannot torture the poor lady further. There is a spot up ahead, next to a small pond with a few trees to shade us. We could spread the rugs out there. The countess can rest, and if you and Jeremy and Miranda wish to go further, I will stay with her and keep her company."

Sam looked back and could not help himself from smiling at the contrast between the limping countess and the woman beside him. She was clearly full of energy and could have continued for hours.

"That is very kind of you, Mrs. Dillon. Are you sure you want to sacrifice your own exercise? I could stay with Lavinia."

"No, no. You go on with the young people. I get out almost every day, and in truth, this sort of day is not one of my favorites. I prefer a few clouds and a bit of wind in my face to this heat."

Within a few minutes they had reached the small pond which bordered the upper end of the High Street.

"This is not as wild a place as we would find on a longer walk, for we are barely onto the Heath," Nora said. "But it is a pleasant spot for a picnic."

Jeremy and Sam spread out the rugs and settled Lavinia under the shade of a small willow. Nora waved the three of them off.

"I will arrange the picnic and keep the countess company. You three go on a bit further."

Jeremy mouthed a thank-you to her, and the three moved off.

For a few moments, while Lavinia caught her breath and leaned against the tree with her eyes closed, all was silent. Nora watched the pond, a steel-blue mirror. The calm surface was disturbed only by the V drawn by a family of ducks, and the silence broken by the warbling of blackbirds hidden in the reeds. They were on the Heath side of the water, so the occasional wagon on the road opposite did not bother them.

When Lavinia opened her eyes, she saw Nora sitting on the edge of the rug, her legs drawn up, arms around them, and her chin resting on her knees. And as the sun glanced through the leaves, one could also see the gray and red highlights in her hair. She seemed so free and faraway, Lavinia thought. And so . . . different. No lady would ever sit like that, yet it was clear she must have originally been from a good family. She and her daughter, Lavinia had to admit, were refined and well-spoken. Perhaps she had married beneath her? thought Lavinia, and without thinking said: "Have you been widowed long, Mrs. Dillon?"

Nora started. "You are awake! I thought you might have wished to nap while we wait. What did you wish to know?"

"How long is it since your husband died?"

"Oh, Miranda and I have been on our own since she was two."

"And have you always written to support the two of you? Or did your husband leave you something?" Lavinia was asking out of genuine interest, and not antagonism, but Nora did not quite trust her.

"No to both. I came to writing a bit later, when Miranda was older. And no, he did not leave me anything."

To ask more would have been ill-bred, so Lavinia only commented she didn't know how it was for Mrs. Dillon, but for herself, while the first grief had diminished, she missed her Charles more as the years went by.

Nora was touched by the real feeling in the countess's voice and was surpised she would be so open with someone who was, in her eyes, some sort of opponent. She said she understood, but did not go any further about her own husband.

"Perhaps we should start laying out the picnic," Nora said briskly, ending the intimacy of the moment, and she began busying herself with baskets, unwrapping brown bread and cheeses and delicate cress sandwiches. There were cold chicken, asparagus vinaigrette, and a "surprise" Nora said, leaving the last basket covered. The meal was simply, yet tastefully done, and required nothing but fingers and napkins.

"Just in time," Nora laughed, as she heard the three wanderers returning. "Could you put these bottles in the pond to keep them cool, Jeremy?"

Lavinia was a bit jealous of the easy relationship between Mrs. Dillon and her son. She knew Jeremy loved her, but she also knew that a certain amount of tension had grown between them since his father had died. She was not sensitive or intelligent enough to see it for what it was: the way Jeremy was able to maintain a certain distance from her. She was by no means a devouring mother, but her helplessness could have pulled him in more effectively than any bullying, had he not distanced himself with his humorously critical stance. Nora, on the other hand, was independent, and, most important of all, not his mother, and so he could respond to her in a way he could not to Lavinia.

"Well, Sam," Lavinia said with a rather forced cheerfulness, the edge returning to her voice, "how was it further on?"

"Delightful, my dear. We have all worked up quite an appetite."

"I hope what I have brought will satisfy it," Nora said. "I did not wish to carry too much, so there is only one knife for the cheese and chicken and bread."

"I am not too polite to hold back," Sam said as he reached for the small triangles of bread and cress and cream cheese, and handed one to Lavinia.

"Would you slice the bread and cheese, Miranda, while I pass around the napkins?"

They were all soon unself-consciously licking fingers from the chicken, and reaching for the softened cheese. Jeremy brought up the two bottles of lemonade.

"I brought only two cups," Nora apologized again, "so we will have to be lost to shame and share. Perhaps the gentlemen will drink theirs from the bottles after pouring."

Lavinia was torn between her enjoyment of the food and her horror of the way it was being served. A picnic usually meant carriages laden with cutlery and porcelain, servants to spread out tableclothes, glassware for the wine and punch, and a menu equal to that of an indoor supper. How could Jeremy contemplate marriage to the daughter of a woman who calmly discussed sharing drinking cups!

"Why does food always taste better out-of-doors?" Jeremy asked of no one in particular.

"It is the exercise that builds up an appetite," replied the viscount.

"I hope you still have room for dessert," Miranda said, as Nora opened the last basket. Inside were fresh strawberries arranged on a bed of mint and decorated with sprigs of hearts-ease. Next to them were two small earthenware crocks, one with sugar and one with butter-yellow fresh cream. Nora placed the basket in the center and even Lavinia had to ooh and aah at the flowers and fruit.

"Again, we will have to ignore convention and dip our

strawberries into a common bowl," she said. "The cream will get sugary and the sugar creamy, but that is the way they taste best." And indeed, the sugar and cream soon became indistinguishable and fingers and chins dripped juice and cream as they feasted.

"Exquisite, Mrs. Dillon," Sam said. "I cannot eat another bite." He stretched himself out along the rug with a satisfied sigh. They all murmured their contentment. Even Lavinia, after her first moue of distaste, had found the berries irresistible.

"Perhaps we should all move out of the city," Sam said. "Living in Hampstead has its own pleasures, despite the pigs."

"Oh, those pigs," Nora laughed. "They are notorious."

"What else is notorious here?" Jeremy queried lightly.

"One of the more famous residents of our village, over a century ago, was the well-known Henry Vane. He was executed by Charles II. I did wonder, my lord, if you are in any way releated to him."

"As a matter of fact, I am," replied the viscount. "He had seven sons and daughters, and our branch of the family goes back to a younger son. I like to think that I carry on his work, since he was a great believer of popular government, as am I."

Nora looked at him with warm approval and Sam found himself unaccountably pleased. "I have always admired him," she said, "for he was consistent but not rigid in his beliefs. He refused to have anything to do with the execution of Charles I, and so he alienated Cromwell. And then his persistence in his republicanism was objectionable to the restored king."

"Lord Erskine, of course, is one of our better-known residents now," Miranda said.

"Ah, yes, he is a great orator, although I do not always agree with him."

"He is one of Prinny's set, isn't he, Sam?" Lavinia said. "I have met him: an egoist, as all small men seem to be. But witty. And most truly heartbroken at the loss of his wife."

"He is quite fond of animals, is he not?" Jeremy asked.

Miranda and Nora looked at each other and laughed.

"He has a pet goose," Miranda said, "that follows him around."

"And two pet leeches," Nora added.

"Leeches!" said Lavinia with disgust as Sam laughed at her horror-stricken face.

"Yes," continued Nora. "He keeps them in a glass vessel and gives them fresh water every day. He claims they saved his life. He even named them after his doctors, Howe and Clive!"

Even Lavinia had to join in the laughter.

"But, Mother, it is not fair to make him out only a figure of fun. He is quite serious in his concern for animals, and I admire him for that."

"As do I, dear," Nora replied. "But I could not resist the story."

"It will certainly make it difficult the next time I meet him socially." Sam grinned. "All I will be able to picture is his good-mornings to Howe and Clive!"

Lavinia, who had been restored by the rest and the food, thought it was time to ask a few essential questions.

"You seem to know quite a lot about your neighbors, Mrs. Dillon. Have you lived in Hampstead long?"

"We all know something about each other," Nora replied, "for it is a small community. And yes, I have lived here quite a few years."

"And where do you come from originally?" Lavinia was determined to get some specifics out of Mrs. Dillon, preferably facts which would confirm her daughter's unsuitability.

"Why, I come originally from Northumberland, Lady Lavinia," Nora smiled.

"Do you still have family there?" queried Lavinia.

"Not as far as I know," Nora replied, and Sam, who was curious himself, saw a flicker of something in her eyes. "I left to get married many years go, and never returned."

"And so you came here with Mr. Dillon?"

"No. We first went to Scotland. I came south only after he was killed."

"Killed?"

"Yes, in a naval engagement." Nora's replies were as close to curt as politeness would allow, and would have discouraged anyone else, but Lavinia persisted.

"How dreadful for you. And you have been raising your daughter alone all these years?"

"Yes. Although I have been supported along the way by many good friends."

"Did you ever wish to return to Northumberland?"

"Never," Nora said shortly, beginning to pick up the crumpled napkins and repack the baskets. She had had enough interrogation for one afternoon—and much good it had done Lady Whitford, for she knew little more about Miranda's background than she had before.

Sam, who had been growing more and more uncomfortable with Lavinia's grilling, even though it did serve their purpose, stood up quickly and said: "Come, Jerremy, let us shake out the rugs and ready ourselves for the walk back." He offered Lavinia his hand, and she stood up, quite happy to be interrupted, for she had gotten no real information and had only succeeded in putting a damper on the whole party.

And that is what I set out to do, Lavinia thought, so why do I feel so guilty about it. Jeremy must be made to see that he cannot marry a girl of no background whatsoever. And this Mrs. Dillon had proved quite elusive, which should make him wonder a bit.

The walk back only added to her sense of discomfort. They went slowly, but Lavinia could feel all the old bruises, plus a new blister coming. By the time they reached the cottage, between her physical pains and her irrational qualms about spoiling a party she had wanted to spoil, she was at her least charming. The querulous tone had returned to her voice and she refused all further refreshment, declaring she only wanted to get back to London and rest her feet.

Jeremy glanced helplessly at Miranda, and she smiled a bit wistfully. They had had no time together during the day and would have to wait until the morrow to discuss and decide whether the picnic could be considered a success or a fiasco.

Sam helped Lavinia into the chaise and turned to the Dillons. "It was lovely to meet you, my dear," he said to Miranda. "And thank you for the delightful afternoon, Mrs. Dillon."

"You're welcome, my lord. I believe it was enjoyable for all of us."

Miranda and Nora watched the party drive off and turned back to the house. They were tired, for the strain of keeping Lady Lavinia comfortable had told on both of them.

"What did you think, Mother?"

"You know how I care for Jeremy."

"But what about his mother?"

"Well, she is still a very attractive woman, and the viscount seems to be very much as Jeremy described him. I think he has been lucky to have him as a godfather."

Miranda seemed to accept these statements at face value, but later that evening she stopped in her mother's bedroom on her way to bed, as she had been doing since she was small. She sat on the edge of the bed and received her good-night hug, and said, in her open, spontaneous way, "Oh, Mother, I am so glad you're my mother."

Nora smiled. "And I am so glad that you are my daughter. But why this sudden delight?" she teased.

"You know I feel that way. I am only rather sad for Jeremy, that he doesn't have a mother like you."

"Lady Whitford strikes me as a responsible parent."

"Oh, I am sure she is. But she is not natural or warm or even very intelligent. . . . I feel disloyal to Jeremy, in some way, but I could not help but compare her to you."

"Well, you are a bit prejudiced, my dear. And used to my ways. But we have lived a very different life from those in society, Miranda, and you will be meeting many more Lady Whitfords, should you marry Jeremy. How do you think you will get on?"

"I don't know," Miranda answered truthfully. "But I know I love Jeremy and that he loves me as I am. I don't think he will want me to change. I will just have to learn to playact a little, is all. Good night, Mother."

"Good night, 'ma wearie dearie,' " Nora replied, rolling her R's, with the phrase that had sent Miranda to sleep over the years.

"Don't ever stop saying that," Miranda whispered into her ear, and whisked off to bed.

Nora sat there, her book lying unopened on her lap. Those were the words she had used over the years, to soothe and say

good-night with. Those, and "my ain wee bonnie lassie."
Somehow the lilting quality of the dialect expressed for her the
inexpressible love she felt for her daughter. For eighteen years
her life had revolved around the rituals of morning and evening
greeting. No matter what hardships she had had to face, Miranda
was the fulcrum of her life, and kept her centered. And now
it was all changing. Although Miranda could not marry the Earl
of Alverstone, she would, in a year or two, marry someone.
And no longer be Nora's "dearie," but someone else's. And
then what? Nora would be free of a responsibility she had
joyously assumed many years ago. "Free." For what? For more
writing, surely. Perhaps she would be able to attempt the serious
novel she had always wanted to write. She had good friends.
But she had been so caught up in living day-to-day, supporting
them, raising Miranda, that she had never thought about a future
without her. And the future was now taking shape and it seemed
to her she was facing emptiness.

My God, I can let her go because it is right, and because I
must. But how will I live without her? How did this come about
without my even realizing it? She turned down the lamp and
slipped under the sheets. Her sleep that night was fitful and she
awoke from a dream, the first in years, in which she was crying
for her mother, who was driving off and leaving her—only in
this dream, her mother had Miranda's face.

8

When Jeremy called on him the day after the picnic, Sam found he was quite sincere in his approval of Miranda and her mother. This disturbed him, for if, on the first meeting, he was favorably impressed, then what, precisely, were his objections to the match? He did, of course, believe in not marrying outside one's class, but was not so rigid as to be termed a snob. He found himself curious about Nora Dillon: was she a lady who had married beneath herself and been forced to live simply because of her widowhood and lack of property and family? Or had she alienated herself from her family by an inappropriate marriage? Perhaps the latter, since she seemed so convinced that separating the young people by force would lead to an elopement.

She was an attractive woman, however, and Sam was pleased he would have the opportunity to see her again. In fact, discussing the next opportunity was what Jeremy had come for.

"What is the best way to introduce Miranda to our friends, Sam?" he asked.

The best way, from one point of view, thought the viscount, would be to have a small, informal outing. In that way, Miranda would not be faced with too many members of the *ton* and be forced to endure their usual inquiries about family background. But since he did not approve of this match, and Mrs. Dillon certainly didn't, he suggested just the sort of gathering that would highlight all of Miranda's disadvantages: a dinner or a musicale.

Jeremy looked dubious. "There are some people whom I want her to meet who have already left town. And don't you think it would be scary for her to meet so many strangers all at once?"

"She seems quite a capable girl to me," Sam replied. "I'm sure she'd be up to the challenge. And it is precisely because

73

it is the end of the Season that I suggest it. There is no time to put together a series of smaller parties.''

''You are right. And this way, I have to ask Mother to put herself out only once. How do you think yesterday went? It was hard to tell, between Mama's sore feet and her rudeness.''

''Oh, Lavinia wasn't that bad.'' Sam smiled. ''I thought it went as well as could be expected, for a first acquaintance.''

''She will like the Dillons better and better as she gets to know them,'' Jeremy said, with an air of determination.

After he had gone, Sam busied himself with his research, distracted occasionally by his memory of Mrs. Dillon's strawberry-stained fingers folding napkins. He decided that after his ride in the park, he would stop at Lavinia's and see how she was feeling.

Lavinia, while she did feel some ambivalence, was less conflicted than Sam. Neither mother nor daughter was as bad as she had pictured, but she did not approve of or trust them. She had liked Miranda—who could not like such a thoughtful, pretty girl? But liking was beside the point. And her mother . . . ? Lavinia had found out nothing about her family background, and had no way to even make an inquiry. Mrs. Dillon might be speaking the truth about Northumberland, but without a maiden name, how could anyone know where she was born and from what kind of family she had come? She could be a farmer's daughter, for all we know, thought Lavinia.

And so, when Sam arrived, she was eager to know how soon he thought Jeremy would come to his senses.

''Did you have no second thoughts, then?'' queried Sam.

''I must admit I found Miranda charming, if still quite ineligible,'' replied Lavinia from the chaise longue on which she was reclining to rest her ''poor tired feet.''

''And her mother?''

''Opaque,'' she answered flatly.

''Yes?''

''I could not get one leading bit of information out of her.''

''Perhaps she thought it was rude to be questioned so soon. She did not, I notice, ask about your lineage or birthplace.'' Sam smiled.

''It is obvioius my background is impeccable,'' Lavinia started huffily, until she saw the twinkle in Sam's eyes. "Oh, all right, I know you think I am a snob, but you don't seriously consider her appropriate for Jeremy?"

"I don't know. Before meeting them, I had no doubts. But I must confess I liked the young lady very much and can understand Jeremy's infatuation."

"And you still think that is what it is? Infatuation?"

"That remains to be seen. After all, he has yet to see Miranda at a disadvantage, which is why I suggested a large dinner party to him. Of course, I know the work involved for you," he continued apologetically, but Lavinia dismissed his apologies and sat up immediately.

"That is just the thing. I will invite Miranda and Mrs. Dillon and the most intimidating of our friends who are still in town. The Dillons will immediately see that Miranda will not do."

"That is just the ticket, Lavinia. But somehow, I feel sorry to have to do this to the two of them."

"Do you really believe this woman has her own objections?"

"After yesterday, I think she is one of the most honest women I've met, although I know nothing of her reasons for disliking the match."

"You sound quite emotional, Sam," Lavinia replied. "Could it be that you are interested in this Mrs. Dillon?"

"Oh, I am interested, but not in the way you mean," replied the viscount.

"She would not do at all for you, even though your taste seems to run to widows."

"Well, do not add me to your worries, Lavinia." Sam grinned. "Maria Hill has seemed quite open to my advances these past two weeks."

Lavinia blushed at Sam's openness and at her own forwardness. Sam's retort had been rather cool, and he took his leave shortly, leaving Lavinia to wonder which was more painful, her jealousy over Jeremy's friendliness with Mrs. Dillon or the fact that Sam, whom she still regarded as a rejected suitor, had never made advances to *this* particular widow.

Miranda and Nora received their engraved invitation to Lavinia's dinner and dance from the hand of her first footman. They looked at each other and giggled after they closed the door, and decided that if they had been able to withstand his haughty look, then they could meet anyone's.

The main question in Miranda's mind was what to wear. Although they certainly were not recluses, and socialized frequently, Miranda's best silk was not appropriate.

"You will have a new dress," Nora said, unwilling to send her daughter out into society looking out of place.

"No, we will both have new dresses, Mama," Miranda said determinedly, and Nora acquiesced. For some reason, despite her usual offhandedness about clothes, she wanted to look her best. It would become clear enough in the course of the evening that they didn't belong, but there was no need to announce it immediately, she thought.

They had no need to travel into London for a modiste, because Madame Didier, a member of the immigrant community of Hampstead, was as much a genius with her needle as Keats was with his pen, Nora remarked. Although they usually made their own dresses, the Dillons patronized Madame's shop for any fabric other than kerseymere and muslin.

They set off down High Street the day the invitation arrived, for it was only six days to the party. Madame Didier, a tall, angular, gray-haired woman, greeted them with surprised pleasure. Her English was excellent, and unlike the English-born modistes, she had no need to pepper her conversation with French phrases. That she was French was clear from her slight accent, and that she was Parisian, from her exquisite taste. She had accepted the drastic changes in her life with grace and strength, and Nora greatly admired her. They were acquaintances rather than close friends, but occasionally took tea together and drew wordless comfort from each other as women in similar positions.

"So, you are to be introduced into society, Miranda," teased Madame.

"Just a small dinner dance, Madame," Miranda replied.

"A small dinner dance could mean over a hundred guests," warned the modiste. "Let me see what I have for you," she said as she started to sift through silks and muslin. "Here is a pale blue silk which would compliment your eyes, Miranda, and I would make it up with an overdresss of spider gauze." Both mother and daughter nodded their approval, and Madame turned to Nora. "But for you, my friend, I must think a bit.

Not blue, although I have an aqua which would be perfect for you . . .'' Madame stood for a moment, gazing at Nora. "I have just the thing," she exclaimed, and disappeared in back, emerging a moment later with a bolt of apricot muslin shot with gold thread.

"Oh, no, I couldn't wear anything so rich," Nora protested.

"Mama, it looks beautiful," Miranda sighed as Madame held the fabric up against her mother.

"But I should be trying to look . . ." Nora paused, searching for the right word.

"Older?" offered Madame.

"Perhaps a turban, Mama," added Miranda.

All three laughed. "You will look old enough next to your beautiful young daughter, my dear. No need to add to your years, only to celebrate them.''

Nora and Miranda selected scarves and gloves and slippers and made an appointment for the final fitting.

"Are you sure you can afford these dresses?" Miranda asked. "I got so excited I forgot to look at the price."

"I received a generous advance for *Cordelia's Conquest,* so do not even worry about them. We have little enough frivolity in our lives, so we may as well enjoy it.''

"It *is* fun, isn't it?" Miranda smiled, giving a little skip as they walked along.

9

The week passed quickly, and on the night of the dinner, both women were dressed and waiting. Nora had intended to hire a carriage, but Jeremy insisted on sending his chaise. When it arrived, the groom, looking as haughty as the invitation-bearing footman, handed them in.

"I feel like Cinderella going to the ball," whispered Miranda. "But Lady Whitford's chaise would not dare turn into a pumpkin!"

When they reached Mayfair, however, Miranda became subdued. She had been to London off and on over the years, but usually for visits to her mother's publishers, to the theater, or to tea with another writer. Their visits had never taken them into the more fashionable parts of town, and so this view of the town houses of the *ton* were her first. By the time they had passed several houses whose steps were crowded with guests, both were silent. When they reached Lady Lavinia's, the crush was not as bad as others they had seen, but there were enough carriages waiting to make Miranda gasp.

"I thought this was to be a small dinner dance."

"I think that 'small' means one thing in Hampstead and another in Grosvenor Square," replied her mother, feeling quite sympathetic to her daughter's fear. She was not looking forward to the evening herself. While she had attended many dinners as formal, the guests had been quite different: literary types like herself, and those of the nobility who were more interested in discussing art or politics than sharing the latest gossip about Prinny.

The butler who greeted them at the front door was much friendlier than any servant they had met so far. He had been with the family since before Jeremy was born and was quite sympathetic to his young master. He had a footman take their

wraps and announced their arrival, watching Jeremy hurry over
with something like a twinkle in his eye.

Nora and Miranda were both so dazzled by the blazing
chandeliers, the jewels and dresses and gleaming boots and
winking diamond studs, that they were almost blinded to the
men and women wearing them. They were able to utter only
conventional phrases in response to attempted conversations.
Unable to take in the whole, they were dazzled by the parts.
They were separated at the table, Lavinia having given in and
placed Miranda next to Jeremy. Nora was on the other side and
quite a few spaces down, between a young man whose shirt
points were so high and cravat so starched that he could not
turn his head more than an inch or two and appeared to be
addressing the elaborate centerpiece instead of Nora whenever
they spoke. On the other side was an elderly gentleman with
whom Nora tried to converse, only to find that he was hard
of hearing. She would have had to shout to make herself understood, and so she gave up. She would have been insulted at
Lavinia's seating arrangement had she not been amused. So she
concentrated on her food and surreptitiously observed those
across from her and attempted to eat only a little of each. How
can they eat so much? she thought as she watched the footman
serve yet another course, the last, thank God.

Across the table and a few places up to her left sat the
viscount, who was obviously occupied with the lady to his right,
an attractive blond. Nora was very happy when the dinner was
over and they could join the ladies in the drawing room. "The
dancing will follow after the gentlemen have had their port,"
announced Lavinia as she led the ladies off.

Miranda seemed to be holding her own with two young
women, although Nora could tell she was nervous by her
subdued expression and lack of gestures. When Miranda talked,
she talked with her eyes and hands as well as her tongue, and
tonight both were very still.

Lady Lavinia started over to Nora, accompanied by a rather
fierce-looking old lady dressed in a bright purple silk leaning
on a silver-headed ebony cane. Lavinia hoped that Lady Harriet
Thomas would help put Mrs. Dillon in her place. She was utterly
at a loss when both ladies recognized each other, smiled, and
moved to embrace.

"Lady Harriet, I am so happy to see you here. I did not notice you at the dinner table."

"Nor I you, my dear Mrs. Dillon."

"You know one another?" Lavinia asked.

"We have met once or twice at Miss Baillie's house," replied Nora. "She is a dear friend of mine, and also of Lady Harriet's."

"I am convinced that Miss Baillie's latest play is a tragedy to rival Shakespeare's," declaimed the elderly countess. "And how is your new novel coming along, my dear?"

"What I write is nothing to compare to Joanna's, as well you know." Nora smiled. "But I am pleased with it."

"Ah, do not belittle yourself, Mrs. Dillon. A good story, an entertainment, is as important as a masterwork. Many's the night a frothy novel has saved me when my arthritis kept me awake. Much as I appreciate Miss Baillie's serious work, I hardly think I would turn to tragedy when my joints are aching!"

Nora chuckled. "So I am better than a sleeping draft, am I?"

Lady Harriet shook her cane. "Now, don't get huffy, Mrs. Dillon. You know what I meant. Come, take my arm and let me introduce you around."

Lavinia was left outmaneuvered and openmouthed in surprise. How could she have known Mrs. Dillon could have met and obviously charmed one of the most intimidating old dragons of society? Instead of being interrogated, Nora was being introduced. So much for her attempt at embarrassment. And once again she was half-ashamed of herself. She did not want this match. Her son, the Earl of Alverstone, could not marry a country nobody, but she had to admit that in her own way, Mrs. Dillon was the equal of anyone here, in manner, if not in birth.

Miranda was being well taken care of by Jeremy, surrounded by his closest friends and protected from the more superficial and malicious young women whom Lavinia had invited. Miranda was still listening rather than talking, but she sat out very few dances.

Nora watched her daughter from across the room. She had been very grateful to the old countess, and had been introduced to several men and women she genuinely liked. But after the first few questions and answers, it was clear there was not enough in common to keep the conversation going. She could hardly, after all, discuss her problems with her latest novel, or trade recipes with women who probably didn't even know where their kitchens were. She could and did answer questions about Miss Baillie, but then someone would remember a piece of gossip and Nora would stand silent, politely smiling as they chattered on about Lord So-and-so.

In the ballroom, she found herself in an in-between position, too young to be keeping the dowagers company and too old to be with her daughter, and ill-at-ease with the matrons her age. She had discovered that the blond lady next to the viscount was Lady Maria Hill.

"Now that Cynthia has remarried, I would not be surprised if Maria becomes his latest widow," was the gossip on the sidelines.

"I wonder why he has never married. He has certainly had the opportunity," wondered one matron.

"For many years, he was traveling, on his own or diplomatic business, and now that he has been more settled, he ignores all the young girls thrown at his head."

"Well, most of the mothers that I know have given up on him."

Nora, who was on the edge of this conversation, smiled to herself. So the viscount was the sort who chose widows, not young girls. That was certainly preferable, in her mind, to setting up serial mistresses from the Fashionably Impure, or marrying some naive young woman Miranda's age. The viscount was partnering Lady Maria in a country dance, and Nora watched them curiously. The widow was certainly an attractive woman and could not be more than twenty-seven or eight, Nora thought, with a slight pang which she recognized as jealousy.

As though he felt her eyes on him, the viscount glanced over to where she was standing a little behind the gossiping matrons in their chairs. I must ask her to dance, he thought. He smiled at the memory of Nora's vigorous strides over the Heath, and the Lady Maria smiled back at him from across the set. Sam had been most attentive and she was quite happy to have been singled out as his next *partie*. He was not the highest-ranking of her admirers, but there was something about him, a combination of strength and a real liking for women, that made him attractive.

Nora watched them smiling at one another and glanced over to where Miranda stood next to Jeremy. He was making sure her first foray into society was successful, and had stayed by her side more than was usually done, in order to protect her from those who might make her feel ill-at-ease. Nora could not help but appreciate his thoughtfulness. As a conspirator, however, she could see her daughter was more relaxed than Nora would have thought she could be. And she was ashamed to admit to herself that she was feeling envious of her own daughter. There she stood with an attentive and protective young man by her side. She was moving out of her old life and into a new one, and Nora would be left behind, never having been able to relax against the knowledge of being loved as Miranda could, did she marry Jeremy. For a moment, all around her fell away and Nora felt herself overcome by a sensation of emptiness, and immediately afterward, as dancers, orchestra, and bystanders fell kaleidoscopically into place, a vulnerability which she thought had gone years ago.

Out of nowhere, it seemed, the viscount was in front of her, asking for the next dance, a waltz, and the moment of openness and receptivity lasted long enough for her to say yes. She looked up at him with a face from which the years had been swept away, the face of a girl, trusting and hopeful. Almost immediately her expression changed, but he thought he had caught a glimpse of someone infinitely vulnerable. He felt a wave of protectiveness sweep over him, which seemed immediately inappropriate as Nora began to speak to him as the competent Mrs. Dillon.

"I am worried Jeremy is going to be successful in thwarting our plans," she began. Sam was, at that moment, far more interested in eliciting that fleeting look than discussing their schemes.

"You and your daughter are looking lovely tonight. In fact, did I not know that Miranda was your daughter, I would have a hard time believing it."

"Thank you, Lord Vane," replied Nora, absentmindedly accepting the compliment, "but I really am worried Miranda looks too much at ease."

Sam glanced down, amused at his failure to entice Mrs. Dillon into a flirtation. The woman in his arms even felt different from the one he had begun the dance with. It was not that she was resistant so much as inaccessible. It seemed as if a part of herself she kept hidden away, but she was so straightforward that Sam would never have guessed at this other self had he not come upon her in that moment of vulnerability.

"Surely Lady Lavinia and I have greater cause for concern, Mrs. Dillon. And I do not think the evening has been as easy as it looks. I know some of the young women and I am sure they have managed to ask an embarrassing question or two and make Miranda feel like an outsider. I must confess, however, that while our objections are quite clear, I still don't understand yours."

"I told you before, Lord Vane, Mirada is too young to make any sort of commitment, however advantageous."

"And that is your only objection?"

"It is enough," replied Nora, quietly closing the subject.

"Well, I would guess neither the picnic nor this dance has been easy for either of them."

"Yet neither a complete fiasco," Nora said.

"Are you reconsidering and thinking we ought to just forbid their betrothal, Mrs. Dillon? For, I must confess, I am now as convinced as you that such resistance would only strengthen their feelings for one another." Sam did not add that he was beginning to wonder if Miranda might not suit Jeremy after all. Of the three of them, he had less reason to object. He cared for Jeremy, of course, but not with the intensity of a mother, and after meeting the Dillons, he felt open to at least considering the betrothal. He believed what was needed was more time: for both families to get to know one another at leisure, and for Miranda and Jeremy to see one another less as secret lovers and more as everyday companions.

"In fact," the viscount continued, "I have decided the next move is mine. I am leaving the city next week to return to Sussex, and I intend to invite you and Miss Dillon and Lady Whitford to join me there for a small house party."

Nora almost lost the rhythm of the waltz, she was so surprised. "Oh, we could never do that, my lord."

The music ended at that moment and Nora was grateful. Although she enjoyed the rare opportunity to dance, she had found it hard to keep time and continue that particular conversation. The viscount led her off the floor and into the refreshment room.

"Come, let us sit down over here. Now, why couldn't you come?"

"My work, for one."

"I promise you, Mrs. Dillon, you could have a study to yourself and all the uninterrupted time you need. I am only talking about an informal visit."

"It just feels too awkward. Lady Lavinia could not want to be with us for that long, and in such intimacy."

"Lady Lavinia and Jeremy will be going to the country soon enough themselves. Since I can't imagine what Jeremy would do without Miranda for those two months, I imagine he would be traveling back and forth, which his mother would like even less. If he chose to remain in town, he would not be happy, for he needs and wants to involve himself in the running of the estates. I have been responsible while he was at school, but now it is time for him to assume control. I suggest that a two-week visit might bring about some sort of resolution."

"I will consider it. But I must be sure that Lady Lavinia does not feel too imposed upon."

"Well, it will be my hospitality you will be abusing, after all, Mrs. Dillon," the viscount replied, smiling down at her quizzically.

"I am sorry. You are right. And since it is your own idea, I suppose I must not be too concerned."

"That is what I like about you, Mrs. Dillon." Sam smiled. "You do not waste time agonizing politely. You apologize as straightforwardly as you do everything."

"I did not know you liked anything about me, my lord," replied Nora, not knowing what to do with such a mixed compliment. Sam was about to reply when Lady Maria and her last partner, the Earl of Hardwich, arrived. Having seen the viscount in the company of an attractive unknown quantity, she decided it would be wise not to leave them alone. The earl sat down next to Nora and Sam and Lady Maria moved off together. Now that their "business" was finished, Nora was left with the most disconcerting memories of their waltz, memories of details she had not been at all conscious of while dancing, like the clean smell of the viscount's cravat, and the feeling of his arm around her waist. The earl had to repeat his request for the next dance twice before she apologized for her distraction.

Miranda was not having as easy a time of it as her mother supposed. Jeremy's presence did make her feel protected, but also, in some ways, more uncomfortable, for not only did she feel out-of-place occasionally, but also had the added burden of knowing he was there to observe how little she and the young ladies had in common. Oddly enough, it was not the shallow little gossips who asked politely phrased but malice-driven questions about the "quaintness" of Hampstead, or who left her out of a conversation only to interrupt their gossip with profuse but insincere apologies, who bothered her. She knew these young ladies would have acted so with any newcomer. She responded with chilly dignity to their attempts to discomfit her, although she was left with a bad taste in her mouth after the encounters. No, she felt most out-of-place with Jeremy's close friends, who went out of their way to make her feel at ease. It was not that she didn't like them. In fact, she was quite drawn to the Honorable Anne Hume, whose plain face was lit by a sense of humor which matched Miranda's own. Miranda would be glad of the opportunity to know her better, for she believed they could become fast friends despite the differences in background. Of the gentlemen, she most enjoyed the young Marquess of Stoughton, a tall, thin, languid young man who looked every inch the bored and boring aristocrat until he opened his mouth. He was a great mimic, and kept the group laughing with his imitations of several guests. Even Miranda's sides were aching, so caught up was she in the general hilarity, although she could not appreciate his witticisms fully. After one dance together, when he queried her with quite genuine interest about her childhood in Hampstead, they continued in animated conversation, for he was a great lover of the theater and was thrilled to learn that Miranda knew Miss Baillie and had even been a guest at several opening nights. They went from discussing tragedy to politics quite easily, and a small excited group gathered about them. At first, Miranda was enjoying herself so much that she did not notice that the group, which was initially ladies and gentlemen, grew smaller as the ladies fell away, and by the end, only she and Anne were left. Jeremy seemed to be watching her with approval, but she became dreadfully tongue-tied as it dawned on her that other young ladies did not seem to be interested, or knowledgeable for that matter, in political questions, and perhaps she was making herself conspicuous. She had become so used to speaking her own mind at home that she had quite forgotten herself. She rejoined the ladies and quietly listened as they traded stories of brothers sent down for pranks at school, or the young women who had been successful this Season in making a match. They did speak quite seriously about music, but here Miranda felt even more left out, for her mother had never had enough money for a pianoforte or for music lessons.

She liked these young ladies and she thought they might come to like her too, but she was beginning to see that life with Jeremy would mean many evenings like this, gossiping, dancing till all hours, and starting all over again the next afternoon. For the first time she began to have doubts about her own ability or wish to fit in. It was not that she felt inferior, but she had had such a different life than all these pampered young people that she felt quite set apart. And she was not sure she wanted to be a part of society if it meant leaving behind the freedom she enjoyed as her mother's daughter.

The only concern Jeremy had that evening, had she but known it, was for her. He was not so naively in love as all supposed, and knew their first attempts to enter each other's lives more fully would be difficult. He loved Miranda precisely because she was not like the other young ladies of his set. No one would ever have guessed how often he had been bored at a rout or dinner party, for he was nothing if not thoughtful and polite with everyone. He had a few close friends, like the marquess and Anne, and he socialized to please his mother more than to please himself. Like his father, he was much fonder of the country than the city, and he knew from early on he would not be happy with a woman like his mother as a wife. His parents had truly loved one another, but he had seen the price Charles had paid every time he was wrenched away from his home and dragged to London. Miranda was used to a simpler country life and Jeremy knew they would both happily settle in at Alverstone when they were married.

He was pleased rather than horrified at Miranda's obvious enjoyment of intellectual conversation. Knowing her as well as he did, however, he was sure she was worried about his reactions. He would, no doubt, need to reassure her that she was all he wanted in a wife. As his countess, she would have certain expectations placed upon her and certain duties to fulfill that would curtail her freedom, but she would be able to assume these new responsibilities without too great a loss of her earlier freedom.

Lady Whitford had also watched Miranda closely all evening and was satisfied that she had felt enough discomfort and awareness of her inappropriateness. Things, as far as she could see, were proceeding according to plan. Jeremy, however, looked not at all disturbed, and she worried about that. All in all, however, she considered the evening a success. As did Nora. And also the viscount, but for quite different reasons.

10

The week after the dinner was uneventful for both families. Lavinia was occupied with her packing and sorting for the visit to Sam's and then their return home. Jeremy continued his old pattern of visiting Hampstead at least every other day, and Sam was busy tying up all the loose ends in town before returning home.

On his first visit to the Dillons after the dinner dance, Jeremy and Miranda went off for a walk through the village, leaving Nora behind to work on her latest heroine's dilemmas. As they made their way down Well Walk, Jeremy noticed that Miranda was quieter than usual.

"Is something wrong, Miranda? You seem not your usual self."

"To tell the truth, Jeremy, although I enjoyed myself the other night, I came home worried about us . . . about you."

Jeremy waited, for he wanted Miranda to speak her worries first. Although he thought he knew what was bothering her, he did not want to anticipate.

"Jeremy . . ." Miranda stopped, and letting go of his hand, stood and faced him. "Are you quite sure after the other night that you wish to marry me? I had never realized how many lovely girls you have to choose from, girls who share the same background and who come from better families. They all seem to know just how to go about in society. I realized too late, I'm afraid, that young ladies do not discuss politics or art, but fashion and music or the latest gossip. Why, Jeremy, it would take me years just to learn who is who in the *ton*, in order to appreciate the *on-dits*!" Miranda was smiling as she said this, but her eyes were shining with tears.

Jeremy grasped her shoulders and shook her gently before he pulled her head down on his shoulder. "Listen, peagoose," he whispered lovingly as she let herself cry a little of her anxiety out, "I don't want to hear nothing but gossip from my wife. I love you because you don't resemble any of those young ladies, not in spite of it. I only worry that you will change your mind because you don't want to be bored by the duties imposed on you as my countess. For we will have to socialize, you know."

"Oh, Jeremy, I was not so much bored as worried that I would disappoint you."

Jeremy lifted his eyebrows.

"Well, maybe a little bored at times." She smiled. "Certainly not with the marquess and Anne. But no other lady talked at length with a gentleman as I did."

"My dear, you don't have to apologize. The marquess is quite jealous, and complimented me on finding one of the loveliest and liveliest young ladies in or around London. He is my closest friend and I was happy to see you so obviously at ease together. And you will find that my other friends, taken in twos and threes instead of in a crowd like that, are quite able to carry on an intelligent conversation," he teased.

"I am not meaning to be critical, Jeremy. It is just I am so used to a different way of living that I cannot imagine what it would be like to have wealth and position, and I'm not quite sure I want it."

"Even if I come along with it?" Jeremy asked his question lightly, albeit with some trepidation.

"Oh, I know I want you," replied Miranda, so warmly and openly that his heart went back to its regular beat. "Only I am beginning to see that love, in itself, does not resolve all problems."

"It may not level all of the differences between us, but it will surely help us negotiate them. And while there are differences, they will not always loom as large as they did the other night. You know I prefer the country, as you do, and you will discover more friendly faces among the crowds. And I do not want you to change, nor to change your life, more than is necessary. But it will be different, you know that, my dear?" Jeremy concluded.

"Yes, I am beginning to realize how much. But if you truly don't want me different, or want someone else entirely, I am willing to do the best I can."

Jeremy leaned down to her pale face and brushed her lips
gently with his. Her arms went quite naturally around his neck
and they found themselves caught up in one of those kisses that
neither wanted to pull away from. Jeremy detached himself first
and said, a bit raggedly, "These kisses are getting longer and
longer and harder to end. I think this betrothal must become
public soon. I want to announce it now and marry you within
a week. I'm not sure I can last the summer."

"Me either," said Miranda shyly, as they reluctantly turned
back to High Street.

Nora watched Jeremy and Miranda closely that week, but saw
no signs, after his first visit, that any rift had been created. They
had started out as good friends, and that friendship seemed not
left behind with the development of romance, but only
strengthened by the addition of desire. And desire was there,
however they were either unaware of it or keeping it private,
thought Nora. The charged atmosphere when they were together
was unmistakable and reminded her of moments she thought
she had forgotten.

She succeeded in hiding her concern for Miranda and Jeremy,
but she had to talk to someone. Miranda could not marry the
Earl of Alverstone, and the more Nora was convinced their
feelings for one another were not merely infatuation, the more
anxious she became. She loved Miranda more than anything
on earth, and was coming to love Jeremy. She wanted neither
of them hurt, and yet they would be hurt. If they did not
back out of their betrothal by the end of the house party, then
she would have to forbid Jeremy Miranda's company. Neither
would understand, for she could give them no reason. And then
it would be terrible to live with what she had done, and perhaps
impossible to live with Miranda.

One afternoon, after the viscount's invitation had arrived and
Miranda had blushed with pleasure and anticipation of two full
weeks in Jeremy's company, Nora could stand the strain no
longer. She had spent two hours trying to get her Lady Cordelia
out of the clutches of one nobleman and into the arms of another,
without success. The silly woman persisted in her attraction to
the wicked Lord Soames, no matter what Nora did. Of course,
a rake could be irresistible at the beginning of a story, but not

at the end. Cordelia must be brought to see the error of her ways *before* she ran way with him and ruined herself. Only Cordelia was naive, trusting, and passionate, so how was Nora to save her from her fall?

As no one could have saved me, she thought in despair. And now look where it has brought me.

She grabbed her cloak, for it was a gray day and spitting rain, and walked down the High Street to Holly Bush. She knew Joanna was probably working, but she had to talk to someone who knew her and cared about her or she would go mad with worry and guilt.

"Miss Baillie has just finished work for the day and is having tea in the morning room." The housekeeper smiled. "She will be pleased to see you."

"Thank you, Mary. I can find my own way."

Nora knocked lightly on the open door to announce herself. Her friend was standing at the French windows overlooking the garden and horseshoe drive. She turned and smiled when she recognized Nora.

"What a delightful surprise. Come in and join me for tea, dear."

"I am glad it is only your tea I am disturbing, Joanna, and not your work. For I confess I would have come, no matter."

"But what is wrong? You look distraught. Come, sit down here and tell me what is bothering you."

Nora sat down next to Joanna and was tempted, for a minute, to bury her head in Joanna's lap and cry all the tears she'd been holding in since Miranda announced her betrothal. Joanna had been something of a mother figure for years, but Nora was afraid if she started to cry, she would never stop. For years she had worked toward independence, her ability to support herself and her daughter. It looked to outsiders like it came naturally. And the mothering certainly had. But the independence had been dearly bought, and had never felt completely achieved. She was afraid the whole carefully built structure of her life would collapse if someone even looked at her with affection. So she got up suddenly and started pacing the carpet. Joanna waited quietly.

"You know my story, Joanna, but no one else does, not even Miranda."

"Yes."

"I think I was wrong about Miranda and Jeremy. I pray I am not, but if I am, then I will have to forbid their marriage."

"Are you quite sure that is necessary?"

"Joanna, she cannot marry the Earl of Alverstone. Or anyone of that rank. She is illegitimate; you know that. I cannot believe this has happened," Nora continued, so obviously distraught that Joanna had a hard time keeping silent. "I stayed here because it was a good place to raise a child. And a safe place. I knew that she would meet someone someday, but here, it would be someone to whom birth was no consequence. There are so many writers and artists who flock here, I thought it likely she'd fall in love with someone from a similar background."

"And would you have told this imaginary artist or editor the circumstances of her birth?"

Nora turned and faced her friend. "No. I know that is wrong, but I would not have felt wrong deceiving someone who was her social equal. Can you understand that, Joanna?"

"Oh, I can understand, dear, but I confess I am a bit amused."

"Amused!" Nora stated, indignantly.

"Yes, for in family background Miranda is more Jeremy's equal than this imaginary suitor's. You are, after all, the daughter of a marquess."

"I know this sounds silly, Joanna, but I never think of that. And quite understandably, since my family disowned me."

"You are not sure."

"My father never replied to my letter asking him if I could come home."

"And, as I have more than once suggested, he may not have received that letter. Or was away when it arrived. And even if his first response was anger, I'll never believe he would have turned you from his door."

"I'll never know the answer," said Nora, "for too many years have gone by for me to go home, even if I wanted to."

Oh, you want to, thought her friend, if you will not admit it to yourself. But you are too proud and too scared. And have to leave that young girl who ran away in the moonlight behind, in order to survive, thought Joanna, wanting with her writer's mind to end the story happily, returning the prodigal daughter to her home, but realizing that life was quite different from fiction.

"If you would be willing to deceive a poor writer, why not Jeremy's family? You have lived here safely for years. They would never find out the truth."

"But I would know I let my daughter marry into a situation where, if the truth were ever discovered, she would be despised. And despise me, and perhaps herself. An earl does not marry a bastard, not to put too fine a point on it, Joanna, and I care for Jeremy enough not to trick him into a marriage he would never have contracted had he known the truth."

"You have more scruples than you can afford, Nora, but I love you for them, for without that sense of integrity, you would not be yourself."

"Thank you for understanding, Joanna. But what shall I do if they do not break off this engagement?"

"You will have to tell Miranda the truth and let her make her own decision. She is almost a grown woman, and she has matured even in the last few months."

"But then I will lose her, Joanna," and the older woman could not bear the agony in Nora's eyes. "She will hate me for ruining her life. How could I have kept this from happening? How could I have foreseen it, when I chose some moments of love over respectability? She will never understand why I did it, why we did not marry immediately."

Nora was lost to her present dilemma, and back in the past, wringing her hands and facing her past all over again. She had been in an awful situation, thought Joanna as she watched her begin pacing again. Yet she has raised a lovely young woman. Joanna got up and stood in front of Nora so she could walk no further. "Stop this, my dear friend. You cannot undo the past. You did the best you could. One cannot control everything, you know. It was not in your power to keep Miranda from running after that child, nor to keep Jeremy from meeting her. Life is like that, you know, full of surprises and beyond our control. Myself, I think you should keep silent no matter what happens, but I understand your scruples nevertheless. Go to this viscount's home and hope it is only calf love. And if it is not . . . well, you will do the right thing, whatever you do, for you are both honest and generous."

Nora took a long, shuddering breath and let herself be calmed by Joanna's common sense.

"You are right, Joanna. I am anticipating disaster. I'll concentrate on that dratted Cordelia and how to keep her away from Lord Soames, and let real life take care of itself for the next few weeks."

"When do you leave?"

"The day after tomorrow."

"If you need me at all before then, I am here, you know."

"Yes, and I cannot thank you enough."

Joanna smiled. "Now, let us sit down and not let these biscuits go to waste."

11

The viscount's estate was between Bury and Arundel. He had inherited one of the family's smaller properties, and despite his frequent travels, he made sure the manor house was kept in good repair and that his tenants were well-treated. Now that he had been fairly settled for the last few years, he was in residence as often as possible.

The viscount had escorted the Dillons, for Lavinia was not able to accomplish her packing by the time Sam wished to leave. The Dillons traveled in his chaise, and he rode next to them. It was a long drive south, so they had been ready before dawn, and slept for the first few hours of the journey. But after a brief stop at an inn midway, to rest the horses and to stretch their legs, both Nora and Miranda were wide-awake and very much interested in the landscape. Nora was able to keep her worries at a distance in the excitement of being on the road. She had not traveled out of Hampstead except to London, and had not been south of Chelsea for years. The rolling downs of Sussex were lovely and very different from the wilder moors of Northumberland and Scotland. She decided that, fall where things may, she might as well enjoy herself, and the tense look about her mouth relaxed.

The viscount joined them in the chaise for a few hours after luncheon, and enjoyed pointing out several landmarks. Since it was close to midsummer night, they had the light till early evening, and even when Sam returned to his horse, they were able to watch the sea-mist-green fields roll by.

"I would like to push on, and have dinner at Fairlawn, late though it will be. Can you ladies stand the wait? We have enough light now, but if we stop for a meal, it will be dark when we come out."

The two women were happy to push on and end the journey

sooner rather than later. They had looked their fill and both closed their eyes and were fast asleep soon after they knew no stops would be made. It was Nora who awoke first when the chaise slowed and the viscount lightly knocked on the window.

"We are passing by Sutton now," he said, "which means we are not far from Fairlawn . . . I thought you might want a little time to freshen up."

Nora smiled sleepily and nudged Miranda awake. Both women shook out their dresses and smoothed their hair.

"Do you see that road off to our right?"

Nora and Miranda saw a long avenue of lime trees.

"That is the entrance to the Duke of Sutton's estate. His grace and the duchess have been invited to join us for a few days later in the week. I think you will enjoy their company."

Nora was too tired to absorb this information. It had grown cooler, and she could smell the sea. "How far are we now?"

"Only a few miles."

"And how far are we from the sea? I smell it in the air!"

"Yes, I always know I am close to home when I smell that." Sam smiled. "We are only about ten miles from Littlehampton. I am hoping for an outing while you are here."

"I would love that," Nora said. "I have not been to the shore since I was fifteen, and the coast here must be very different from the north."

Fairlawn sat on a hill facing east, and as they drove up, the sun had set behind it, leaving the front in shadow and lighting up the side windows as if they were made of gold. It was a small Georgian mansion with a circular drive, and they pulled right up in front of the door. Miranda and Nora were a bit overcome. If this was a "small estate," then what would Alverstone look like? they wondered.

The housekeeper greeted them warmly and led them up to their rooms, where she had hot baths and a light supper waiting. The two women were so happy to be out of the chaise and so eager to bathe that they almost forgot to bid good night to their host.

He smiled understandingly as Nora turned in the middle of the stairs to thank him for his escort.

"Never mind, Mrs. Dillon. I will see you in the morning. Sleep in if you wish. I am usually up for an early-morning ride

before breakfast, but there will be servants in the morning room
until ten.''

Nora awoke early the next morning as the sun poured through
her light muslin curtains. She had forgotten to pull the draperies
over them, but since she was usually an early riser, she did not
mind. She and Miranda were in adjoining rooms with a connect-
ing door, and she peeked in, knowing that she would find her
daughter still asleep, since Miranda tended to be more wide-
awake after nine P.M. and to sleep late in the morning. She was
happy to let her sleep, and dressed quickly. Her own routine
was to breakfast early, write for a few hours, and then take some
exercise.

The viscount was there at breakfast when she came down.
He was obviously surprised to see anyone up this early.

"I hope I do not disturb you, my lord?"

"Not at all. I am merely surprised to see you up after such
a tiring day as yesterday," Sam replied. "Is Miranda up also?"

"Oh, no." Nora smiled. "I am the early bird in our household."

"Well, please help yourself to eggs and ham and cereal. It
is all there on the sideboard. I usually serve myself in the
mornings," he added apologetically, "and did not think to have
a footman ready till later for you."

"I assure you, I am quite used to serving myself breakfast,"
said Nora. "And cooking it too. I have become quite accustomed
to living without servants, you know."

Sam filed that remark away. If Mrs. Dillon had *become*
accustomed to doing without servants, then did that mean that
she had once been waited on? She gave so little information
about her past that Sam was intrigued and certain there was a
small mystery involved.

"Do you ride, Mrs. Dillon? If you would like to join me
tomorrow, I can pick out a mount for you."

Nora's face lit up at the prospect before she realized that
accepting the offer was quite out of the question. She had not
ridden in over eighteen years, and of course had no habit.

"I am afraid I have not been on a horse for many years, my
lord, and I could hardly ride in my morning gown," she said

with such regret that Sam was determined to have her on horse-back in the next few days.

"Let me see if I can remedy that," replied the viscount. "There are trunks of old clothes in the attic and I will set Nellie the task of digging through them. I'm sure there must be a habit or two—outmoded, of course, but that would fit you and Miranda."

"As much as I would love to ride again, I am not sure I should," Nora said. "It is almost easier to do without than to have a little taste of pleasure, knowing it is only for a short while," she said wistfully.

Sam was sure, from this simple statement, that this was the way Mrs. Dillon had survived: not by rationing luxuries, but by doing without them altogether. He felt a sudden desire to give her something, anything, to make up for her years of deprivation, and determined that whatever happened between Jeremy and Miranda, he would see that she could ride whenever she wanted, even after she returned to Hampstead.

"If Miranda married Jeremy, then you both would have every opportunity to ride," Sam said, curious to get her reaction.

Nora looked up from her eggs and toast to see, if she could, what lay behind that statement.

"But Miranda will not marry Jeremy," she said quietly, unable to fathom Sam's expression. "That is what we are here for, isn't it, to convince them their marriage would never work?"

"But what if it convinces them of the very opposite? Have you thought of that possibility, Mrs. Dillon?"

Of little else, thought Nora. "If that happens, then I will forbid Miranda Jeremy's company," she replied.

Although it was what she had been saying all along, Sam was surprised. If her daughter's heart was truly given and Jeremy's also, what reason could she have for such a harsh step? Her objections on the basis of age did not make sense either. She could ask for a longer betrothal, surely, so Miranda had time to mature, rather than severing all ties. And if, as Sam was beginning to suspect, the bond between the two young people was genuine and strong, then such an extreme response could send them off to Gretna.

"And if you cost Jeremy and your daughter their happiness?" asked the viscount.

"It would cost far more if they ever married," replied Nora. Knowing she had said too much and wishing to distract the viscount, she said quickly that she had changed her mind and would like to try riding again, and would seek out the house-keeper herself and help her search the attic trunks.

Sam had no choice but to let the subject drop. He was not willing to push her further, but knew, from her vehemence, there was some other, more serious reason for her objections to the match than age or difference in station. He found himself wishing he could win her trust and get her to share her burden with him, to let someone help her for a change, instead of shouldering it all herself. Perhaps this little house party had been a good idea for more reasons than the original one, he thought as he wiped his mouth with his napkin, pushed his chair from the table, and excused himself.

Nora happily let him go. She was determined not to let the viscount push her toward revealing any more than she had already. He was so genuinely friendly that it was difficult to go against her own tendency to be open with people. She had liked him almost from the beginning, and found herself attracted to him. He was quite tall, and a bit thin, and his face was interesting, with light blue eyes a startling contrast to his dark complexion. And his springy black hair looked like it would . . . Nora caught herself up short. She did not want to wonder what his hair might feel like, or to notice him at all as a man. He was someone who was being kind and hospitable under difficult circumstances, but they would never see each other again after these two weeks.

She finished her breakfast and went back to her room, ready to wrestle with Cordelia and Lord Soames, which would, she hoped, keep her from dwelling on another lord.

12

It was due to luck that Nora had gotten some work done in the morning, for Lady Whitford and Jeremy arrived that afternoon and the household was at sixes and sevens, as the viscount's servants got her settled. Nora was able to pull Nellie aside for a moment and mention the viscount's suggestion. The housekeeper smiled and said they could meet at the attic stairs when Lady Lavinia was taking her nap, and she was sure there would be suitable habits in one of the trunks.

And there were. Although both were outmoded, she and Nellie found two broadcloth habits, quite simple, with none of the frogs and epaulets of the modern style. The dark blue could be altered for Miranda, and the black fitted Nora almost as though it had been made for her. Nellie was sure that they could be aired and pressed and altered by the next afternoon.

Dinner that evening was a bit strained, since Lavnina was tired and therefore at her most annoying. She could not ignore their guests, but she certainly kept them ill-at-ease, with her complaints about the long journey for such a short visit, and her reminders that she and Jeremy would need to unsettle themselves again when they returned home. The fact that Alverstone was only ten miles away and that they would have been making a journey from London anyway was one that Sam wished to point out, but decided, from long experience, that it was easier to let Lavinia get all her irritation out, no matter how unpleasant. After dinner, he suggested a few hands of whist, not wanting to burden the Dillons with Lavinia the first evening. He volunteered to watch, but Nora immediately said, "I am a very frustrating partner, as Miranda will attest, my lord. I tend to get distracted and start throwing away my trumps rather recklessly."

"I must warn you that she is not merely being polite."

Miranda grinned. "I would be happy to have you as a player, my lord."

"All right, for this time, but I must insist that you play on another occasion, Mrs. Dillon."

"You will regret it, but I promise. And now, if you will just point out the way to the library, I will, with your permission, find a book for this evening."

The viscount escorted Nora, and lit the candles in the library himself. She was delighted with his overflowing shelves and assured him that she would be happy for hours, so he returned to the card room. Miranda was no woolgatherer like her mother, and he and she were soon joking together like old friends as they proceeded to win one rubber after another.

"That is enough," protested Jeremy after an hour and a half. "We yield, don't we, Mother?"

"I am too tired to attempt a comeback," replied Lavinia, in a far more relaxed tone than anyone had heard from her all day. "I think that I am off to bed." She excused herself, and the viscount looked at Jeremy and Miranda, who looked not tired at all. Ah, youth, he groaned to himself.

"I am going to see if your mother was able to find something in the library. And then, I think, it is time for us all to retire, for I understand you have a riding lesson, young lady?"

Miranda smiled in anticipation, and Jeremy waited impatiently for Sam to leave so he could pull Miranda down on the sofa with him. They were drawn immediately into an almost involuntary embrace. Miranda pulled back first. "The viscount will be returning, Jeremy."

"I know," he groaned. "I was so looking forward to these two weeks, but now I realize we will be able to snatch only a few moments alone together."

"Perhaps that is all to the good," Miranda said, blushing a little.

"You are probably right, but I cannot wait until we are officially engaged."

"Are you certain, Jeremy?" Miranda asked seriously.

"About what?" he asked, surprised at her tone.

"About an official betrothal. If this is what is described as a small estate, I shudder to think what Alverstone must be. Neither mother nor I am used to any of this: servants, housekeepers, libraries, and stables and . . ." Miranda waved her hand in an arc to sum up all the rest. "How can I become a countess and run a household larger than this? It quite terrifies me."

"I would be there to help and support you, and once you become a bit used to it, you will make a wonderful countess. I truly have no doubts at all, Miranda."

"Then I will try to ignore mine."

When Sam arrived at the library, he expected to find Mrs. Dillon engrossed in a novel, or perhaps already gone up to her room. What he had not anticipated was that he would come upon her curled up in the corner of the leather sofa, sound asleep, her book in her lap. She looked very young, he thought, relaxed and vulnerable, and he was tempted to lift her and carry her up to bed, as he might have done with Miranda. She must have dozed off just before he came in, for she stirred as if she felt his eyes on her, and opened hers, which were glazed with fatigue.

"Oh, dear, did I fall asleep?"

"Whatever book you chose must not have been too stimulating." Sam smiled down at her, and she immediately became conscious that her feet were tucked under her, her dress rucked up, and her hair, no doubt, all over the place. She sat up, and put her stockinged feet on the floor, searching with her toes for her slippers, and smoothing her dress.

"No, no, it was not the book, but the hour. I keep quite early hours at home, my lord, and am used to reading myself to sleep in bed. I must have done just that here. I apologize."

"No need, Mrs. Dillon," said Sam, offering his hand, "but we should get back, for I have left Miranda and Jeremy alone for a few moments, and although we can be rather informal in the country, I would not want the servants gossiping."

"Of course not." Nora could not find her left slipper, however, and in her embarrassed fumblings, had sent it under the couch. Now she could not reach it.

"Let me, Mrs. Dillon," said the viscount, smiling to himself as he realized her predicament.

"No, no, I can get it. You don't have to get down on your hands and knees, my lord." They both found themselves down on the floor in front of the couch at the same time, reaching for the slipper. Nora got her hand on it first, but not before she had brushed his. The shock was electric, and she stood suddenly, like a jumping jack, leaving him on his hands and knees, watching her shaking hands replace her slipper and admiring her trim ankles.

She was almost out the door before he caught up with her.

"Do you ever let anyone do anything for you, Mrs. Dillon, or are you always so self-sufficient?"

Nora was confused by her reaction to him, and by her realization that any other woman would have let him do that small service of retrieving a slipper. What did that mean about her, if she could never let anyone help her?

"I have become used to it, I guess," she replied, her voice shaky. Sam saw that he had upset her in some elemental way by his teasing words, and followed her thoughtfully down the hall.

13

The next afternoon, the viscount had two of the gentlest horses in his stable saddled and Miranda had her first riding lesson. Nora, who was following behind her, beginning to feel at home again on a horse, marveled at her daughter. She seemed to have a natural seat and sense of balance, and very little fear after the first few minutes.

Miranda went back after an hour, accompanied by Jeremy and the viscount, and Nora decided to continue with the countess. After a gentle canter down a tree-lined lane, the two women pulled their horses up and gave each other the first natural smiles since they had met.

Nora was prompted by the moment of friendliness to say:

"Lady Whitford, I know you are not happy with the present circumstances and I know you were not sure letting Jeremy and Miranda be together was the right way to handle them. I wanted to tell you I appreciate your willingness to have us here."

"It is the viscount's hospitality you are enjoying, Mrs. Dillon," Lavinia answered.

"Yes, but you might have kept away."

"But I was convinced, although I admit I had my doubts at the beginning, that forbidding the betrothal would be the best way to intensify the attachment."

"And I still believe that myself," Nora said with a sigh, "but I am not sure I see any signs they are having second thoughts. Miranda has spoken to me about her fears that she could never manage a household the size of Fairlawn, let alone Alverstone. But she said Jeremy had convinced her she would make a fine countess." Nora smiled ruefully.

"I must tell you, Mrs. Dillon, that before I met you and your daughter, I was convinced you could be nothing but vulgar fortune-hunters. But although I am still opposed to the match,

104

it is only because of the differences in station. Miranda is a lovely girl, and you can be proud of her. But she is not the wife I want for my son,'' Lavinia finished, almost apologetically.

"I appreciate your plain speaking, Lady Whitford. And I stayed to ride with you precisely so I could reassure you, as I have the viscount, that a wedding will never take place. Should Miranda and Jeremy not end their betrothal, I will forbid it. I agree with you. The Earl of Alverstone could never marry an unknown.''

Lavinia should have been pleased, but as they kicked their horses into a slow trot, making further conversation difficult, she had to admit she was beginning to feel some sympathy for the young lovers. Miranda was lovely, and one would never have guessed she was not wellborn. It was a shame, she thought to herself, she is not from a good family, for I would not have minded her as a daughter-in-law were things different. Lavinia smiled at herself at this about-face. Mrs. Dillon most certainly seemed sincere about her intentions to forbid Miranda Jeremy's company, and provided with that assurance, Lavinia was able to relax her own objections and imagine what might have been. Well, we must have been right to begin with, she realized, if such categorical statements make one immediately consider the opposite possibilities.

The two women returned home almost in charity with one another, and certainly without the tension that had been present in their first two encounters. Lady Lavinia, having rested and ridden, two of her favorite occupations, was her most charming self at the dinner table. And she is charming, thought Sam, remembering his *tendre* for her. Nora caught the look on his face and wondered if the viscount's devotion to Jeremy's interest came from a devotion to his mother. She felt a pang of something like jealousy, but dismissed it so quickly that she gave herself no time to examine it or wonder why she should feel jealous of the countess.

The next day, the riding lesson was in the morning, for the duke and his family were to arrive for luncheon. Miranda rode in the paddock only, so Jeremy could correct her seat, her hands on the reins. "Everything,'' she said despairingly, "I'm doing everything wrong.''

"No, no, you have wonderful balance, you are a natural rider, and will be quite accomplished in short order."

"Well, then, give me only one thing at a time to concentrate on, Jeremy, I can't keep it all in my mind at once," she replied with some asperity.

"I'm only trying to help," he said, with some justifiable annoyance.

"But you are 'helping' too much."

"If that's the way you feel, then I don't know how I am to teach you."

Sam, who was watching the lesson, tried to hide his grin as he stepped in.

"Jeremy, would you make sure the groom has cleaned out the right stalls for Simon's team? I will watch Miranda while you do."

"All right, but don't bother trying to help her, for she'll just ignore you," Jeremy grumbled as he stalked off.

Miranda pulled her mare up short, and watched him in amazement and anger.

"I didn't ignore him, my lord, truly, but he kept giving me ten directions at once, and I am, after all, only beginning. I never knew he could be so infuriating!"

"Well, I learned a long time ago never to try to teach anything to one you love." Sam smiled. "I think I had better take over the riding lessons. Now, let me see you go around once more."

By the time Jeremy had found the groom and discovered that "Of course everything is ready for 'is grace, m'lud," Miranda and Sam were walking back to the house. She was moving a bit stiffly, and Jeremy, grinning in sympathy, caught up with them.

"I say, Miranda, I am sorry for browbeating you."

Miranda smiled at him. "That is all right, Jeremy. The viscount and I decided he would take over the lessons to keep us friends."

"I remember your father and me vying for the privilege of teaching your mother to drive a pair. We had her in tears one day, until she finally got the Baron Blakeney to do it, leaving us behind." All three were laughing at Sam's reminiscence as they walked up to the house, and Nora, who was just coming down the stairs, was almost ready to declare her plan a fiasco, then and there.

14

The duke and his family arrived about an hour earlier than expected, and only Nora was around when the coach pulled up. She watched as a small woman, rather plain-looking, got out and lifted out a little girl. The child was about two, and had the palest of skin, and dark red curls. Nora guessed the small woman was the child's nurse and waited with some curiosity to see what the duke and duchess were like, but the only other person to step out of the coach was a tall, rangy man dressed comfortably in corduroy, who seemed to be looking off to the left of the house. Unless they had sent their servants ahead of them, this appeared to be the duke and duchess.

The duchess picked up her little girl, who had immediately squatted down to examine the stones in the driveway, and then gave her arm to her husband. As they moved up the stairs, Nora realized with as shock that the duke, who had been handed a cane by his groom, was using it as a guide to the height of the steps. The viscount had never mentioned the duke's blindness. Now, added to her trepidation about dealing with high-ranking intimates of the family was added the worry of how to act with a blind person.

She quickly realized she was the only one available. The viscount had ridden off on an errand, Lady Lavinia was having one of her many beauty naps, and Miranda and Jeremy were bathing and changing from the riding lesson. She could not let the duke and duchess go to their rooms without being greeted by someone other than a servant, so she went down the stairs to the front hall.

The duchess looked up at her, and then, with that extra sense that mothers have, turned to her daughter, who was just about to pop a bit of driveway gravel into her mouth.

"No, no, Sophy, give the pretty stones to Mama."

The child surrendered them happily and the duchess oohed and aahed over the treasures before she folded them up in her hand.

Nora walked right over to her and without thinking said, "How old is she? Just about two, I would guess, or she would not have surrendered so easily!"

The duchess smiled. "I have heard that the third year is a stormy one. You sound experienced, Mrs. . . . ?"

"Oh, goodness, I am sorry. I am Honora Dillon and am visiting with my daughter Miranda. I am afraid my experience with small children is way behind me," she replied wistfully.

"I am Judith Ballance, and this is my daughter Sophy, and my husband, Simon."

Nora turned to the duke, who had his hand extended. She shook it and said:

"I must apologize, your grace, for being the only one to greet you, but I believe the viscount was expecting you a bit later."

The duke smiled. "Yes, I know, but Sophy was up early this morning and we wanted to give her lunch and put her down for a rest before the adults sat down. We find ourselves following her schedule more often than not. I fear we are too indulgent, and we apologize."

"Not at all," Nora replied. "The viscount has ridden over to a tenant's, and everyone else is resting or recuperating from my daughter's riding lesson. Nellie, could you show the duke and duchess to their rooms," Nora said to the housekeeper, who had come up behind her.

Judith murmured her thanks and the family walked up the stairs slowly behind their daughter, who was ascending by herself, leading always with her left foot, thus slowing down the process even more. Nora remembered Miranda's insistence on climbing alone, and marveled at the couple's willingness to allow their daughter so much freedom. As soon as they got to the top, Nora hurried down the hall and knocked on Miranda's door.

"Come in, Mother. Was that a carriage I heard in the drive?"

"Yes, the duke and duchess are here."

"So early?"

"Yes, they seem to follow the little Lady Sophy's schedule! I suppose that is what one must call her," mused Nora, "Lady

Sophia, although they do not seem to be high in the instep.''

"What are they like?" Miranda asked nervously.

"The duchess is small and rather plain from a distance, although she is much more attractive close up. The duke is tall and quite good-looking . . . and blind," Nora added.

"Blind?"

"Yes. The viscount didn't tell us that, did he? But from the little I saw, they paid no heed to it. I would think the best way to go on would be to ignore it, unless it is necessary to do otherwise.''

Luncheon was quiet, and after introductions and a few moments of stiff politeness, it became clear it was not necessary to stand on ceremony with the duke and duchess. Lady Sophy was in bed. "For a few hours, if we are lucky," commented her mother, thus the duchess was able to give her attention to her meal and to her husband. Although, thought Nora, aside from a quiet description of the table and the location of food on his plate, there was no need to hover over him. It became increasingly clear that he was uncannily good at identifying speakers and looking at them as though he could see, and he had none of the mannerisms that Nora had seen in people blind from birth. She soon forgot about his limitations and found herself enjoying his conversation, which ranged from the weather and the state of the wheat to mutual acquaintances in Hampstead. The duke and duchess began discussing politics at one point, but Lavinia vetoed the topic immediately.

"I know you are eager to continue, but can we not have one meal with merely frivolous conversation?" she said lightly, and Nora caught a glimpse of the charmer she must have been twenty years ago. Simon apologized, and Sam promised that they would confine their talk to the library.

"Do you have a nurse for Lady Sophy, your grace?" Nora asked, intrigued by the fact that the duchess seemed to take responsibility for her daughter.

The duchess looked blank for a moment and then laughed. "Oh, dear," she confessed, "I wasn't sure of whom you were speaking. I am so unused to hearing her called by her title. Why, yes, we do have a nurse. But when we are at home, I tend to rely on her less than I do in town, when I am so much busier entertaining.''

"You are wise, I think, although perhaps not fashionable," Nora said, "to spend so much time with her now, for these early years go by so quickly. It seems such a short time ago Miranda was that age.''

The duchess agreed, and wondered to herself about Mrs. Dillon. There was something about her that suggested she came of a good family, and yet, as the viscount had described her in his letter of invitation, she was only the widow of a naval lieutenant. It will be an interesting visit, Judith thought.

After the first day, it was clear the house party was to be successful. Depending, of course, on one's definition of success, thought Sam ironically. Mrs. Dillon and Miranda became quite comfortable with Simon and Judith. They rode and picnicked and entertained some of the viscount's neighbors. Jeremy and Miranda were getting on famously, and Miranda became more and more comfortable with the size of the house. Judith was partly responsible for this, for she and Miranda became quite friendly. Although the duchess and Nora had motherhood as a common bond, Miranda and Judith were closer in age, and had similar futures in front of them. Nora found herself drawn into conversation with the viscount and the duke. It was clear they were political allies, and their views were close to hers. And the duke had quite won her heart after dinner one night when he said he'd heard she was a novelist.

"Yes, your grace."

"Would I have come across one of your works, do you think? My wife and I are avid readers, you know. Do you write under your own name?''

"Yes, although at one time I was tempted to become 'Artemis Meade.' ''

Simon could not help himself. He laughed out loud and then immediately apologized. "I am sorry, Mrs. Dillon, but from the little I know of you, 'Honora Dillon' fits you better than 'Artemis Meade.' But I know many authors use pseudonyms.''

The duke's comment reminded her that "Honora Dillon" was also a pseudonym, and she was silent for a moment.

"You are not offended?" Simon asked anxiously.

"Oh, no, your grace. And since my novels are of the Minerva Press variety, I doubt you and the duchess have read them."

"Ah, a writer of romance, then? Well, we have an expert on romance in our household, Mrs. Dillon. My reader, Mr. Wiggins, devours them. I will have to ask him about you when we return to London. I understand you have met quite a few literary well-knowns. My wife and I would love to hear your views on them. We envy you your literary life," Simon said, and Nora could tell he was uttering only a slight exaggeration of the truth. It was clear that the duke and duchess had a real love for literature, and would probably enjoy a literary evening over a ball.

The duke and Nora found time for many such conversations, for when out riding, he tended to keep her company.

"I know what it is like to be a slow-top," he joked.

"I hate to hold the rest back, but I have not ridden for so long that I wish to start slowly. Of course, my daughter has not ridden before at all, and there she is, outriding her mother," Nora said with great pride mixed with a bit of jealousy. "But do not feel you have to stay back with me."

"I do not mind in the least," replied Simon, and she knew he was speaking the truth, "as long as you do not mind the lead line?"

"Of course not. If I am not being too forward, have you always been blind, your grace?"

"No, only for the past three years. It happened at Waterloo," Simon replied quite naturally.

"I am sorry. I shouldn't have asked."

"Not at all. It is natural to be curious, and I would rather have people be straightforward with me than pretend they haven't noticed at all."

15

Nora not only admired the duke for his independence but also had come to want him for a friend. She found herself wishing she did not have to separate Miranda and Jeremy; that the two families might continue to see one another, and perhaps occasionally socialize with the duke and duchess. She had not that many friends near her own age. Joanna was a dear, but was more like an aunt or a mother. The younger women of Hampstead were acquaintances, for despite Nora's willingness to overlook class differences, they were, she knew, very real. Bess Barker, the village woman to whom she was closest, was a good friend, but the only interests they shared were to do with the raising of children. Nora's work meant spending hours alone, and when she was eager and free for a walk or a conversation over tea, Bess was helping her husband in the tavern or keeping one of their four boys in line. So these evenings spent in animated conversation on topics ranging from emigration to Mr. Scott's latest novel were nourishment to Nora's starved spirit.

Of course, with Lady Sophy around, child-rearing was bound to be a topic of conversation. Nora admired the duke and duchess as parents. Although they let the viscount's housekeeper act as a nurse when needed, the duchess was more likely to skip a ride, if Sophy awakened early from a nap, than leave her with Nellie.

The relationship between the father and daughter was quite touching. Simon had infinite patience with her and let her pull him here and there, despite the fact that he often ended up barking his shins or banging his head.

She was at the stage where she wanted to know what everything was, and would point or bring things to her mother or father, asking "Dis? Mama?" waiting for the name of the object. She seemed to know that she could not just point with her father, and would bring him things to feel, and wait patiently while the duke ran his hands around a pebble or sniffed a flower.

Sam was enjoying the visitors also. As he had hoped, the duke and duchess were able to put all the members of the party at ease. The viscount, who was older than the duke, had gotten to know him well in the past two years through their political alliance, and the two had gone from being acquaintances to fast friends despite the disparity in age and experience. Even Lavinia had relaxed, and in one private conversation had admitted to Sam that against her will she was beginning to ponder if Miranda would be such a bad match for Jeremy. "Perhaps there is some way, if they still seem sure at the end of the summer, to *create* a background for Mrs. Dillon?"

Sam laughed. "Lavinia, you never fail to surprise and delight me." She looked at him, nonplussed. "Here you are, on one hand, softening from your position, and on the other, trying to concoct some romantic story about Nora's . . . I mean Mrs. Dillon's past."

"Well, you must admit there is some mystery there," Lavinia replied huffily. "She is clearly a well-bred woman. Even I have to admit that. So what is she doing, living in Hampstead and writing novels for a living?"

"I don't know," Sam admitted. But I intend to find out, he continued to himself.

Sam had watched Miranda becoming more at ease, and Nora relaxing in the company of Simon and Judith. In fact, he found himself becoming less and less interested in Miranda and Jeremy; it was becoming clear they would probably make an excellent couple. Lavinia was becoming resigned, and despite her mysterious adamance, Nora would surely have to give in. So he quite often found himself watching Mrs. Dillon. As she held Sophy on her lap, he could see the young Miranda and Nora. She spoke as naturally and expertly to Simon on thumb-sucking as on the poems of Byron. She was winning over Lavinia without trying, was a wonderful counterbalance to his mother for Jeremy, and Sam realized he could very easily find himself falling in love with her.

One evening, well into the second week of the visit, they were all gathered in the drawing room. Most nights they talked or

played cards, but this evening Lavinia had wandered over to
the pianoforte and started to play. She was actually the only
one of the ladies who did play, an unusual fact, given that
women were expected to have a little music, but none of the
other women had had the time or money for lessons.

Lavinia played several etudes and then went into folk songs,
"for I have not heard you sing in such a long time, Sam, and
you have such a lovely baritone." Sam smiled down at her,
remembering evenings around the piano when Charles was still
alive. They all sang songs familiar to everyone, challenged each
other to remember every verse of "Barbara Allen," and then
Sam began to sing, letting Lavinia follow him, finding her way
after the first verse.

> The provost's daughter went a-walking one day
> Oh, but her love was easy won
> And she heard a Scots prisoner a-makin' his moan
> And she was the flower of Northumberland.

Sam was good at dialect, and rolling his R's, he continued
the story of the maiden who ran off to Scotland, only to be sent
back at the border by the man who had used her. It was a favorite
of his, and he quite forgot about the unsuitability of the subject
matter until he was halfway through, at which point it was too
late to do anything but pretend he had forgotten a few lines,
the ones where the lover referred to the lady as a "brazen-
faced hoor," and at the end apologized. "But for all that it is
crude, it is one of my favorites," declared the viscount, "for
the tune and because in this version the maiden is welcomed
back home. In too many of these ballads, the wronged maiden
kills herself!"

They all laughed except for Nora. Sam had not looked at her
directly while he was singing, for he had been concentrating
too hard. Now he noticed that her face was white and her eyes
suspiciously bright. As the others begged Lavinia for more,
Nora left the group and sat down in the corner. Sam immediately
followed and drew up a footstool next to her.

"Are you all right, Mrs. Dillon?"

As Nora looked up, Sam saw a tear rise and spill over. He

had almost put his hand out to brush it gently away when he realized what he was about to do.

"I thought it was a rather happy ending myself," he said, trying to tease her out of her sadness.

"Oh, but I know that song, and the story does not always end that way. In some versions, the parents are not as eager to welcome home the prodigal daughter." She stood up, visibly shaken, and said quietly, "I fear I am indisposed, my lord. Will you let me slip away this evening and give my excuses to the others?"

"I will never sing again if it affects you this strongly," Sam replied lightly, trying to get her to smile, and she did, fleetingly, before she went away, leaving him there puzzled and concerned.

Nora had not heard that song for years, and she was as taken aback by her own reaction as the viscount. At fourteen or fifteen she had heard it sung by an old ballad singer at a fair and had romantically imagined herself as that young girl whose love was "so easy won," just as she herself had imagined herself as Lady Margaret when hearing the story of Tam Lin. What a foolish young woman I was, indeed, she thought despairingly as she undressed and climbed into bed. But once she had blown the candles out and pulled the covers up, the song would not leave her, and she could only cry for that poor young maiden, knowing, of course, she was crying for herself.

16

Nora took breakfast in her room the next morning, since her face and her puffy eyes told all too well the story of the night before. She reassured Miranda that she was just tired, and sent her down for her ride. After the maid had removed the tray, she sat for a while, determined to face her dilemma. It was obvious Miranda and Jeremy were not in the throes of calf love, but quite committed to one another. Nora had had great hopes, after the visit to Hampstead, of Lady Whitford, but underneath her snobbery, there was a good-hearted woman who wished her son happy. Her manner had softened so much over the last two weeks that it was clear that, while she might yet protest the match, in the end she would give in. And the viscount? Nora was really rather annoyed with him. He seemed to have lost his hostility toward her and her daughter almost immediately, and had been acting in ways which could only encourage the connection. Why on earth did he have to invite such lovely people as the duke and duchess? They were unlikely to intimidate anyone, and it seemed the duchess herself, although of good background, had married above her station quite successfully. Well, there had always been a risk, thought Nora. And so I am left to forbid the official betrothal. Thank God we are leaving tomorrow.

When she finally dressed and went downstairs, she found everyone gone out, to her great relief, since she was not up to answering solicitous questions. She slipped out the French doors of the morning room into the small garden at the side of the house. Someone had planted informal herb beds, which reminded Nora of her own garden. She loved the wild look of the bergamot and spearmint and rue, riotously growing behind hip-high borders of lavender. As always, anything green soothed her, and she was lost in the heady scent around her as she walked

toward the stone bench at the end of the path. She was startled
to find she was not alone. The duke was sitting there already,
while Sophy played in the path, using twigs and stones to build
small houses peopled by iridescent dead beetles.

Simon looked up as he heard her approach, and Nora quickly
identified herself. The duke smiled as he heard her kneel down
and question Sophy about her house and her babies. The little
girl babbled away, and again Nora was caught by a memory
of her own Miranda, so happy and so good, playing the same
game on a dusty country road as they waited for the public coach
to bring them one more stage of their journey from Edinburgh.
Nora got up, and brushing her skirt off, sat next to Simon.

"I am always amazed at how well she can entertain herself," said the duke as he listened to his daughter's "conversations."

"Yes, I was just remembering Miranda at that age." Her
voice trembled, and Simon could hear the distress lying under
her polite response. She had left the group very early last night
and had not been down in the morning for the first time since
their arrival, and he wondered what could be troubling her.

"Sophy?"

"Yes, Papa?"

"Could you take your babies in to show Nellie?"

Sophy nodded, and Nora smiled at the thought of the housekeeper's response to three desiccated insects!

"Come, take Papa's hand, and Mrs. Dillon and I will bring
you to her."

Simon took Nora's arm and they walked back to the house,
where Nora rang for Nellie and saw Sophy safely in her charge.

"Thank you, Nellie," the duke said. "Now, Mrs. Dillon. . ."

"Nora, your grace."

"Oh, I may be informal, but you may not?" quizzed Simon.

"I am sorry, Simon. I am a little preoccupied this morning."

"Would you come for a walk with me? I did not want to ride
this morning, but I'd enjoy some exercise. Or were you seeking
privacy in the garden?"

"I would be delighted to accompany you, as long as it is not
too much of a ramble. I am really not dressed for the woods."

"I thought we could wander down the path at the back of
the house. That will only take us across lawn, as I recall."

They were quiet as they walked, commenting only upon the weather, until they reached the end of the path.

"I could spread my coat and we can rest from our exertion," Simon suggested.

"Oh, no, the grass is dry," Nora said. "And that was hardly a long walk for me."

"I was teasing, Nora," Simon replied gently, knowing that Nora must indeed be upset, since they were usually quick to respond to each other's joking.

They sat for a few moments in silence, and then Simon broke it.

"Something in your voice makes me think that you are upset. I don't mean to pry, but is there anything I can do to help?" Simon was not sure how, or indeed whether, to continue. He and Sam had had a long conversation, and he was well aware of the purpose of the Dillons' visit. He felt, from what he had come to know of them, that Jeremy and Lavinia would be very lucky to have them part of the family. Sam had mentioned Nora's objections, but surely such a loving mother would not, in the end, interfere with her daughter's happiness?

Nora had become so in the habit of shouldering her own burdens that she rarely experienced the desire to let them all go. But after watching Miranda and Jeremy for two weeks, not only did she realize it would be up to her to sever the connection, but that she might be hurting her daughter beyond repair. She had, with some success, pushed her concern to the back of her mind, and acted naturally. But last night had brought home to her what must happen, and she was unable to ignore the duty ahead of her. And she was also, it seemed, unable to handle it alone, for as soon as she heard the sympathy in Simon's voice, she started to cry.

"Oh, dear, I seem to have been crying the clock round," she sniffed.

"How can I help?" Simon asked.

"No one can, Simon. That is the problem. I am only reaping the results of a mistake I made years ago, and Miranda will be the one who suffers most. Oh, I tried so hard to protect her," she said despairingly. "How could I ever have foreseen this?"

"You must tell me," Simon said, struck by the depth of her feeling.

"Can I trust you? . . . Yes, I do feel that I can . . . but how could you ever understand?" Nora took a deep breath and became more coherent. "If I tell you my story, your grace, it must be kept a secret. I know you are a good friend of the viscount's, but no one must ever know of this. I shouldn't tell you . . . but I *must* talk to someone."

Simon reached out, found Nora's hands, and held them. "I promise that unless you give me leave, I will never repeat what you tell me."

"Did you listen to the song the viscount sang last night?"

"Yes," said Simon, wondering at this seeming change in direction.

"Well, I am that 'maiden.' Or rather, I *was* that maiden," said Nora with a tinge of bitterness in her voice. "When I was seventeen, I ran away with a handsome young Scotsman, just like the provost's daughter. Actually," she added with a strained humor, "he was a charming Irishman, but he lived in Scotland, and my love was 'easy won.' We were to be married at Gretna . . ."

"Of course," murmured Simon.

"Somehow, we never got there. We went directly to Edinburgh. We did not keep apart from one another, Simon," Nora said in a low voice. "And it was not Breen's fault. I was as much to blame. But I became pregnant . . ." Nora could feel Simon stiffen, and was almost unable to continue. "I am not Mrs. Nora Dillon, widow of a sailor, but Lady Honora Margaret Ashton, and Miranda is illegitimate. Now you know why she can never marry the Earl of Alverstone," and Nora pulled her hands out of Simon's and turned away.

Simon sat back, trying to absorb what he had just heard. The mystery was solved. Nora was indeed from a good family. But she was right. Illegitimate daughters did not usually marry into highborn families, no matter what their background. And yet, he thought, surprising himself, must it come out?

"And this man, Breen, is he really dead?"

"Oh, yes, he died in a tavern brawl after someone accused him of cheating at hazard. We were to have been married that week." Simon was silent and Nora continued.

"I am sure you have lost all respect for me, your grace, but when we eloped I loved him so much . . . and was . . . so physically drawn to him, that we seemed to be living in another world, one where it didn't matter whether one had said one's vows in public, if one had in private. And then we were in Edinburgh only a short time before he was killed.''

Nora's embarrassment at speaking about physical desire was palpable, and Simon, who knew gentlewomen were supposed to be passionless, yet reveled in the passionate nature of his own wife, knew not how to address the question. It was not a subject to be discussed, except in the privacy of the marriage bed. Or with a mistress, thought Simon inconsequentially.

''And when Breen was killed? Why did you not go home?''

''I wrote to my father and he never answered me. Breen's uncle and aunt helped me for a while, but I did not want to be too dependent so I took Miranda and came south. Hampstead seemed like a good place to bring up a child, and so I stayed.''

''How did you support yourself at first?''

''I had a very little I had kept for such an emergency. It got us to Hampstead. And then I worked as a barmaid.''

''Who watched Miranda?'' Simon asked, shocked to hear how difficult Nora's life had been.

''We were so lucky, Sam. The owner of one of the local taverns was understanding and his wife had two children of her own, so Miranda would play with them and sleep upstairs while I worked.''

''How did you manage to stand such a job?''

''Oh, I was young, and I had no other choice.''

''But didn't it leave you open to all kinds of . . .'' Simon wasn't sure how to continue.

''Offers? Of course. But one learns to laugh away drunken proposals. You are shocked, your grace?'' Nora asked somewhat coldly.

''No. Yes. Well, also utterly astounded by how much you have coped with.''

''I had to. I never thought much about it. I just did it. And Miranda . . . well, she was the joy of my life. I tell you, Simon, I have never for a moment, until now, regretted my choice, for I had her. And my regret now is not for me, but that I must bring heartbreak to her.''

Simon sat quietly, trying to absorb all he had heard. He *was* a little shocked at what she had revealed. He didn't know what he would have felt had it been Judith's story. Would he have married her had she been Nora, or Miranda? He thought not, although he was ashamed to admit it. *Am I that conventional?* he wondered. He thought back on the past week. There was nothing in either mother or daughter that was not fine, intelligent, and honest. If he hadn't heard this story, would he have objected? No. Now that he had? He still could not object.

"If Breen is dead, and no one knows your secret, then why not just let Miranda marry Jeremy?"

Nora looked at Simon in surprise. "Why, how *could* I let them, knowing what I know? If I didn't care about Jeremy . . . and his family, it would be different."

"What does Miranda think?"

"She doesn't know," Nora replied flatly.

"Nora, how can you forbid her marriage to Jeremy without telling her her history?"

"I can't. That is why I am so overset. She will hate me for causing her so much heartbreak." Nora knew if she let one more tear fall, she would never stop crying, so she sat there rigidly controlling her emotions.

"You are well-named 'Honora.' But as much as I admire honesty, I still believe it best in this situation to lie . . . or at least, not reveal the truth. I am surprised to hear myself say that, but as a friend of the family, and as, I hope, your friend, I cannot see the use in opening up the past."

"I must tell Miranda," replied Nora. "More and more I am convinced she has a right to know. She can then make her own decision, and I would abide by it."

"Tell me, Nora, if Jeremy were to agree to the marriage, having heard the truth from you or Miranda, would you feel honor-bound to tell anyone else?"

"I suppose it would be enough for me that *he* knew, since he is the one most closely concerned."

"Can I at least persuade you to give him a choice? To tell Miranda and Jeremy and see how he reacts?"

"All right, I will do that," Nora promised.

"Come, we had better get back before Sophy has exhausted Nellie," Simon joked. He stood up and reached his hand toward Nora. She took it and he pulled her up. He reached down and felt gently for her face, wiping away the traces of tears with his thumb. "I wish I could be more of help, Nora. You have had a hard enough time, without this."

"You have helped, Simon. I am relieved to have told someone."

Simon let her take his arm, and they walked slowly back to the house.

17

Simon was not the only one who had noticed Nora's absence from breakfast. The viscount had wondered whether she was truly tired, or upset by something. He was unusually quiet during their morning ride, although Miranda assured him that Nora was only tired and would be down by the time they returned.

The Dillons' visit was drawing to a close, and although Sam had not had much direct conversation with Lavinia, he knew she could be persuaded to the marriage. When they returned to London, he was prepared to let Jeremy place a notice in the *Post* and make the betrothal official. In fact, for his own reasons, he was happy to have Miranda brought into the family. It meant he would have reason and opportunity for seeing Nora on a regular basis.

He had laughed at himself, over the course of the visit, as he realized what was happening to him. Here he was, an old bachelor mothers had despaired of, who had been content to form a series of fairly long-termed alliances with available gentlewomen, falling in love with an unfashionable widow who was anything but dashing. He had long ago diagnosed the state of his heart: given once, years ago, in calf love, and afterward, disillusioned by his first *tendre,* kept protected and never fully given again, until now. He was not a cold man, and had had genuine affection for his mistresses, but not one had drawn from him the response Nora did.

He was feeling younger than Jeremy, as he watched himself hoping Nora admired his seat on a horse, or his intelligent and witty comments on politics. He had sung last night with great feeling, knowing his voice was good and hoping to impress her. Instead, he had, it seemed, driven her to bed!

She had shown no real signs of interest in him. But she seemed comfortable with him, which was a start. He sensed he would have to go slowly. The few times in the last two weeks he had offered to do the smallest service, she had refused, lightly, of course, but he felt a reserve and guardedness that went beyond independence.

He knew none of the details of her life, but it could not have been easy to support herself and her daughter. He wanted her to tell him her story. He wanted her to allow him to give to her. But he was nothing if not patient, and was willing to win her trust slowly.

Nora was not as indifferent to the viscount's presence as he thought, although she was certainly not in love with him. She *had* noticed how well he looked on a horse. In fact, she had been surprised that someone that tall had such a good seat on a horse. She had noticed the viscount's observations in their political and literary conversations. Simon was slow and detailed in his arguments, while Sam tended to sit quietly and then dazzle them with a comment that synthesized the whole discussion. Somehow that surprised her, and after she thought about it, she realized she associated wit and brilliance with physical attributes. She had taken Breen to be more intelligent than he was because of his good looks and charm. The viscount was not really handsome.

Yet she often found herself focusing on his long fingers and the battered signet ring he wore on his right hand. Once, when she had taken Sophy for a morning, saying it made her feel like a mother again, he had offered to carry the little girl upstairs for her nap. She had looked up to refuse him, and then quickly down again, at Sophy, half-asleep in her arms, for his offer to help had caused a melting sensation she refused to acknowledge.

She had met a few attractive men since Breen, but the feelings she had had for him were dead and buried long ago, or so she believed, until Sam had begun to sing. The old ballad made her remember the bittersweetness of that reckless passion, and opened the door to a room she had bolted long ago. Sam's voice, sweet and strong, took her by surprise, but she refused to attribute any of her feelings to the present. With Miranda's situation, it was natural she should start remembering. But that was all it was, memory. She had not found anything trustworthy in Breen, and she could not trust herself not to be deceived again by her own feelings. And so, whenever she found herself more conscious of the viscount's presence, or his humor or intelligence, she would immediately shift her attention to something else, thankful that after this visit she would never see him again.

The Dillons were to return to Hampstead in the viscount's coach, this time with only a groom to escort them. Nora would not hear of either Sam or Jeremy leaving just for them. Their thanks were given and their farewells made the night before, for they would leave early in the morning. Jeremy, of course, was up to see them off, as was the viscount. While the two young people stood murmuring on the steps, Sam lifted Nora into the coach.

"I am afraid our plan did not succeed," he observed, looking back at Jeremy and Miranda.

"Thanks to you, I believe," Nora replied tartly. "Why ever did you invite such a lovely and unassuming couple as the duke and duchess? We all had such a comfortable time together that Miranda and Jeremy are more than ever convinced their love will easily surmount their differences."

"And are you *not* convinced?" Sam asked. "I am, and when I talk to her, I am sure Lavinia will agree to the betrothal."

Nora paused. "Yes, I do think their love for one another is more mature than I first thought. But I have had my own reasons all along, and I will still forbid the marriage, my lord."

Sam's eyebrows lifted questioningly, but luckily for Nora, Miranda was almost to the coach and there was a flurry of goodbyes with no time for further conversation. The coach pulled off and both women looked back at the two men waving them off. Nora turned away first, although she was conscious of an unreasonable feeling of sadness. Of course I will miss Jeremy, was her reasoning, but she knew the feelings had as much to do with the fact that it was the last time she would see the viscount again.

18

Nora awoke the next day with a leaden feeling in the pit of her stomach. She could put if off no longer: this morning she must talk to Miranda, the sooner the better. This morning Miranda slept later than usual, so Nora was dressed and in her study by the time her daughter was up. She called out a greeting and asked Miranda to join her whenever she finished eating.

She was trembling by the time Miranda came in, looking charming in a dusty-pink wrapper, her eyes still sleepy and her face open and relaxed. How can I do this to her? Nora thought. But she had to.

"You wanted to speak with me, Mother?"

"Yes, Miranda, sit down." Nora was silent for a moment, unsure of how or where to begin. Finally she leaned forward and looked into her daughter's face intently.

"You know I love you more than anything else in the world, and I would do nothing willingly to hurt you?"

Miranda was taken aback by her mother's intensity. "Why, yes, of course, I know that," she replied slowly.

"You *are* going to be hurt by what I have to tell you—and you are perhaps going to hate me for it." Miranda's eyes widened, and her mother continued quietly.

"Miranda, you cannot marry Jeremy. Your father was not Harry Dillon, a lieutenant in the navy. There was no Lieutenant Dillon."

"I don't understand," whispered Miranda.

"When I was sixteen, my mother died. My father, the Marquess of Doverdale, brought home a new wife little more than a year after my mother's death. I was very lonely, Miranda, and my father seemed to have forgotten both my mother and me. The summer after he remarried, a young man called Dillon Breen came to Northumberland. He was visiting distant cousins, our neighbors, and I fell in love with him almost immediately. My father forbade the marriage and so we ran away together. To Scotland.''

"To get married?" questioned Miranda hopefully, unable to comprehend yet that her father was not the mythical navy hero.

"That was what we had planned. But it never happened.''

"Why not?" Miranda asked, almost harshly, as she began to realize what this meant to her.

"I was romantic, foolish, and thought that our exchange of loving promises in private was enough until we reached his family in Edinburgh. There, I was understood to *be* his wife. And then I discovered I was increasing.''

"Did you not wish your child to have a name?''

"Yes, Miranda, of course. But he was killed in an argument over a card game the week we were to have been married.''

"Why did you never return home?''

"I wrote to my father when Breen died, begging him to forgive me and asking him to take me in. He never replied.''

Miranda heard the break in Nora's voice. "And how did we come here?''

"After you were born, I took what little money I had put aside and came south. I thought we would be safe here. I never desired to enter society, and thought you might eventually meet someone to whom family would matter less than one of the *ton*. How could I ever have foreseen you would instead meet the Earl of Alverstone?''

Miranda was sitting very still, looking blindly in front of her. Not looking at Nora at all, she asked in a dead voice, "Does anyone else know of this?''

"Joanna, of course. And Simon.''

"The duke?''

"He saw me upset, and was so sympathetic that I had to tell him.''

"Why did you let me go to Sam's if you knew it was impossible? You let me believe we were betrothed!''

"Unofficially. You see, Jeremy's mother and godfather were against the marriage also. We feared a blunt refusal would cause you to do something reckless.''

"Like run off to Gretna," Miranda said, in a tone that Nora had never heard from her before.

"Yes. We hoped it was calf love, and if you were allowed to be together, you both would see the unsuitability of the attachment. Instead . . ."

"Instead, you saw we do know our own minds, are aware of the difficulties, and still wish to make our lives together. Oh, you know me very well, Mother. I was terrified at the party and at the viscount's. But I became less afraid. Judith helped me tremendously, for she married above her station also, and made me realize that it was possible. And Jeremy—he cares nothing for the difference in rank. But in truth," continued Miranda, "there *is* no difference in our positions. If you are truly the daughter of a marquess, then I am his granddaughter," she said wonderingly.

"The illegitimate granddaughter."

Miranda seemed to shrink from the words. "Why did you never tell me? Why did you have to tell me now?" she cried.

"You have to know the truth, my dear. I could not forbid the marriage and not give you the reason." Nora watched as her daughter rose, and turning a blank face to her, said: "Yes. Well, thank you, Mother, for telling me at last," and left the room. Never had Miranda looked like that. Nora sat paralyzed by her daughter's repudiaton, until she began to sob. Her tears came from a place deep inside, and she found herself on her knees, almost retching, as she knelt there crying for her daughter and herself.

When Nora finally finished crying, she stood up and half-consciously wandered out to the old apple tree in the garden. She sat down, back against the trunk, as she had many times before, as though leaning back into her mother's arms.

She awoke a few hours later, stiff and damp, and was struggling to her feet when she saw Miranda coming down the path. She could not see her daughter's face clearly and did not want to, if it still held the same expression. She gave Miranda enough time to get inside, and then, shaking her skirts out, she went in through the kitchen door, only to find her daughter pumping water for the teakettle. Nora could not bear to look up and was about to walk out the door and keep on walking until she could go no further, when her daughter turned and saw her.

Miranda felt she was seeing her mother for the first time, this woman who had only, until today, been "Mother." The hands, the face: so familiar and yet so strange. Once, years ago, Nora had been her age and fallen in love. Miranda could understand how love could change the way one looks at things. She loved Jeremy, and her mother was right: she might well have agreed to an elopement. The woman facing her had been herself first, before she had become Miranda's mother. And as Miranda's mother she had done nothing to be ashamed of. Indeed, she was a woman to admire. She had taken a small child on a long, arduous trip south. She had taken the work she needed to keep a roof over their heads. She had carried heavy trays and ignored drunken advances so that eventually they could have a home of their own. She had begun to write in short periods of time, snatched here and there from her duties as a mother. She had lived happily a life which had given her back very little, compared to the one she was raised to.

She looked so small, standing there. How did I ever fit in her lap? Miranda thought irrationally.

"Mother . . ."

Nora looked up, afraid of what she might see in Miranda's face.

"Can you forgive me?"

"Forgive you for what?" Nora whispered.

"For the way I acted. For not realizing what you have endured."

"Oh, my dearest, it is for you to forgive me," replied Nora. "Can you?"

At the old endearment, Miranda moved toward her mother, and Nora opened her arms. She murmured soothing noises and smoothed back the blond hair. She was comforting her little girl again—and she was not. For this lovely young woman had her own decisions to make. She might return to her arms from time to time, but this morning had marked a turning point. Never again could they be mother and daughter in quite the same way.

"Come, let us sit down and talk of what we must do." Nora led Miranda into the morning room and sat her down on the sofa. Sitting next to her, she said:

"I was afraid you would hate me forever."

"I almost felt like I could, for a moment or two. I found myself walking toward Joanna's. She helped me to understand so much, Mama," Miranda said.

"Miranda, it is impossible for me to regret my past when it brought you into my life. The moment I begin to say I am sorry for causing such sorrow and pain, I realize you would not have existed, had I not loved Breen. A painful and joyful paradox, I know."

"Mother, what did the duke say when you told him your story? Both Joanna and I wondered."

"At first he suggested I tell no one, not even you."

"Truly?"

"Yes, I was surprised myself. I think he was shocked, but could not see the point of hurting so many people. I told him I thought the deception had gone on long enough, and whatever happened, you had to know. He could understand that." Nora paused.

"Did he have any solution?"

"He suggested if I had to tell you the truth, I leave the final decision to you and Jeremy. I promised him I would."

"I think I must be the one to tell Jeremy," Miranda said, after a few moments.

"Yes?"

"And I also think, since it is his life and mine, that we must decide together."

"I think Simon hoped you would say that."

"Did he? Then I am sure it is the right thing to do, for he is clearly someone to trust."

"I think you should let me help tell Jeremy. It is, after all, my deception that is responsible for all this. Then, give him time to think, for if he marries you, he will be continuing that deception. I do not believe anyone else is owed that information, and I will no longer stand in your way, if Jeremy still wants the marriage. I have come to love him too, you know." Nora smiled.

"Thank you, Mother. I will write to him today, asking him to pay us a visit. And hope that he loves me enough . . ."

19

Jeremy and Lavinia had left the day after the Dillons, but not before speaking of the betrothal.

Jeremy approached Sam first, the evening of Miranda's departure.

"I would like to make my betrothal public and official, Sam. Do you see any reason why I should not?"

Sam got up and went over to the decanter on the table and poured each of them a glass of port.

"Here, sit down, Jeremy, and let us talk."

Jeremy unbent a little, and sat down opposite the viscount.

"I would like to hear your observations on Miranda's suitability as your countess," Sam said. "Have you had any second thoughts over the past two weeks?"

"None. Oh, I know it was hard for her, in London, and I know it will take her a while to get used to managing a large household. But, you know, Sam, my heart has always been in the country. I will not be demanding she live in town and become the great hostess, after all. Not," said Jeremy, after another swallow of port, "that she couldn't do it. Don't you think she is lovely?"

"I do. And I must admit," replied Sam, "Miranda would be good at whatever she set her mind so. Will you truly not be bothered by the difference in family background?" Sam queried. "It will be remarked upon, at first."

"I respect Nora almost as much as I love Miranda."

"Well, then, here's to your engagement and marriage," Sam said, lifting his glass.

Jeremy flashed him a smile and they toasted each other.

"I knew you could not resist her, once you got to know her. That's why I agreed to this unofficial engagement. Oh, I know you and mother hoped I would change my mind, but I think even Mother has come around."

"Yes, well, so much for careful planning. But there can be no public announcement until your mother is also in agreement."

"Can we call her in now, Sam?" Jeremy asked eagerly.

"Why not? We might as well settle it all tonight." Sam would have preferred to tackle Lavinia first, but he was confident she had come around enough. And perhaps Jeremy could make the better argument after all.

He rang for a footman. "Please ask Lady Whitford to join us in the library."

"Very good, m'lord."

Lavinia, who had only been in the music room, was soon at the door.

"What? I am invited to share a cigar and have some port with you?" she teased. The two men grinned at her sally.

"Come in, Mother, and sit down. *Would* you like a glass of port?"

"Why, yes, why not?"

"Sam and I have just come to an important agreement about the betrothal, and I wished to have us all together."

Lavinia was not a stupid woman, nor was she hard-hearted. She had observed Sam's growing approval, and she had watched Miranda and Jeremy closely over the last two weeks, as well as held a heart-to-heart with the young duchess. Jeremy and Miranda were deeply in love; that she could see. And Miranda and her mother were quite different from what she had envisioned. She knew she could live with the marriage, even though it was not what she had wished for her son.

"You have not decided to break it off," she asked with very little hope.

"Why, no, Mother. Would you still want me to?"

"I never said anything of the sort," protested the countess.

"You didn't have to," replied her son. "I knew you were both against it. But now that you know her?"

"I must confess she is a lovely girl. Not what I have wanted for you," she said quickly, "but I must admit I do not think it would be such a bad match."

"Would you approve of an offical betrothal and a wedding soon to follow?"

Sam looked at Jeremy in surprise. He had expected a longer betrothal.

Lavinia was a bit taken aback. "Do you think that is wise?"

"Yes. I want Miranda to come to London for the Little Season as my wife. It will be the easiest way to introduce her into society and will be less of a strain for her. And then we can have our first holidays together in Alverstone."

Sam and Lavinia turned to each other almost automatically and shared a private look of amusement at Jeremy's eagerness. Each knew just what the other was thinking: How like Charles.

"My dear, aside from Miranda's lack of family, I could not imagine a lovelier daughter-in-law. I would wish it a longer betrothal to lessen the gossip, but I will go along with whatever you wish."

Sam's smile of approval was almost worth the capitulation, thought Lavinia. He had not looked at her with such warmth in many years.

Lavinia had sat up a little straighter, and smiled back in her most appealing way. He laughed to himself as he realized that for the first time in years he was free of both his automatic resistance to her and his slight disdain. He could finally see her limitations, yet appreciate her for what she was: a warm but rather shallow lady who had been a good friend for many years and who would always remain one. Someone, moreover, who had allowed him to develop a relationship with Jeremy which was the closest thing to fatherhood he was ever to get.

"Sam, do you agree?"

Jeremy's voice pulled him back into the conversation.

"What?"

"That an August wedding is a possibility?"

"Jeremy, it seems that we are all in agreement. But I remind you that you have not yet spoken to Mrs. Dillon or Miranda yet."

"But of course she will approve. We get along splendidly."

"I have some reason to believe she may have her own objections. Do not publish any announcement until you have met with her in person."

"Of course not," Jeremy replied, insulted that Sam would think he would do such a thing. "I intend to spend a week at Alverstone, and then I will ride to Hampstead to see Miranda and her mother. What objections could she have, after all?"

Sam merely nodded. He would not offer any more cautions, for, confronted with Jeremy and told of Lady Lavinia's approval, perhaps Mrs. Dillon would abandon her mysterious scruples. And an August wedding would mean he would be seeing Nora sooner than he had hoped.

20

It took longer than a week for Jeremy to get his mother settled in and to resolve the most pressing estate problems. Miranda had written to him, requesting a visit, but he was not able to set off for London immediately. Although her note sounded strangely formal to him, he was not overly concerned by her summons. He had planned to visit as often as his home responsibilities allowed, and he was pleased she missed him as much as he missed her after their two weeks of steady conversation.

When he finally reached London, he sent a footman off with a note to Miranda telling her to expect him in the morning. Nora was the one who answered the door, and she handed the note wordlessly to her daughter, who opened it with trembling fingers.

"He will be here tomorrow."

"Good. I know you are terrified, but it will be better to have this ordeal over as soon as possible. I cannot stand to watch you go through another week of waiting." Miranda, who was easygoing and even-tempered in contrast to her mother's more up-and-down temperament, had scared Nora this week with her frozen face and lack of energy.

She is strong enough to take his rejection. She won't be devastated by it, Nora would try to convince herself, and then look at her daughter and want to cry all over again for the pain she had caused her.

Neither woman slept well that night, and the next morning found them at the breakfast table pale and heavy-eyed. Miranda pushed her food around and took only a few sips of tea and a bit of toast. Nora went out into the garden after breakfast, and so, when Jeremy arrived, she didn't hear him. She was weeding as ruthlessly as though she were the Judgment Day Angel separating the wheat from the chaff.

Miranda called to her from the kitchen steps, and she went up the walk slowly, her heart beating as though she had just run across the Heath. What would her life be like if Jeremy rejected her daughter? How could Miranda *not* blame her in the long run?

Jeremy and Miranda were in the morning room, Jeremy on the couch and Miranda, at the window, her back to him, waiting for her mother.

Jeremy stood up as Nora entered, and she gave him her hand. "It is good to see you, Jeremy, and kind of you to answer Miranda's note."

"But of course I would. I would have been up soon anyway. Miranda should have known that." He looked toward Miranda, who at last was facing him. The look on her face startled him, and he got up and stepped toward her. "Is anything wrong, my dear?"

Miranda put up her hands as though to push him away.

"No . . . yes. Please sit down, Jeremy. There is something I must tell you. It concerns our betrothal . . ."

"Well, that is just what I wanted to talk about! Although I did intend to speak with your mother first," he added quickly. "Both Sam and my mother have agreed to an official engagement, and I want to put the announcement in this week, if I have your mother's permission," Jeremy said. "You have no objections, do you, Nora? Sam said he thought you might, but I don't know where he would have gotten that idea."

"No," replied Nora slowly. "I have no objections. You are, in all ways but one, just the man I would have wished for Miranda."

"Which one?" Jeremy quizzed. "Not spectacularly handsome, or not as rich as the 'Golden Ball,' " he joked.

"You are the Earl of Alverstone," replied Nora.

"I know you are rather republican in sentiment, Nora, but surely you forgive me an accident of birth," Jeremy answered lightly. "After all, I had no choice in the matter."

"It is really a matter of my birth," interrupted Miranda. Her tone made Jeremy look up in alarm.

"What do you mean?"

"What Miranda wants to say is—"

"Let me, Mother," Miranda said firmly. She had never sounded quite so adult, and Nora knew some crucial shift had taken place. She was speaking not just as Nora's daughter, or as Jeremy's Miranda, but as herself, a grown woman.

"Jeremy, I can't marry you."

Nora, who was about to protest these words, to her own surprise was silenced by a flashing glance from her daughter.

"What do you mean? We are betrothed."

"Yes, and I am thankful that it has not been announced. When I told you I would be your wife, I knew nothing of my own background."

"I don't understand," Jeremy said, looking around questioningly, as though to see how her background had miraculously changed. "You are Miranda Dillon, daughter of Lieutenant and Mrs. Dillon. I know there is a difference in our status, but it means nothing to me, you know that."

"Our positions are more alike and yet more different than we had thought. It seems I am not Miranda Dillon, but Miranda Breen. Or perhaps Miranda Ashton. I am not quite sure which would be correct, since my mother never married Mr. Breen."

"Of course not, she married Lieutenant Dillon," replied a thoroughly confused Jeremy, who wondered whether Miranda was suffering from a high fever.

"Jeremy," interrupted Nora, "I have been living a lie for many years. Miranda knew nothing of this until last week, when I had to tell her, for your sake and for hers. I had hoped none of it would need to come out, that you were both in the throes of calf love . . ."

"You did not approve either? You were as much opposed as Sam and my mother? Why?"

"Because I am not Nora Dillon. I am Lady Honora Margaret Ashton. I ran away with one Dillon Breen when I was only a little younger than Miranda. I had her when I was eighteen and I never married her father. Miranda is illegitimate."

Jeremy turned to Miranda as though waiting for her to deny all of this. She merely nodded and said softly: "So you see, knowing this now, I could never become the Countess of Alverstone.''

"Because your mother forbids it?''

"No. Because it would not be right to ask you to bear the disgrace.''

Jeremy's head was too full of conflicting facts. He had not yet assimilated the change from Miranda Dillon to Miranda Breen or whomever. He had not even registered the information that Nora was of the nobility. His heart, however, needed to assimilate none of it. He heard himself say what he knew to be the truth for him, beyond any careful reasoning:

"Why would anyone else have to know?'' he asked.

God bless you, Jeremy, thought Nora.

He turned to her. "Is this Breen really dead, or is that another lie?''

His tone was cool, and Nora flushed as she answered. "No, he is truly dead.''

"Then there is no way for the truth to come out,'' he said with relief in his voice.

"Jeremy,'' protested Miranda, "the Earl of Alverstone cannot marry a . . . bastard.''

Jeremy was next to her in one moment. He took her by the shoulders and shook her gently and said, "I never want to have you use that word again.''

"But that is what I am,'' she answered.

"You are an intelligent, lovely woman, and the circumstances of your birth have nothing to do with you. Do you think so little of me that you believe my love could be extinguished by just one word?''

"Oh, no.'' Miranda lifted her eyes to his. "It is only that I love you too much to hold you to a marriage that would be abhorrent to you. That would be beneath you.''

"Then you would have sent me away, and all for your lack of trust?''

"No, you don't understand,'' protested Miranda, the tears she had been holding back for a week beginning to fall.

"I *do* understand,'' said Jeremy softly. He kissed her gently on the forehead and folded her into his arms. "But what you don't seem to understand is I loved you the first time I saw you, and could never stop loving you.''

Nora did not stay. She slipped out the door, leaving Miranda and Jeremy their private moments, and walked blindly down the path toward the Heath. She should be happy for Miranda; she *was* happy for her. She had prayed Jeremy was who she thought he was, and he had not disappointed her. For, once she had revealed the basis of her objections, she had found herself wanting for them the ending she had never had to her own romance. She had had no true consummation, no growth of love, but only a slow realization that she had thrown herself away for a fantasy. She had been surprised by her daughter this week. Miranda had made a decision in silence, a decision to release Jeremy. A decision that reflected her maturity. And as Miranda came to her decision, Nora had hoped, against all her own reasons, that Jeremy would prove worthy of her daughter. And he had, in a way that erased all of Miranda's doubts. Had he *thought* about it, had he taken any time over it, she knew Miranda would always have been insecure in the marriage. This way, she knew he had no hesitation; that he loved her for herself.

Then why was her relief not unalloyed? Why was she seized by an almost palpable unhappiness? For herself. It had nothing to do with Miranda. Or maybe it did, after all. She kept walking faster and faster, as though to outrun her jealousy. For that was, after all, the feeling that tore at her. Her daughter was loved in a way that she herself had never been loved. Her daughter had found a man, grown-up. Breen had never grown up. And perhaps I never have, thought Nora. Oh, I have in some ways; I have taken on responsibility and raised a child. But there is still a part of me who is that seventeen-year-old looking for a knight in shining armor, she thought. And that young girl has just seen someone else who has been granted the reality, not the fantasy. And she is dying from it.

Miranda had grown up. And she would marry Jeremy, and would drive away, leaving her mother behind, the young girl in her awake at last, finally facing what she had lost and knowing what she had never had, an adult passion. She had thrown it away for blue eyes and bright hair. And now the fulcrum of her existence was being removed. She sat down suddenly, as though all her energy had drained out in one moment, and opened her mouth in a long silent cry.

21

After a while Nora composed herself and walked slowly back to the house. Miranda and Jeremy were sitting hand in hand on the old bench in the garden. Nora approached them slowly. Jeremy had sounded so cold when he had heard the truth, and she wondered if she had lost his respect. In Miranda, he had nothing to forgive, for she was an innocent. But my story must have shocked him, thought Nora. And I am not an innocent; I am responsible for all of this.

The lovers looked up at her approach, and Miranda got up, and taking her hand, brought her over to sit down on the bench.

"We were worried about you, Mother."

"I just went for a walk, my dear. It seemed to me that you did not need a third person. Am I to wish you happy?"

Jeremy, who had as yet given no sign of welcome, smiled at her question and nodded. "Yes, and we are glad you are the first. The notice will go in in a few days, and we are planning an August wedding."

"So soon? Why, that is little more than a month away," protested Nora.

"I want to introduce Miranda as my countess in the fall," replied Jeremy. "That way she will have the support of her position, and any gossip about her background will have died down by the holidays."

"I see," Nora said slowly, dazed by the events of the morning.

Jeremy looked at her and saw more clearly the tracing of wrinkles around her eyes. He had enjoyed Nora as a welcome contrast to his own mother. He had idealized her as an independent woman who had survived widowhood without falling into the vaporish states that Lavinia did. She had almost seemed like an older sister, Miranda's and his.

When he heard the truth from her, he had initially been shocked and disillusioned. But after he and Miranda talked, he had begun to try to imagine what it must have been like for Nora. Miranda could not tell him anything about Scotland, but she did remember some of the early years in Hampstead, and Jeremy wondered at Nora's courage. She was the daughter of a marquess, yet she had worked as a barmaid to support herself and her daughter, and then managed to establish herself as a writer. He knew he might not have been capable of that. He had been raised in luxury, and though he worked hard on his estates, he did so because he chose to. Like Miranda, he was seeing Nora for the first time, and wondering about that seventeen-year-old. Who had she been? Not this capable woman, but a romantic girl.

Jeremy turned to Nora and said, "I have always admired you, Nora, but never so much as this morning."

Nora blushed.

"Thank you, Jeremy," she said, looking straight at him. He looked back at her and she knew he was accepting her past and did not despitse her for it.

"And, Jeremy," she continued, "I would not wish for any other son-in-law, even though you *are* an earl."

Their laughter eased the tension as she had hoped it would. Suddenly they were all chattering about details: how would Miranda put a wardrobe together, who would pay for it (Nora insisted on the responsibility for the wedding dress), who would be invited? As they talked, Nora felt herself to be two people: one, the excited mother, the other, a woman who was beginning to realize how alone she would be in just a few weeks. Her whole life was about to change overnight.

22

During the next few weeks Nora felt the split even more. She accompanied Miranda to Madame Didier's to choose the material for her dress. They found an ivory silk, and decided upon a pattern that was a bit old-fashioned but which suited the material better than the wider skirts that were coming in vogue. The silk hung gracefully, and needed little embellishment. Madame produced a cache of freshwater pearls, with which she embroidered the sleeves and neckline, and Nora, unbeknownst to Miranda, visited a jeweler's in London to have the rest of them strung into a delicate choker. The pink-tinged jewels emphasized Miranda's pale rose complexion. Nora was convinced by Madame to wear a certain shade of blue-green that complemented her darker coloring to perfection.

Once the announcement went in the *Post,* there were gifts to be opened, cousins and aunts to visit, and, of course, Lavinia to be included and entertained. The city was fairly empty, but since one of Lavinia's sister's lived near Richmond, there was some socializing that could be done.

Sam did not return to the city until a week after the announcement. He had been detained by problems with one tenant, and a long-promised visit to Sutton. Simon and Judith had been happy to hear of the betrothal, as was the viscount himself. Whatever Mrs. Dillon's objections had been, he said to the duke and duchess, they must have been overcome by the obvious rightness of the match. The duke agreed, but wondered to himself just what had transpired. He assumed Nora had left the decision up to Miranda and Jeremy, as he had advised. Perhaps he would find out at the wedding.

When Sam returned, he immediately rode out to Hampstead with Jeremy. The little house was in an uproar, what with putting the trousseau together and packing up Miranda's personal belongings. Nora seemed at ease with Jeremy and caught up with the excitement. Yet there was a difference in her Sam could not put his finger on. She was involved and removed at the same time. He felt some part of her was just not there. At the same time, that air of self-sufficiency was subtly changed. He had a glimpse, from time to time, of the vulnerable girl she must have been.

They had no chance on that visit to talk alone, so Sam could not ask what had erased her objections, or even joke about the failure of their scheme. He watched her as she helped her daughter, and realized, with some surprise, that Miranda appeared the calmer of the two. Nora was flustered and disorganized, picking up a book in one room to bring to another, and returning with it still in her hand. Or putting something down, like her scissors, and ineffectually searching for them, and summoning Miranda, who found them immediately. From the joking comments between them, Sam decided that while Miranda seemed a naturally calm person, Nora drew on her writing and gardening to center what was perhaps a more . . . passionate nature? He hoped so, for the more he was with Nora, the more he appreciated her and desired her. These little glimpses of absentmindedness intrigued him, for they were the first break he had seen in that independence of hers. Although he imagined that it might, in the long run, be exasperating, he found himself wanting to be the one she turned to to ask anxiously: "Now, where did I put my scissors? I just had them." He was ever on the verge of saying, "Damn, the scissors, woman. Come here and let me love you."

At any rate, this was the first chink in her armor he had seen so far, and it gave him hope she was not as self-sufficient as she appeared. He wondered if she had had any offers of marriage over the years. It was possible she was one of those people who loved only once. As it seemed I was, Sam thought to himself as he recalled the years he had kept his heart intact even with the most charming and lovable of mistresses. But if he could now feel as excited as a young man on seeing his love, then why might not Nora feel the same about him? There would be plenty of time and many opportunities to woo her, thank God, now that she was in the family. He would go slowly and carefully, he decided. Nothing too obvious.

Nora was fleetingly aware, from time to time, of Sam's gaze, and when she lost her scissors for the third time that morning, she was conscious that his look of amusement was also a look of affection. She put her head down as she felt herself blush. Luckily there was nothing else to show how flustered she became. No on had looked at her with that kind of appreciation in years, and she opened herself up to it for only a moment before remembering that it was just that openness which had brought her all the pain of the past few weeks. She closed off her awareness of Sam's lean frame lounging against the bookcase as he watched them put the finishing touches on Miranda's going-away dress. She *would not* let herself imagine what his hands would feel like on her shoulders, she would not let herself be betrayed by her body again. She managed to pull herself back to the task at hand: hemming Miranda's dress, and finding herself very relieved when the viscount's visit came to an end. It was difficult, but not impossible, to put him out of her mind, for much of her time was taken up with getting ready for the wedding.

23

The weeks before the wedding went very quickly. Jeremy stayed in town, and visited Hampstead almost every day. The viscount occasionally accompanied him, but more frequently purposely stayed away, despite his desire to be with Nora. She was too busy, and he knew there was no progress to be made when she was in this distracted state.

Miranda and Nora would again travel south, this time to stay at Alverstone. The wedding was to be informal and take place at the parish church. A few intimate friends of the family, like Simon and Judith, would be there, as well as family and contemporaries of Jeremy who lived close enough to make the journey in one day. Lavinia, who had not yet had the opportunity to plan a ball or dinner to celebrate the betrothal, decided a formal dinner on the eve of the ceremony and a wedding breakfast would satisfy her need to entertain.

Although Jeremy had described it to them, neither of the Dillons was prepared for Alverstone. If the viscount's house had at first seemed intimidating, this was even more so. As they drove up the long driveway and caught their first glimpse of the house, a long mansion which obviously dated back to Tudor times, but had been added to over the years, Miranda looked at her mother with sheer terror in her eyes. Nora knew at that moment her daughter was ready to flee home to the cottage.

The servants were all lined up to greet them, and Jeremy proudly introduced Miranda to each one. The unreality of the past few weeks was broken, and Nora felt like a mother again, and not an actress playing a role. She spent the next few days reassuring her daughter that, yes, she was doing the right thing, that she could handle her responsibilties and would not be bringing some sort of disgrace upon Jeremy by marrying into his family.

Nora herself felt a bit intimidated. Although she had been

the daughter of a peer, their family, which numbered a few Catholics in the background, as did many in Northumberland, had lost land and homes over the centuries. They had held only Moorview, the small estate in Cumberland, and a town house in London. The luxury that surrounded them here was overwhelming, and Nora wondered that Jeremy had managed to grow up such an unspoiled young man.

The viscount did not arrive for two days. Nora found herself looking forward to his arrival, for although Lavinia was not looking at her with hostility, Nora knew this was not the marriage she wanted for her son. And Lavinia was clearly being her most dignified, as befit the mother of an earl and groom-to-be: the relatives who had arrived were all Lavinia's contemporaries and as unremittingly polite as she was.

There were opportunities to ride, thank goodness, and Jeremy offered Nora a lovely little mare as a present to his soon-to-be mother-in-law. It would be hers for whenever she came down, which he hoped would be often. Nora was delighted with her, and on the morning Sam arrived, was returning from a ride, when she heard hoofbeats behind her.

She was relaxed, and so happy to see someone with whom she could converse in more than polite monosyllables that she gave him a heart-stopping smile as he slowed down to a walk beside her.

"I see Jeremy gave you his present early," Sam said, speaking casually but wanting more than he could have thought possible that smile of welcome to have been for him as a lover rather than as a new friend.

"Yes, and she is a love. Perfect for me and my rusty riding skills," Nora said. "Gentle, but not an old plug. Did you ride all the way?" she queried.

"Yes. My chaise is behind me, with my luggage and presents." The viscount smiled. "And how have you and Miranda been surviving?"

"May I be frank?"

"I have never known you to be otherwise," teased Sam.

"I think we were both ready to run back to Hampstead at the first sight of the house. I have had to reassure Miranda that she will indeed make a fine countess. And the guests who are here do not make it any easier."

"Ah, I would venture to guess that you have met Lavinia's side of the family."

"Yes, and they are so . . . well, I should not be so critical," said Nora shamefacedly. "But the formality is chilling. How did Jeremy ever become who he is?" she asked, without thinking of the insult implied to Lavinia.

Sam laughed out loud. "I can always count on you to get to the heart of the matter, Mrs. Dillon. It is a shame you never knew Charles."

"Jeremy's father?"

"Yes. He was a delightfully unassuming man. Jeremy is much like him. He preferred the country, and only his love for his wife got him into town for the Season. He was good for Lavinia. He loved her very much, and she needed the security of that. It was as if her better self emerged when she was with him. When she lost him, she lost the one who strengthened her weaknesses. But she is a good woman underneath all her super-ficiality, and deserves much credit for Jeremy also."

"Oh, I do not doubt it." Nora hesitated before asking hesitantly: "She must have been quite beautiful when she was young?"

"Yes, she was. She had many men in love with her, but was fortunate and wise enough to pick Charles."

Nora heard something in the tone of Sam's voice, and without thinking, blurted out: "And where you one of the young men in love with her?"

Sam turned and smiled ruefully. "Why, yes, how did you guess?"

"I don't know. Something in your face occasionally when you look at her, and something in your voice just now. Please forgive me. It was unspeakably rude to ask such an intimate question." Nora was feeling miserable, embarrassed by her outspokenness, and unhappy, for some reason, that the viscount had once been enamored of the countess. Was perhaps still enamored. Well, she would not make herself the complete fool and ask him that. She was happy when they came in sight of the house, and began to chat about inconsequentials. Sam could tell she was embarrassed. If she fell to wondering about his feelings for Lavinia, which her questions indicated she might be, he was not at all displeased.

24

Sam's arrival seemed to speed up the days remaining till the wedding. More guests arrived, including Simon and Judith, and the unending formal dinners were a thing of the past. Conversations became stimulating, indeed, *occurred,* thought Nora, and Miranda had another woman to allay her fears. Nora was a little jealous, but on the whole very happy that Miranda had made such a good friend in the duchess.

They had left Lady Sophy behind with her nurse, and Judith was obviously suffering from her first real separation.

"We knew that this would be too much for her, and I still worry she will think we abandoned her. She was crying so when we left that I almost turned back and let Simon come alone."

"They are terrible, aren't they, those first few moments when you leave," agreed Nora. "But I remember whenever I left Miranda with anyone, she would tell me that Miranda stopped crying almost immediately, and went happily about her play. I think the mothers suffer more than the children."

"Perhaps you are right, but I will be happy to get back," sighed Judith, and then immediately apologized. "It is not that I am not delighted to be here for the wedding, you understand?"

Nora and Miranda assured her that they did, both thinking what a nice person she was, and hoping that if she had managed to survive becoming a duchess, perhaps Miranda could survive the changes in her circumstances also.

The dinner was a great success. The whole county came, or so it seemed, and Miranda was exhausted after the first hour. Jeremy stayed close by her, and Nora was thankful for Sam's presence, for were it not for him and Judith and Simon, she would have felt even more peripheral than she did, for it was clear Jeremy would now be Miranda's intimate and her support.

Nora and Simon sat out a few country dances together. She expressed admiration for his dancing, having marveled at the way he and Judith waltzed together, as though he were sighted.

"I would offer you a waltz," Simon replied, "but I fear I am too used to my wife's guidance to risk it with anyone else at such a large gathering."

"You partner each other as well off the dance floor," observed Nora.

"Yes, I am very lucky."

"And the duchess . . . she is very lucky too."

Simon smiled. "I am glad you think so, Nora. I value your opinion. And your friendship, which I trust I have?"

"Indeed."

"Tell me, did you ever speak to Miranda and Jeremy?"

"I followed your good advice. She surprised me, Simon, for she herself told Jeremy she couldn't marry him and why. It was he who convinced her. We all decided her background would remain a secret. I still have doubts, though," Nora murmured.

"You shouldn't. It would do no good for anyone else to know. I think they are meant for a happy life, and I am pleased if I had any small part of that. But what of you? Won't you be a bit lonely now?"

Nora was touched by Simon's concern. "Of course, but I cannot imagine me living in Miranda's pocket. Although they have offered me a lovely little house on the estate. But I could never live this kind of life."

"You did once."

"Not really. Northumberland was different. My family's estate was small compared to this, and perhaps because of the wildness and the weather, things were a bit less formal there."

"Well, things are a little less formal at Sutton, and you must come for a long visit."

"Thank you, Simon. I promise I will after I have settled a bit into my new life."

"You are looking very serious, the two of you," said Sam, who was returning Judith after a dance. "Come, Nora, let me have this next waltz."

Nora touched Simon on the arm in farewell, and moved off with the viscount. She could not relax, however, for she was too conscious of Sam's arm around her waist, of his height, his own now-familiar smell, the small scar at the corner of his mouth, which she realized added to the quirkiness of his grin.

Sam could feel her tension and wondered if it was only from the events of the past weeks. She had seemed happy to be with him over the past few days, but she might like him, yet feel no attraction. He did his best to relax her by making amusing comments about some of the guests, but he could feel the distance that she placed between herself and him. She held herself just a fraction of an inch further away than was necessary for propriety. Of course, he could console himself by imagining that some reaction was better than none. Surely were she indifferent, she would be less conscious of their closeness? He certainly hoped so.

25

The next morning a heavy fog shrouded the countryside, and Nora feared it would last all day, casting a pall over the festivities. But by nine it had burned away, to her great relief, for she wanted the day to be perfect for Miranda in every way.

Nora's hands shook as she helped her daughter dress. The ivory silk hung perfectly and she thought that with her pale-rose complexion and the pearls, her daughter looked beautiful, as though all the colors that are inside a shell had taken on a woman's shape. Nora herself looked lovely, but she was not even aware of it. The viscount was, however. He watched her pale, set face as she emerged from the carriage and knew that she must be in the grip of conflicting emotions: happiness, pride, anxiety, and perhaps sadness as she remembered her own wedding? He wondered if she still felt bound to the dead lieutenant.

For Nora, the ceremony and the breakfast that followed were a blur. Sam was, in part, correct: she was not only happy for Miranda, but also felt she had completed the work that had been given to her. Miranda was a lovely young wife, more mature than she herself had been at the same age, and Nora had no doubts about the rightness of this match. But the tears that had risen when she and Jeremy exchanged vows were not just tears of happiness. They sprang from a deeper source, for she had never uttered those solemn words to anyone, nor had anyone wished to commit himself to her for life. And now that part of her life was over, and she could not feel the unalloyed happiness for Miranda she should. She was ashamed of herself for it, but there it was.

And so, back at the house, when the viscount brought her her second glass of champagne and asked her solicitously if she had been reminded of her own wedding, she almost lost control.

151

She turned the beginning of what she knew to be hysterical laughter into a cough, and gripped the glass so tightly that it broke in her hand. She looked, as though from very far away, as a drop of blood welled up from her finger and turned the dripping champagne pink. Sam rushed off to get a napkin, and she stood there holding the broken glass in her hand, feeling she herself had been broken. She took a deep breath, telling herself that all she needed was to get through this day, see the young couple off and return to Hampstead in the morning, where she could seek the comfort of her bed. She would crawl into it and never get out.

"Let me see your hand, Nora."

Sam's return startled her and she stuck out her hand to him without thinking and then drew it back, exclaiming that it was nothing, just very stupid of her to be so nervous, but it was her daughter's wedding, after all.

"Stop being so damnably independent and let me see that finger. There might be glass in it." He examined it carefully and pronounced it clean, and Nora brought her hand automatically to her mouth, sucking at the cut and looking at it for all the world as though she were little Sophy and not a grown woman, thought Sam. He wanted the right to comfort her and the opportunity to make her forget that dead husband of hers. But today is not the day for that, he thought, and he offered his arm and led her to the table.

Nora managed to get through all the well-wishing and Miranda's departure. They were going to spend a few days on one of Jeremy's small estates in Cornwall.

"It is by the sea, Mother, so we will be able to take long rambles by the shore." This was not, of course, a fashionable honeymoon, but Jeremy himself had suggested it. "We will travel to the Continent soon," he had told her, "but for these few weeks I want you to myself."

Miranda had turned to her mother at the last minute and held her close, whispering, "I don't want to leave you."

"But you must, 'ma dearie,' and I will always be home for you to come and visit."

"And you will visit us here?"

"Of course."

"I must go, Mother. I will see you soon." And she turned toward Jeremy and her new life. Nora watched them drive away, and remained for a long time after the carriage had disappeared from sight. She felt an arm around her shoulders. It was Joanna, who had, as her closest friend, been invited to the wedding.

"She will do fine, Nora."

"I know."

"I think it is good we are going home together. And I do wish you would stay at my house for your first night alone."

"Thank you, Joanna, but I must get used to it sooner or later."

26

In the weeks after the wedding, Nora alternated between feelings of intense longing to have Miranda restored to her as a little girl, and a complete lack of feeling. She had the house and garden to keep her busy, and even managed to guide Lady Cordelia to the successful conclusion of her adventures by the end of the summer. This was, of course, a good thing, because she needed the money and had promised the novel to her publisher by September. On the other hand, the emptiness which accompanied the completion of a book, the feeling that she had lost another child, most certainly did not help her state of mind.

She was very much alone in August. Miranda was on her honeymoon. Joanna had left after the wedding for a visit to Scotland. Nora made a point to get down to the village more than a few times a week, just to have some human contact, however trivial, but for the most part her days fell into a rhythm of writing, walking, and gardening without an exchange of words with anyone.

In some ways she was reminded of the weeks after her mother's death. She found herself again in a sort of limbo. Indeed, there were moments, working on her herbs, that she felt herself a shade, someone who was not her mother's daughter or her daughter's mother, hence no one. Luckily, these moments were infrequent and fleeting, or she would have been concerned for her sanity. But she felt lost in Dante's dark wood, with no guide at all.

And so, at the end of the month, when she heard someone on the walk early one afternoon, she gave the viscount a welcome that would have at least satisfied an old friend, if not a new and hopeful lover.

"What a surprise," Nora exclaimed.

"I am sorry for barging in like this without permission," Sam said at the same time.

"Please do not apologize, my lord. I am delighted to see you. Although I always seem to be full of dirt when you arrive." Nora laughed, looking down at her hands, which she had just been washing, and at her old blue dress, which was worn at the knees and splashed with water and soil.

"Perhaps I should come back another time?"

"No, no. Just go into the parlor and give me a moment to change and get the kettle on. Have you seen Miranda and Jeremy? I am so eager to hear everything." Sam smiled as she paused for a moment to hear the answer, and was gone an instant later, saying over her shoulder. "Don't answer now. Wait til! I am proper and can hear the news at my leisure."

Nora was back very quickly, having grabbed the first clean dress she could find, a faded sprigged muslin. Her hair was all flyaway about her face and her hands and face were red from the cold water, but to Sam she looked lovely.

"The kettle is on, so we will have our tea in a moment," she said as she sat down. "Now, give me the news."

"Miranda and Jeremy returned two days ago, and since I was returning to London early, I promised I would come and give you their love."

"How did she look?"

"Radiant. I must say I cannot help but be reminded of my first visit here, and am thankful that our 'best laid plans went agley.' "

Nora's face changed subtly at the reminder, but the shuttered look passed almost immediately, and she agreed, quite sincerely, Sam thought.

"When will they arrive in London?" she asked eagerly. Sam got a hint of the lonely month she must have spent.

"They need a while to unpack and close up the house before they repack for the Little Season. They hope to be here by the third week in September."

"Three more weeks," exclaimed Nora.

"I am afraid so," Sam replied, automatically reaching out to cover her hands with his in sympathy.

Just as a thrill went through her from his touch, the kettle started shrieking, and Nora jumped up, confused by her reaction and thankful of the interruption. Sam was busily cursing the fool who had invented singing kettles, tea, and boiling water for good measure, as she ran out to the kitchen, but had calmed himself down by the time she returned with the tea and biscuits. They chatted away as though nothing had happened.

Well, nothing had happened, Sam thought, and he took his leave shortly thereafter. He rode toward the city and realized he was quite pleased, after all, with his visit, despite cups of tea and howling kettles, for why would a woman start up as though she'd been scalded if there was not some response to a man's touch?

Nora was left feeling not quite so pleased. She felt rather foolish, in fact. She had jumped up like a nervous schoolgirl, startled more by her own reaction than by the damned teakettle. She did not know why she had these fleeting but strong reactions to the viscount. What did she know about him, after all? He was Jeremy's godfather, a seemingly intelligent man. Serious about his work in politics. But aside from his brief reference to his travels, she had no idea what his life had been like for the past eighteen years. He had been in love with Lady Whitford, but had never married. Well, that didn't mean anything, she thought, since most men occupied themselves elsewhere, married or not. The viscount, she knew, had had a mistress or two; perhaps Lady Maria would be the one to bring him to the altar . . .

Nora caught herself up short. One of the hazards of being a novelist, she had found, was the tendency to write stories in one's head about friends and acquaintances. She really had no idea about the viscount's past or present *chères amies,* she told herself, and what did it have to do with her anyway?

27

The viscount visited Hampstead twice more before Miranda and Jeremy's return. On one visit, he accompanied Nora on a long walk on the Heath, marveling at her knowledge of flowers and birds and small animals, and at her stamina. Their conversations were always comfortable, and the informality of a day outdoors loosened both their tongues. Sam talked about his travels in India, and Nora was fascinated to learn that a country she had pictured as only steaming jungles and dry plains also had lakes and snow-covered mountains.

"My travels took me up north, and I cannot really describe to you the beauties of Kashmir. We have no scenery quite so majestic in Britain."

"What did you think of the people?"

"They are very different in thought from ourselves. I do not share my compatriots' distaste for darker-complexioned peoples. I was lucky to spend some time with a Nawab and his family, and came to understand something of their culture. I suspect our policies there will one day cause us much embarrassment, if not tragedy. I returned because I could not stomach them."

The viscount continued with some thrilling tales of his adventures among the mountain peoples, and Nora realized that behind his rather ordinary exterior was an adventurous risk-taker, who in order to become more familiar with a country had gone where most Europeans did not. He had begun his travels soon after Lavinia married Charles, and Nora imagined his journeys over the years must have been quite effective in helping him forget his heartache.

She was glad of his company, for she was still suspended, waiting for Miranda. When she and Jeremy finally arrived one morning in late September, Nora flew down the path, meeting an equally eager Miranda halfway. They both cried and laughed and cried again.

"Let me look at you. Why, you are magnificent," said Nora, rather in awe of her daughter, who was dressed in the height of fashion.

Miranda smiled. "My wardrobe, Mama, would have dressed and fed us for several years. I confess it is hard to get used to."

Jeremy, who had been standing by the carriage, allowing mother and daughter their private reunion, came down the path and very naturally slipped his arm around Miranda's waist.

"Is she not a beautiful countess?" he asked Nora.

"She quite intimidates me," replied Nora, only half-joking.

She was aware, over the course of the morning, of many small and natural gestures of affection between the young couple. She had always known, and indeed was happy, that a strong physical attraction accompanied Miranda and Jeremy's love, but before the marriage, she had never seen that many signs of it. Oh, she suspected that they embraced privately, but since she had not seen it, it was easy not to think about it. Now, however, she had to let the fact in; her daughter was a married woman, with all that meant.

What it seemed to mean for Nora, over the next weeks, was a deepening feeling of loneliness, as well as the reappearance of that awful jealousy. As Miranda's mother, she was invited to private family dinners as well as some of the social events that Lavinia had planned for the Little Season. She was not inclined to go often, but realized if she didn't, she would hardly see her daughter. Miranda had been pulled into a social whirl almost immediately. It was her duty as Jeremy's countess, and although she preferred the country, and missed the quiet times she had hoped to have with her mother, she could not help but enjoy her social success.

The viscount was present on most of the occasions that Nora was invited to. He did not monopolize her, but always made sure that he had his chance to escort her to supper or claim a waltz. She was too grateful for his familiar face and the easy conversations with him to think much of his attention. He paid equal attention to Lavinia, the young ladies, and various widows, after all.

At home, especially after a dinner at Lavinia's or a night at the theater, Nora wandered about, all the old habits and patterns gone, now that Miranda was not there. There was no one to laugh with over the latest black-pig episode and no one to listen to her difficulty with a character. Worst of all, there was no Miranda to put her arms around in a good-night hug, no Miranda interrupting her at her work, no Miranda needing the comfort of her presence.

Sam continued his occasional visits, and could not help noticing Nora's low spirits. She was clearly going through the motions when she socialized with the family. Her eyes would come to life only when she was with her daughter, but on her own, standing with Lavinia and the other matrons, or even discussing a play with him, he sensed a lack of vitality. He imagined she must be very lonely. After all, she and Miranda had been companions for eighteen years. But he did not feel he had the right to ask her.

He wished Nora would turn to him as a companion. She clearly enjoyed his visits, but he did not feel she looked upon him as anyone central to her life. He was plagued by doubts that she would ever see him as more than a family connection, but he knew—he was not sure how—that he must not push her.

By the middle of the Little Season, it became clear to Nora that Miranda's marriage meant the end of their close relationship. She had, of course, anticipated changes, and the separation that would occur when her daughter married, but in the normal course of things, Miranda most probably would have married someone who lived in Hampstead or one whose London residence was more informal. The mothers in the village were able to drop in at all hours upon their married daughters. Having a daughter who was a countess, however, meant she saw her only on formal occasions, for even "intimate" dinners at Lavinia's were formal. Miranda had of course visited her mother for lunch or tea, but it felt to Nora that these were flying visits, and that her daughter was preoccupied by the tightness of her schedule. The two women never seemed to get beyond small talk.

Nora had never wanted to be an interfering or clinging parent, so she never met Miranda with anything but a smile and the most amusing tidbits of news from Hampstead or the publishing world.

Had Nora known it, Miranda herself felt a sense of loss. It had been hard to leave her mother and start such an unfamiliar existence, but the weeks in Cornwall and Sussex had been lovely. Jeremy and she had become even closer, and she felt the pain of leaving her old life disappear. But in London, that cherished time with him was less. It was not fashionable to have one's spouse in one's pocket, no matter how recent the wedding. Jeremy certainly spent more time with her than the other husbands did with their wives, but it was inevitable that they would be together less. Miranda had become close to Ann Hume, and there was Judith, but she missed her mother. She was too embarrassed to tell Jeremy or Nora. Her mother seemed to be surviving quite well without her. She always seemed happy and full of the latest local gossip. And of course, she had her writing. Miranda would never worry about Nora, for she knew as long as she could write, she would be happy. But she did find herself looking forward to the holidays at Alverstone, when they would all be together and she would have the time to spend with both her new husband and her mother.

28

Joanna had returned from Scotland in mid-October and was concerned, though not surprised, at Nora's state of mind. She had known that the change in such a close mother-daughter relationship would be difficult, but she only now realized, as Nora had, what Miranda's change in position meant.

One afternoon, a few days after she had returned, she walked up to the cottage. Nora greeted her warmly, but there was a lack of energy that was beginning to worry Joanna. After they had chatted inconsequentially for a few moments, Joanna decided to come to the point.

"My dear, I am worried about you."

Nora immediately began to deny any reasons for concern.

"No, no, don't put up your guard with me, Nora. Is it Miranda's marriage?" Joanna asked with such sympathy that Nora, who had been denying her state of mind for weeks, felt her eyes fill with tears.

"You are right. I am miserably lonely. I never realized how much distance this marriage to Jeremy would put between us. Miranda never has time for more than a short visit, and when I go to visit her, we have so little privacy that I leave quickly myself. I am so ashamed of myself, Joanna, for I never wanted to be one of those clinging females who would never let their children go. But Miranda is gone with a vengeance." Nora laughed shakily.

"I can hardly picture you as clinging, Nora. In fact, that is precisely your problem. You try so hard to be independent that you deny yourself even the common feelings of loss that a mother would feel."

"Oh, I know, we have been over this before. But I am afraid to feel them. If I really cried over Miranda, I fear I would cry myself away, leaving only an empty shell. And sometimes she gets so confused with my own mother. Or rather, I get confused and wonder who it is that I am missing, my mother or my daughter. And who am I, between the two of them?''

''You are a lovely woman who needs a life for herself now, and a different kind of companionship than that between parent and child. Has the viscount been to visit?''

''Why, yes, but what has that got to do with anything?''

''I rather thought he was interested in you, my dear. And he is just what you need. I liked him very much from what I saw at the wedding.''

''I don't need a man in my life, Joanna. I have my friends, my writing, and when things calm down, Miranda, although in a different way.''

Ah, but you do need someone like the viscount, thought Joanna. Someone to help you learn to trust yourself again. A man very different from that wastrel Breen.

''And anyway,'' continued Nora, ''the viscount and I are just good friends. I doubt he is interested in me in any other way. He has plenty of opportunities to find female companionship. I am sure he has innumerable widows setting their caps for him.''

Joanna smiled to herself at this last. Nora's tone had changed subtly, and Joanna was sure that underneath all her denials, there was some interest, however nascent. But there was something that held Nora back from allowing those feelings to develop. Something more than the habit of taking on all the responsibility herself.

Joanna had often thought over the years, and mentioned it from time to time, that Nora should revisit her home in Northumberland. Nora had always reacted strongly, claiming that there was nothing there for her. After all, her mother was long since dead and her father had virtually disowned her.

''Nora, I know you get upset with me whenever I mention this, but perhaps it is time to go back to Moorview. You yourself are saying that Miranda's leaving brings back the loss of your mother. Even if your father did turn away from you, people change. He has a granddaughter he has never seen. Miranda has family and a heritage that she has only found out about. Would you deny her and yourself one last change at reconciliation? You are a grown woman now, not a penitent young girl.

Surely you could speak very differently for yourself today than you could eighteen years ago?''

Joanna was leaning forward, hands clasped in front of her to keep from pulling Nora into her arms. She knew that she was on dangerous ground, but somehow felt that it was at last the right time to say this. Nora, who had stiffened at Joanna's words, gave a shudder and suddenly relaxed.

''Perhaps you have been right all along, Joanna. I know I could not have gone back before,'' she said in a low voice, looking down at the floor. ''But now? . . . Oh, Joanna, I feel so lost. Without Miranda, my life seems to have collapsed around me. Even writing has become empty. I am sick of my Lady Cordelias and Lord Soameses. I never want to describe a ball dress again!'' Nora looked up with a smile, but with tears in her eyes.

''If I did go back, what would I do? Just walk up to the door and announce myself? My father could be dead, for all I know.''

''I think you could decide when you get there. You may find it is enough to be there in the countryside of your girlhood. You may wish to spend only a day or two, and visit your mother's grave.''

''I will consider it this time, Joanna,'' said Nora, getting up. ''Perhaps it *is* time for me to go home.''

''And to forgive yourself.''

''Forgive myself?''

''Yes. I think that your new life cannot truly start until you stop doing penance.'' As Nora started to protest, Joanna put her arm around her shoulders. ''Hush, and listen to me, for what good are all my years if I cannot pretend to be wise! I know that you have said that you have no regrets about the past, for it brought you Miranda. But I think you feel something deeper than regret—a shame that you let your passionate feelings blind you to the truth of Breen's character. My dear, you were seventeen, you had just lost your mother, and, it seemed, your father. From what you have told me, Breen was charming, handsome, and, I think, loved you as much as he could have loved anyone.''

''Oh, but my love was so easy won,'' replied Nora sadly.

''Yes, because you are a loving person. But you cannot spend the rest of your life alone in fear that you will make the same mistake again. Don't say anything now," added Joanna, as Nora started to continue her protest. "Think about my words later. And if you decide to go, let me know."

Nora turned and hugged the older woman. "Whatever I decide, thank you for your affection, my good friend. I do not think I would have survived without you these past years."

"It has been a mutual joy, Nora," replied Joanna, kissing her on the forehead. "Now, be sure to let me know if you need anything should you decide to go."

Nora wrapped her shawl around her and stepped out into the High Street to see Joanna on her way. The weather was beginning to get colder, and it occurred to her as she walked back into the house that did she decide to make the journey, she must do it soon, or have to wait to spring.

I will sleep on it, she decided. In the morning, things will be clearer.

That night she dreamed of her mother, a rare occurrence, for she had often wondered why she never had the comfort of her mother's presence in dreams. In the dream, she was a child again, perhaps six or seven years old. She was walking down a dusty path, lost, and knowing she was likely walking in the wrong direction, but not knowing what else to do but keep on walking. She was crying as she walked, and did not hear the carriage wheels behind her. Before she knew it, she was being enfolded in her mother's arms as her mother crooned to her and said, "Oh, Margaret, I've been looking everywhere for you. Let me take you home."

She awoke with dry eyes and that tight pain in the chest which occurs when one has been sobbing in a dream and the crying has not broken through into the daylight. Oh, Mother, if only you could take me home with you, she thought, and then slipped into a deep sleep.

In the morning she awoke knowing she must go to Northumberland, and having decided, lost no time in making preparations. Luckily, she did have a small amount of money set by. Miranda and Jeremy had been very generous and given her several dresses, so she had not had to use her own funds for her recent socializing. She had enough to hire a chaise, but as she sat and thought about it, she decided she would go by coach. It was the way she had come south, after all, and it would bring back the past more vividly. It also left her with more money for accommodations, and to hire a private parlor when they stopped for refreshment.

There was an old valise in the back of her closet, the same one she had used when they left Edinburgh. It took her a while to find it, and she was just brushing the cobwebs off it and out of her hair when she heard someone coming up the walk. By this time, she was so thoroughly energized by her decision, and the rising sense of excitement combined with anxiety, that she was quite distracted in her greeting to the viscount.

"I seem to have come at a bad time," he said, looking at the small piles of folded clothes. "Would it be better if I returned later in the week?" he asked politely.

"Yes," replied Nora without thinking. And then: "No, no, I won't be here later in the week, so you may as well come in now for a moment." She was not so distracted as not to register that Sam had caught her once again with her clothes and hair in disarray.

"I am obviously disturbing you," he said a bit stiffly.

"Well, yes," she admitted in a friendly tone, "but I am ready for a cup of tea, and I *am* happy to see you," she added as if in afterthought, "for I have a letter to Miranda that I can send back with you. So you are welcome, but I will have to ask you to put aside your dignity"—she smiled—"and join me in the kitchen, since the parlor is too cluttered for us to be comfortable."

Sam sat at the old deal table and watched her pump water, fill the kettle, and slice a loaf of plum cake. Very soon they were sitting cozily over cake and tea, the thin slices of cake disappearing into Sam's mouth at the rate of three to Nora's one.

"You were hungry, my lord?" she teased.

"Have I finished all that?" Sam exclaimed. "I fear I've demolished your plum cake, but it is so good."

"That is all right. It won't be left to get moldy when I am gone."

"Yes . . . then you are going somewhere?"

Two cups of tea had given Nora a becoming flush, but she warmed even more as she said, "Yes, I am going home."

"Home?"

"Northumberland."

"This week?"

"Tomorrow."

"Forgive me, I know I have no right to question you, but is this not a sudden decision? What of Miranda and the rest of the Little Season? What of the holidays?"

"Oh, I will be back for Christmas, of course. That is why I am leaving now. I will have to go right away, or the weather will be too wild to go before spring. And as for Miranda, she is coping well, it seems to me, and after all, has her husband to support her."

"Is there some family emergency? I was not aware you had family left up north . . ." Sam's voice trailed off as he realized he had no real right to question Nora about her personal life.

"No emergency, my lord. Just a strong desire to revisit my childhood home."

And to revisit the scenes of her early days with her dead husband, perhaps? Had she met him in Northumberland? Had Miranda's marriage turned her thoughts back to her own youthful happiness? Sam was amazed at the strength of his own reaction. He had envisioned an autumn of slow and relaxed courtship. Visits like this, waltzes which brought them close. And a leisurely few weeks at Alverstone to ensure a positive answer to his proposal. And now she was just stuffing a few dresses into an old bag and going north. She really is an outrageous woman, he thought. No wonder I love her!

"How are you intending to travel? Have you asked Jeremy for the coach?"

"I haven't even told Miranda or Jeremy yet. That is the letter I want you to carry back for me. And of course I wouldn't dream of using the earl's coach."

"Why not? You are his mother-in-law, after all."

"Why, so I am," Nora exclaimed, momentarily distracted by the thought. "Oh, dear, I never pictured myself as anyone's mother-in-law."

Sam couldn't help but be amused by her consternation. "Well, you don't seem like one to me either. But back to my question. Do you wish to borrow my chaise instead? With whom are you traveling? Joanna? Didn't she just return from a long trip?"

"I am going alone. And thank you for your offer, but I am going by public conveyance."

"Are you mad! You can't go alone by coach! Let me drive you, then, and we will hire an abigail."

"I do not see what gives you the right to question my arrangements, Lord Acland," Nora replied coolly.

"I am your . . ."

"My what? We are not really related by marriage, you know, though you are Jeremy's godfather. It would be most inappropriate for us to travel together. And I am quite capable of traveling by myself. It is the way I came to Hampstead."

"I hoped I was your friend," Sam replied with almost superhuman control, since he was ready to throttle her. "I made my offer as one."

"I do consider you one, my lord," Nora said in a warmer tone. "And I thank you. But I have been making my own decisions for a number of years and am very used to acting independently."

"Too damned used to it, I think," replied Sam, irritated beyond endurance. "You must do everything yourself and you will not let anyone in behind that wall of self-sufficiency, will you?"

"I do not know what you mean," Nora said, rising from the table. She could feel her legs shaking from the shock of Sam's attack. "If you are a friend, then you should appreciate that quality in me, not condemn it. But perhaps you prefer women to be more like the countess, always leaning on someone."

"It would do you good to do a little leaning, Mrs. Dillon."

"I think we have both said enough, Lord Acland." Nora was horrified she had said so much. "You will, I hope, be kind enough to give my letter to Miranda." Nora walked out of the kitchen, clearly dismissing him. He followed, furious at himself for losing control, and at her. They stood in polite silence at the door, and Nora handed him the envelope.

"Nora, I don't know what came over me . . . I hold you in the greatest esteem. I am grateful for your friendship . . . indeed, I had hoped . . ."

"Yes, my lord, you had hoped what?" She was standing straight, her shoulders back, with that air of self-sufficiency.

There it is again, that wall, Sam thought despairingly. And in almost the same instant: I won't let her hide behind it again.

"I had hoped that your feelings were beginning to go beyond friendship. But I can see you are quite happy to live in your romantic memories of your saintly husband, Lieutenant Dillon. Well, I wish you well, my dear. A ghost is, after all, cold comfort in bed. Good afternoon, and may your tryst with the past keep you warm for the next few years."

Nora was speechless. She watched Sam walk down the path, mount, and ride away without a backward glance. She felt like she was seeing him for the last time and for the first. Although she had felt attracted to him, she had imagined it all one-sided. The idea that he might feel more than friendship had not occurred to her. No, to be truthful, it had, but in denying her own feelings, she had denied the possibility of his. His parting words finally penetrated, and she shut the door and began to laugh quite hysterically at his mistaken notion that she was still mourning her saintly husband. If he only knew! Her laugh turned to tears, for if he had known, his interest in her would have died. She wiped her eyes and immediately got herself busy. Finishing her packing kept her from dwelling on what Sam's feeling might mean to her.

The next morning she was up by four and prepared a light breakfast by candlelight. The cottage looked different so early in the morning. She looked around as though it were a stranger's dwelling, although it had been home for many years. She would be returning, of course, but somehow she felt she was saying good-bye to it.

She wrapped her cloak around her, and picking up her valise, stepped out onto the front porch. She locked the front door and walked down the road without a backward glance. Very quietly she approached Joanna's door, leaving the key under her mat as they had agreed the day before. And then she was truly off, free, and on her way to meet the northbound coach.

29

Sam had not gotten back to London until late the previous day. He had no engagements that evening and had originally planned to spend a few quiet hours reading, but after his scene with Nora, he found himself pacing the carpet, unable to concentrate on even the most frivolous read. He knew Miranda and Jeremy were attending the Sefton ball, and was intending to deliver Nora's note in the morning. Impulsively he decided to walk to Grosvenor Square on the off-chance Simon and Judith were home. If they were, he might just ask Simon's advice, and if not, well, at least he would have walked off some of his restlessness.

Cranston looked at him calmly, as though there were nothing untoward about his arriving at a time when most London couples would be dressing for the evening's rout, and ushered him into the library. No, his grace was not going out, and yes, he would announce his lordship's arrival.

Sam was there only a few minutes when he heard Simon's steps in the hall. The duke stopped and said, "Sam? Cranston told me you were waiting?"

"I fear I have disturbed you," Sam said, smiling to himself at the duke's rather disheveled appearance. His hair was pulled into elf-locks and his cravat was half-untied.

"Not at all. Why do you think so?"

"Well, you look a little *en déshabillé,* if I may say so."

Simon ran his hand over his head. "Oho, my daughter has been at me again. We were just putting Sophy to bed and I tend to get a bit rumpled," Simon said, sheepishly straightening his cravat, a Mathematical gone wrong.

"Perhaps this is not a good time for a visit? Are you and Judith planning to go out?"

"As a matter of fact, no. We are both rather fatigued and decided to stay home this evening."

"Then I should go. I am disturbing you both."

"No, no, Sam. I admit I am not wishing to make a late night of it, but while Judith reads to Sophy, we can have a drink."

"If you are sure?"

"Yes. Something must have brought you out, after all."

Sam sank down into a chair and groaned. "Yes. Something did."

"What can I do?"

"Well, you can listen and tell me all the kinds of fool I have been, for one thing. I think I am in love, and isn't that ridiculous for a bachelor of thirty-nine?"

"Who is it who has captured your heart after all these years?"

"Nora Dillon."

Simon raised his eyebrows inquiringly.

"You don't seem surprised," continued Sam.

"Nora is one of the most appealing women I have met in a long time. If it weren't for Judith, I might have developed a *tendre* for her myself," Simon teased.

"Well, up until today I have been trying to establish a comfortable friendship. I have been in the habit of dropping in on her once in a while, taking tea, going for a walk on the Heath. I think she likes me well enough, but I feel a certain air, one that reminds me of young debutantes who are frightened by any physical contact. Since she is not an untouched maiden, I can only surmise that she has kept that part of herself safe, out of loyalty to Dillon."

"Hmmmmm. Perhaps," said Simon as noncommittally as possible.

"You are usually very perceptive about these things, Simon. What do you think?"

"I think that while your conjecture might be true, her stand-offishness may merely be the way she has kept herself safe these many years. After all, she is alone and unprotected by family or position."

"Well, that may be true, but today when I arrived, I found her packing for a visit home."

"Home?" Simon did not have to pretend surprise. He wondered what had brought Nora to this decision.

"She has not been there for many years, and wishes to revisit the countryside of her childhood, or so she says. For myself, I think Miranda's marriage has brought back memories of her own romance and that she returns out of some reawakened feeling for this Dillon, her 'sainted husband' as I believe I called him today. I felt so jealous of this attachment that I lost control and accused her of living in her romantic memories."

Simon could hear the pain in Sam's voice, but could not help being secretly amused at his misconceptions. For whatever reason Nora was making this journey, it was certainly not to revisit happier times. Since he knew Nora's story in confidence, he was not free to set Sam's mind at rest. Indeed, he was not sure what the viscount's reaction would be. But he could, at least, make some general reassurances.

"You hardly made a formal declaration of your feelings, Sam, and I don't think today will ruin the friendship you already have," Simon said. "I don't believe she is attached to Dillon's memory. Nora's journey will give you both the time you need to forget today's contretemps."

"If she is not attached to her husband, then why do you suppose she has never remarried, Simon?"

"She has hardly been living in a situation which would expose her to many eligible suitors. And she strikes me as a rather independent woman. Maybe she never met anyone who made her want to give up her independence."

"She is too damned independent, if you ask me," replied Sam, all his frustration and anger resurfacing. "I have never met any woman who so elicits my desire to help her and who so frustrates that desire. She has been on her own for so long that she only knows how to do for herself."

"She is very different from your usual *partie*, isn't she?" said Simon, thinking of Sam's old history with Lavinia, and his latest, very feminine widow.

"Don't remind me. I have been quite content for years to enjoy the comfort of a mistress's attentions, have always been able to keep things light, and never thought to fall head over heels ever again."

"Nora Dillon is not the sort of woman a man can take lightly, I agree."

"She won't even take advantage of Jeremy's position and

borrow the coach. Or my chaise. She intends to travel all that
distance by public conveyance. You should have seen her valise.
It looks like it hasn't been used in twenty years.''

"How long does she intend to be away?''

"I don't know. She did say she will return for the holidays.
She would have to, or stay in Northumberland all winter.''

"It occurs to me this must be a difficult time for Nora.
Miranda must be very caught up in her new life. And to go
from what must have been a very quiet and cozy existence to
being the mother-in-law of an earl and the parent of a countess . . .''

"I had hoped my . . . friendship would compensate for her
loss,'' Sam replied.

"Oh, I am sure your friendship makes a difference.
Unfortunately, I have no way of knowing whether you have
a chance of getting her to accept more than friendship. You will
have to hope this visit to her old home will bring a change to
her state of mind.''

"I suppose you are right. There is nothing I can do but wait.
And I do have a letter to Miranda to deliver. Perhaps her mother
has told her more.''

Miranda was very much surprised by her mother's brief note,
which explained no more than did Nora's conversation with the
viscount.

"She has already gone?''

"Yes. She has left this note for you. I assume it explains her
reasons.''

Miranda opened the folded pages slowly. The outside was
blank, and inside Nora had written only a few lines of
explanation. She wished her daughter well for the next few
weeks and informed her that it seemed time for her, at last, to
return home and see if there was anything still there for her.
Miranda knew that there was quite possibly an unforgiving
marquess still alive in Moorview. She herself, once she had told
Jeremy of her background, had put the story behind her, as she
had assumed her mother had. Her new life was so full and
exciting, she could not imagine what effect her leaving had had
on her mother's life. Why would her mother want to visit Northumberland, which could only hold painful memories?

"She does say she will return for the holidays," Miranda said, lifting her eyes from the note. "And wishes me well. But she does not offer any explanation for this trip. It seems rather sudden to me. How is she traveling?"

"By stage," replied Sam.

"Why didn't she ask me for the coach?" Miranda exclaimed. "Can we send it around?"

"It is too late, I'm afraid. I offered my chaise, but she seemed determined to go by public conveyance."

Miranda was torn by affection and amusement at her mother, and anxiety and anger at this precipitate, unexplained behavior.

"What shall I tell Lavinia and Jeremy? There were a few dinners and other entertainments to which Mother was invited."

"Make her excuses and tell them it seemed very important to her to return home. They know, after all, that she is from the north, although she has spoken very little about family." Sam's voice rose questioningly.

"There is no family left . . . although perhaps my grandfather is alive," murmured Miranda, not wanting to sound completely ignorant, but unable to say more.

"I have often wondered if your mother perhaps married your father against her family's wishes. Would it be a breach of that sort she wishes to mend?"

"Perhaps. My mother has not spoken much to me of those early days." At least, that was true, thought Miranda.

"We shall all be curious to hear the story when she returns," Sam said as he took his leave. "I would not be too concerned," he added reassuringly. "Your mother is nothing if not capable of taking care of herself!"

30

Nora had not traveled by public conveyance, except for short trips into London, since she and Miranda had settled in Hampstead. She had forgotten how noisy and crowded the coaching inns were, and how crowded the coach itself. For the first leg of her journey she was seated between two stout country people, one woman who kept checking her basket as if to make sure that no one had stolen anything. But where would anyone go with it? wondered Nora, amused and irritated at the same time by the woman's nervous movements. The other was a young man who was either getting a cold or in the habit of sniffling.

Her journey with Miranda had been quite different. Her daughter had been such a delightful child that she had transformed her fellow travelers into almost-friends. Nora had benefited from it, one woman taking Miranda on her lap, another clucking over her sympathetically about her widow's status. Traveling alone, however, as a middle-aged single woman of no obvious class or occupation, elicited only suspicious glances.

Reading was impossible, and sleep seemed equally out of the question, but Nora realized she must have dozed off several times, not into a deep sleep, which relaxed, but into that border between dream and thought. She would awake from time to time, head jerking up as she became conscious that her jaw had fallen open or that she was beginning to drool on the hand she rested on. How embarrassing, she would think, and then doze off again.

She was glad, therefore, she had decided to spend her money for a private parlor and bedroom. The inn at York was old, but well-kept, and despite her status as a single woman alone, the landlord was friendly enough. The bed was a bit lopsided. It seemed as if all the former inhabitants had slept only on the left side of the mattress, probably for the same reasons I want to, thought Nora, to be near the window and away from the thin wall which separated her from the next bedroom, the occupants of which must be newlyweds, she decided as she tried to block out their gruntings and creakings and, at the same time, not roll out of bed from the decline in the mattress. She did sleep, albeit fitfully, and was awakened by the rooster in the courtyard.

It was cold, and the water in her basin was sealed off by a thin skin of ice, so she barely splashed herself awake. She was glad she had worn kerseymere and that her cloak was lined, for it would only get colder.

One more night in another moderately satisfying inn, and she was on the last leg of her journey. She had paid for a seat to Hexham, and for the last day, to her delight, she was able to sit near the window and watch as the countryside turned wilder with every mile. No wonder she had chosen to live by the Heath in Hampstead—it was the closest she could come to the moors of home.

When they reached Hexham, it was late in the afternoon, and Nora stepped down from the coach in a daze. She had not planned further than arrival, and realized as she looked about her that she would have to get herself a room for the night, or hire a chaise and drive directly to Moorview. And since she hadn't really decided whether she would indeed go home, and she was exhausted from the past thirty-odd hours, she picked up her valise and headed for the Lion's Head, an inn she remembered from her childhood and which she prayed was still in existence.

It was, and she stood in front of it for a moment, remembering how her father had, from time to time, taken her into Hexham so that they could have a lemonade at the table near the window and listen for the mail coach.

''Can you hear it, Meg?'' he would say, and she would listen for the rumble of wheels and the sound of the yard of tin. Out ran the innkeeper, and with no hesitation he would reach out and grab the mail pouch. It took only a minute, but the sight never failed to thrill her. Then they would return home and she would excitedly tell her mother how she had heard the coach even before Papa this time.

The inn had changed very little and she bespoke herself a room and the front parlor for her supper. Cold and tired as she was, she decided just to smooth her hair and wash her face before going down immediately to the parlor, where there would be a fire. She ordered a mulled wine, ignoring the stares of the hostess, and let the warmth of the fire and the drink reach her inside and out. She was able to remove her shawl by the time supper was served. The vegetable pie was heavy on onions and carrots, but the crust was flaky and light. She finished with an apple custard and hot tea, which woke her up enough to get herself to her bedroom, but did not completely counteract the wine's soporific effect. She fell almost immediately into a deep sleep.

She dreamed she was in the graveyard, looking for her mother's grave, sure it would be neglected and hard to find. Instead, she came upon a beautifully tended plot, planted with flowers, and with two stones.

My father must be dead, she thought, but why did they not just add his name to my mother's stone? She moved closer and saw both stones were exactly the same, the engraving reading "Honora Margaret, beloved wife," and "Honora Margaret, beloved daughter." Her father wasn't dead; she was. Long dead, and long-forgiven, or why "beloved daughter?"

She awoke in the morning, calm and knowing exactly what she would do. She would go to the door and announce herself to whomever was still there, her father, his wife, or perhaps her second cousin, who had inherited by now. She would not first visit her mother's grave, as she had originally intended. After the dream, she did not have the courage to find the grave neglected, or her own tombstone. Better to find out first whether her father, still alive, refused to see her, or, dead, had forgiven her.

The inn had only an old pony and cart for hire, since their chaise was being repaired. Luckily, although it was cold, it was clear and sunny, and she drove slowly, recognizing this tree or that granite slab, passing the path leading to the hill where she and Breen had first declared their love.

The driveway of Moorview was in good condition and the shrubbery clipped. There must be someone here, she thought, and she noticed the roses had been covered with burlap for the winter. There was some noise from the stables, but the front of the house seemed very still. Perhaps only the servants were about?

She tied the pony to the ring in the mouth of the stone lion and patted his head as she had always done as a child. Shaking out her skirts, she started for the door.

It opened before she got up the steps, so someone *had* been watching the stranger up the drive. It was Jackson, their butler, who had seemed old to her twenty years ago and whom she never thought to find here still. But at sixteen, forty-five looks old, and at thirty-six, sixty-four is not so far away, and so he looked remarkably fit to her.

"May I help you, madam?" he asked. She did not know what to say. He would hardly recognize her, yet she wanted him to, immediately. Her whole body was trembling along with her voice as she said:

"You do not remember me, Jackson? It is Meg."

The old man took a step back, as though someone had pushed him.

"Lady Margaret has been dead these eighteen years."

It was like her dream, only worse. Did it mean her father had declared her dead or believed her dead?

"Nonetheless, it is I, Jackson," and Nora smiled shakily.

The butler looked closer and lost his composure, disgracing himself as the expressionless servant as he realized this small woman looked like . . . maybe . . . nay, *was* the seventeen-year-old girl he had last seen almost twenty years ago.

"Lady Margaret? We all thought you dead. Your father only heard from you once. He wanted to bring you and your daughter home, but his letter was never answered . . ." He was unable to say any more.

Nora stood there as speechless as their old servant. He *had* cared, he had tried to find her, had, indeed, it seemed, forgiven her. But his letter had never reached her and she had been too hurt and proud to give him another chance. She had never sent any but the first letter.

"Is my father . . . still alive?" she asked hesitantly.

"Why, yes, he and Lady Evelyn live very quietly now that Lord Richard is away at Oxford."

"Lord Richard?"

"Yes, the marquess's son."

"My half-brother . . . ?" Nora said wonderingly.

"Why, yes, I suppose he is. May I announce you to Lady Evelyn first, my lady? I think that it would be too great a shock for your father to hear unprepared."

"Is he not well?"

"He has occasional spells with his heart. Nothing serious yet, the doctor says, but he must be careful."

"Thank you, Jackson. May I sit in the morning room and wait?"

"Of course."

Nora sat down on one of the Sheraton chairs, not wanting to relax on the sofa or feel too much at home. She heard the rustle of Lady Evelyn's gown and stood up as she entered the room.

"It *is* you, Meg. I could not believe Jackson at first."

"Yes, Evelyn, it is. I am so sorry to have disturbed you. I wasn't even sure myself I would come, so I didn't think of writing ahead." Lady Evelyn looked very different from what Nora had remembered. She was no longer a young bride, but a matronly-looking woman whose hair had turned gray. She did not look unhappy, thought Nora, but perhaps a bit worn. She is past forty-five, after all, and has a right to look older. And how must I look to her?

Lady Evelyn kept looking at Nora as though to reassure herself she was not conversing with a ghost or prankster.

"Why did you never answer our letter, Meg?" she asked finally. "Your father answered yours, asking you home."

"I never received it. I thought his silence meant he had not forgiven me. So I was determined not to beg again."

"He was distraught that first year after hearing from you. At first, he would reassure himself that you had just gone somewhere else. But finally, it was easier to think you dead than alive somewhere and lost to him. Where have you been? Did your child live?" Lady Evelyn asked hesitantly.

"We lived in Edinburgh at first. When Breen died, I decided to leave, and when I didn't hear from Father, Miranda and I headed for London. We settled in Hampstead and have lived there these sixteen years."

"How on earth did you support yourself, or did Breen leave you a little money?"

Nora smiled at that. "No, he was a gambler, and played almost all our money away. I waited on tables at the local tavern." Lady Evelyn winced. "I admit, it was not something I had ever imagined myself doing, but it was preferable to the poorhouse or to walking the streets. Then I discovered I had a small talent for writing, and so I have made our way by writing."

"You write novels?"

"Yes. Not great ones, but I am competent. It has brought in enough to buy a small cottage and keep us in comfort."

"And Miranda? Why did you not bring her with you?"

"That is, I suppose, the reason I came home. She has just become the Countess of Alverstone." Nora had to laugh at Lady Evelyn's expression, a mixture of surprise and pleasure.

"Did you . . . ? Oh, I shouldn't ask, but did you marry Breen after all?"

"No. And Miranda and her new husband know that. They are the only ones who do, but I felt I owed them that. And you, Evelyn, you are also a mother now?"

Her stepmother's face brightened. "Yes, and Richard has been the joy of our lives. He almost consoled your father for your loss. He is up at school now, but you must meet him; he is your half-brother, after all."

"And Miranda's uncle."

"Yes! What a lot of changes to absorb in just a few minutes' time."

"May I see my father?" Nora asked suddenly.

"Of course. I think I should prepare him first, however."

"Yes. Jackson told me that he has 'spells with his heart.' "

"Nothing terribly serious, but the doctor says he must not exert himself as much as he used to and should be protected from sudden shocks. I am quite sure the doctor would count the appearance of a long-supposed-dead daughter as one of those. Why don't you wait here. I'll talk to him. He is in the library now. I'll send for you when we are ready."

"Thank you."

Nora settled herself on the sofa, more relaxed now that the first hurdles had been jumped. Lady Evelyn had been surprised and a bit shocked, but not hostile. She could only hope her father proved as welcoming.

After a fifteen-minute wait, during which every creak of the floor made her jump, Jackson knocked and offered to escort her to the library.

"I think I remember the way, thank you." And she walked slowly down the hall, drawn to this meeting and dreading it at the same time.

She gave a light knock and heard Lady Evelyn say, "Come in."

Nora entered, and for a minute or two stood there hearing and seeing nothing, only remembering afterward that Lady Evelyn quietly excused herself and left father and daughter alone.

31

An old man was standing by the window, his back to her. He was smaller than her father, his neck and shoulders thicker and his legs thinner. His hair was almost completely white, and here and there a bit of scalp showed through. His hands were behind his back, the left one twisting the old silver signet ring on the right. She realized this old man was her father.

He turned just as she cleared her throat and said, "Father?"

He was not her father and he was. All these years she had held a picture of the handsome, virile marquess who had hardly aged. And now she was looking at a familiar stranger.

She was frozen. But when he said her name, his voice was the same and the timbre of it shook her to the core. They approached each other slowly.

"Meg," he said, grasping her hands hard, as if he were afraid she would disappear again. "I cannot believe it is you after all these years. Are you sure you are not a ghost, come back to haunt me?"

"No, Father, not a ghost. At least I know few ghosts who have grown daughters after their demise." She was desperate to make him smile, to keep them both from crying. "Come, sit down next to me on the sofa. I am sorry for coming back unannounced. I would have written, but it was a very sudden decision to come north and I wasn't even sure I would come to the house."

"Yes, Evelyn told me. All these years I thought you dead, and you thought me unforgiving, all because of an undelivered letter. I suppose I had got the address wrong or some such thing."

"Or perhaps Breen's relatives did not know who Lady Honora Margaret was. To them I was Nora Breen."

Her father winced at the name and flushed with anger. "Breen! That scoundrel."

"Hush, Father. He was someone to be pitied more than hated, and he is dead. And, Father, it was my choice to go," she added quietly.

"You always were a passionate child, Meg. Your mother and I worried about you. If your mother hadn't died, all this would not have happened."

And had you not married so soon afterward, thought Nora. But she was unable to accuse her father. And indeed, now that she was older, she had more understanding of why he had sought comfort.

"I miss her more than I could tell you, Father, but had she not died, I would not have Miranda. I do not wish to shock you, but were I offered a choice, I would choose my daughter. I never knew till now I felt that way," Nora continued after a moment's silence, "but I do."

"You speak as a true parent, my dear," replied her father. "But come, tell me how you came to settle in Hampstead, and of my granddaughter."

Nora told him at length of her life in the village, her writing, and the events of the past year.

"What is she like, this granddaughter of mine?" asked the marquess, terribly moved by Nora's story, but unable to ask her anything but surface questions.

"She makes a beautiful countess, Father. She is quite different from your hoydenish daughter, however. Very calm. Very womanly. And very happy in her marriage. Jeremy is almost as dear to me as she is."

"Evelyn tells me that you never did marry Breen." Her father looked at her almost apologetically for asking that question.

"No, I never had the chance, for he was killed soon after we arrived in Scotland. But you must accept that I gave myself to him willingly. He did not set out to deceive or ruin me. I think he even loved me."

"And the earl's family? Do they know that Miranda is . . . ?"

"Illegitimate? No, only Jeremy knows that she is the granddaughter of the Marquess of Doverdale. The dowager countess believes Miranda to be the daughter of a deceased naval lieutenant, for that was the background I created for myself.''

"It hurts me to think that all these years you might have been cared for here; that I would have seen my granddaughter grow up; that you had to struggle so hard . . . '' her father said, in a voice filled with emotion.

"It was hard at times. But I don't know but that it was better after all. Perhaps that is the sort of philosophy we hold on to after something is too late to change." Nora smiled. "But I know I learned much in those years alone. And my writing is a part of me I never would have discovered, living here as your daughter.''

"Ah, yes, your writing. Evelyn told me, and then went immediately to the bookshelf to pull out one of her favorite novels by one Mrs. Honora Dillon. I think she is as thrilled to meet a favorite authoress as she is to have you home.'' The marquess laughed.

"And you, Father? How have these years been for you?''

"Good ones, my dear, aside from the pain of losing you. Evelyn has been a wonderful wife and mother, and Richard is an heir to be proud of. I hope you don't feel displaced?" he asked anxiously. "Now I know you are alive, I will make sure you receive the settlements which would have been due you on your marriage. And you will still inherit a comfortable sum. But the estate is entailed, so it would have gone to your second cousin anyway, you know.''

"Father, please do not apologize. I did not come for my inheritance, but to see you. I am excited to find I have a half-brother. Perhaps you all will consider coming to London in the spring? I would so love to have you meet Miranda and Jeremy.''

"And how would you introduce me? As a distant relative, or as her grandfather?''

"Oh, dear, I hadn't thought that far ahead. I really don't want anyone to know Miranda's background. Well, we will have to come up with some story of an estrangement due to your dislike of the lieutenant. I think they have assumed something of the sort already.''

" 'Mrs. Dillon' ought to be able to concoct some sort of tale, though,'' her father said.

"Why, yes, indeed, she should,'' said Nora smiling.

did not know what to do or whom to turn to. My first advice,

32

After that first day, the succeeding ones were more and more comfortable both for Nora and for the marquess and his wife. Nora refused all suggestions for socializing, however.

"I know you would like to kill the fatted calf, Father, but I do not think I could take all the curious stares and questions. Let us keep this a quiet family visit, and perhaps in the summer I will come home after you have told people of my return."

Nora spent her days exploring old haunts on foot or horseback. The riding at Sam's had been a good way to regain her seat, so she was ready for some wild gallops across the moors, which made her feel seventeen again until she had been sitting for a few hours afterward. Then every additional year made itself known to her as she walked down the halls, hip stiff or knees creaking.

One afternoon, she and the marquess drove to St. Anne's. They stood by her mother's grave quietly. It was well-tended and the rosemary that the young Meg had planted years ago was now a small tree, with a gnarled and twisted trunk.

"I did love her so, Meg. You know that?" said the marquess suddenly.

"Yes, Father, I do." Now, she added silently to herself.

"I could not have lived alone. She understood that very well. I am not sure you did?"

She knew that this was the closest her father could come to asking for forgiveness.

"I understand now, Father."

The marquess's hand sought hers and they walked back in silence to the carriage, closer than they had been since Nora was sixteen.

That night she had a hard time getting to sleep. The visit to her mother's grave had brought her full circle, for the last time she had stood there it had been with Breen, as a young woman who was suffering from the loss of her mother. Now she was a grown woman who was, in a sense, suffering from the loss of her daughter. As she tossed and turned, it felt to her like something in her had never lived these past nineteen years. That in some strange way she was still standing with Breen by her mother's grave, fallen into a trance. That she had awakened from a strange sleep and found herself in a grown woman's body, with a daughter and no recollection of the intervening years. These feelings so disturbed her that she forced herself to concentrate on her breathing and finally fell asleep.

She was nineteen again, and at the bottom of a steep hill. She knew she must climb to the top by herself. All around at her feet were boxes and bags that also must get up the hill. And a baby. A small, laughing little girl: Miranda at two. The baby, the boxes, and all must go up, and there was no one else to help. She, Meg, had to do it herself. She started pulling boxes and bags together, and was finally able to fashion a haversack that fit on her back. She slung it over the shoulders, and thought she would go over backward from the weight and the incline of the hill. But when she picked up Miranda, the little girl's weight counterbalanced what was on her back, and she started to climb. Every few feet she would stop, and wanted to sit down and cry and wait for her father or mother to find her. And then she would remember: her mother was dead, her father didn't love her, and she would start up again. The little girl gurgled and laughed and stroked Meg's face, but Meg felt nothing. She could not afford to feel anything if she wanted to get to the top of the hill. And so she climbed, and stopped, wanting her parents, and shutting them out, knowing she could not go on if she remembered them. She was close to the top when she saw someone waiting, someone tall and thin, who "helloed" her and asked if she needed any help. She sat down, knowing that she could not take another step and also knowing that she could not let this stranger help her. She had to get to the top and she was not going to make it, and she woke up, torn by the unresolvable conflict.

The nightmare had been so vivid it had thrown her back into

her childhood, and she found herself crying out as she had as
a little girl, "Papa, Papa, Papa."

And miraculously he was there, as he had been for her when
she was nine or ten.

"Meg, Meg, my dear, what is it? I was unable to sleep and
heard you cry out."

"Oh, Papa. I am so tired. I can't do it all myself anymore.
But I have to, I have to get Miranda to the top."

Her father put his arms around her and pulled her head onto
his shoulder.

"Hush, hush, my dear. I know you are tired. Where do you
need to take Miranda?"

"To the top of the hill. But I have this heavy bag on my back
and I can't carry it all by myself. But Mother is dead and you
are gone and I can't just ask a stranger to help."

The marquess stroked his daughter's hair, realizing for the
first time just what these past years had been like for her on
her own.

"Yes, your mama is dead, and I am not there . . . ?"

Nora was sobbing like a child, freely and without self-
consciousness. She was still half-asleep, and the marquess hoped
she would stay that way, for, awake, he suspected she would
never have revealed so much.

"He asks me if I need help. But I have to do it myself."

"Why, Meggie?"

"I don't know, Papa. I just do. If Sam helped me, I would
just give up."

"Go to sleep now, dear. It is only a dream," whispered the
marquess.

Nora's crying stopped, and after a few shuddering sobs she
slid under the covers, pillowing her head on her hand, just
as she had done as a child. The marquess stroked her shoulder,
feeling disoriented and very old. He hoped he had done the right
thing, coming into his daughter's room. He hoped he had said
the right things. And he knew they must talk in the light of day.

Nora remembered only a little of the night before. She thought
she had had a nightmare. She thought her father had come in
to comfort her, as he had in the old days. But maybe that was
a dream too? She felt exhausted and empty, and was too

embarrassed to go to breakfast with her father and Evelyn, so she had it brought up for her, sending the maid down with her apologies. She fell asleep over her roll and chocolate, and awakened close to noon.

The weather had changed. It was colder, and an icy rain was beginning to fall. She realized that she would have to start home soon. She dressed in her old kerseymere and went downstairs to seek the warmth of the library.

Her father was there, working at his desk. She smiled hesitantly, still not sure what had transpired last night.

"Did you sleep well after your nightmare, Meg?"

Nora flushed. "Then you did come in. I thought it part of my dream. I am so embarrassed, Papa. I never lose control like that."

"But this has been an unusual week for both of us. It is understandable you would be affected by it. Come, sit down by the fire." The marquess moved from behind his desk, and sat opposite his daughter.

"I think you needed the dream. And perhaps me to comfort you. Do you remember any of it?"

"Just the feeling I had to climb and climb and everything was so heavy."

"And who is Sam?"

"Sam? How did you know his name?"

"He seemed to be someone who was wanting to help you. Who is this Sam?"

"He is Jeremy's godfather. A friend. A good friend, I thought, but . . ."

"But . . . ?"

"It seems he wants more than friendship."

"And you?"

"Me? I don't know, Father. I am quite happy with my life as it is."

"Nora."

Nora looked up, surprised.

"You *are* Nora, you know. A grown woman, no longer my little Meggie. Why would you be so determined not to let this Sam into your life?"

"You don't understand, Father."

"You are right, I don't. But I am trying to."

"I do like him. I have to admit that. But I cannot feel that way, ever again," she continued vehemently. "Look what happened when I did with Breen." Nora was staring at the fire as though her gaze were all that kept it burning.

"Nora, I am not the one who should be talking to you. Your mother would have known far better what to say. But I am the one who is here, so I will do my best. My dear, you made one mistake, many years ago. You are older now, not the same impressionable, lonely girl. And you said yourself, had you not been with Breen, you would not have your lovely daughter. I forgave you, if that is what you returned for, years ago. And I suspect I need to ask your forgiveness for leaving you so alone after Margaret's death. Can you forgive me and yourself?"

Nora, who had felt so empty, who believed she could never shed another tear, felt them pouring down her cheeks. She turned to her father and said: "Oh, Father, can you forgive me?"

•   The marquess reached out and took her hands in his.

"My dear daughter, you are so welcome here and have been in my thoughts for so long. You have done so much with your life and I am so proud of you. But you must not keep yourself from human love because you think yourself too 'loving' or believe you need my forgiveness."

"So I'm 'welcomed back to Northumberland,' " said Nora. "Sam sang that one evening, and I think it must have started me on my way home. He has a lovely voice," she said shakily.

"Ah, yes, the old ballad," said the marquess. "The parents do welcome her home, don't they? A rare happy ending for one of those old songs." He smiled. "And is your love still so 'easy won'?"

"I'm afraid at least my passionate feelings are," replied Nora, embarrassed to be talking with her father about such matters. "But I have not let my attraction for Sam grow into love. I have been too scared."

"Do you think you can love him?"

"I don't know, Father."

"Well, much as I hate to let you go, you shall have to return home and find out, won't you?"

"I suppose I will." Nora squeezed his hands, crushing the signet ring against his fingers until he winced.

"Your heart!" she said, frightened the strain of her return had brought on an attack.

"My fingers," he replied, and she let go, and they both laughed, breaking the unwonted intimacy between them.

Nora stayed only a few days more, and left Moorview one morning smiling and crying at the same time. Her father and Lady Evelyn, as well as many of the servants, stood by the door to wave her off. She had gotten the marquess to promise to visit London during the Season. Her half-brother would be able to join them, and Nora looked forward to meeting him and introducing Miranda to her newfound relatives.

She went in her father's coach; he had insisted, and she had not protested. It would make for a more comfortable and restful ride. In fact, it seemed to her that she slept much of the way home, napping in the coach, or much of the time in a daze that felt like sleep. Often, even on short journeys, she found herself using the time to plot her next book, letting the voices of her characters rise and fall like waves. But on this trip her mind was blank as she gazed out the window for hours, watching the countryside roll by, watching the rain run down the window, or looking at the innyards with little interest, despite the comings and goings of travelers, which usually stimulated her imagination.

When she finally reached Hampstead, she felt she was being pulled back into a life she hardly remembered. She sent the coachman and groom back immediately, and then crawled under the quilts of her own bed and slept the rest of the day and the night through.

She awoke to the sound of wind and rain. She was glad she had returned right away, for the rain beating at the cottage was mixed with ice. In Northumberland it would have been snow. She huddled under the quilts for a while, letting herself become accustomed to being home. Yes, it *was* home. Moorview welcomed her, but here was where she had found a life, had made her own way. She pulled on an old wool wrapper, thrust her feet into worn shearling slippers, and went downstairs, feeling more awake than she had in days.

She brewed herself a pot of tea and unwrapped the remnants of a small loaf of bread she had carried from the last inn. She had to drink the tea black, because she had no milk in the larder.

She would have to brave the weather later on and get milk and butter and vegetables. At the moment, however, she was delighted to be here in her own kitchen, warmed by the fire and the drink in her hands.

She wandered through the house later, opening the shutters and tossing out some flowers that she had left in vases, in her rush to leave. By midmorning, however, she was ready to go out, whatever the weather. She pulled on her oldest brogues and her heavy wool cloak that was almost waterproof and made her way to the village, happy to be filling her basket at the market. She also bought a ready-made loaf and buns at the baker's, since she knew she wouldn't get to any baking until tomorrow.

On the way home, she turned into Holly Bush. Joanna was sure to be in, and she wanted to tell her friend she was back and that the trip had been, after all, the right thing to do. Joanna's housekeeper pulled her in out of the rain and sent her right into the morning room, where a fire burned warmly in the grate.

"Miss Baillie's writing, but I'm sure she'd want to see you, Mrs. Dillon."

Before Nora could protest, she was gone and a few minutes later Joanna was with her, enfolding her in a warm hug.

"It is so good to have you back, Nora," she said as she let go.

"It is good to be back," and as she said it, Nora realized just how much she meant it.

"Come, sit down and tell me all. I will ring for some sherry in honor of your return."

The sherry warmed Nora and relaxed her as she told Joanna of her travels.

"You were right, Joanna," she said after she had recounted the essentials. "It was important for me to go home. I was very moved to see my father again. I understand his actions and my feelings better than I did twenty years ago. He *did* mourn my mother, although he married again, and he *did* love me, although I didn't feel it at the time."

"I knew there had to be some explanation for your not hearing from him."

"Who knows what my life would have been had I received his letter asking me to come home?" mused Nora. "I most certainly wish I'd known he wanted me. But what would I have been there but a dependent daughter? I have made my life here, and, you know, Joanna, I feel it no tragedy that my life was changed by a misdirected letter.''

"No, you've grown into a fine woman, one who found her calling as a mother and an artist."

"Hardly an artist, Joanna," protested Nora. "I am content to be a plain novelist. My work is hardly comparable to yours, after all."

"We shall see what happens with it in the future, my dear. Now, what of Miranda? Do you think she will be eager to meet her new family?"

"I think she will be thrilled with her new grandfather. Their visit in the spring should ease the way for all of us to go back for a few weeks in the summer."

"It is satisfying to have a happy ending in life," exclaimed Joanna, "particularly since I am often writing tragedies!"

"Well, this is all your doing, Joanna. Had you not encouraged me, I should never have had the courage. I feel like I have had a piece of my past returned to me. I will still miss Miranda, but feel more prepared to build a new life for myself."

"Do you see yourself alone in this new life?" Joanna queried. She was curious about Nora's feelings for the viscount. She was aware of his frequent visits, and whenever she had seen them together, had been struck by their apparent compatibility.

"Oh, I imagine so," Nora answered, blushing for some strange reason. "I am too old for romance."

"One is never too old for romance, my dear. I had rather thought the viscount was becoming a good friend."

"He is, Joanna, but nothing more," Nora replied, suddenly very busy with smoothing her dress as she got up to leave.

Well, well, we shall see, thought Joanna as she stood at the window and watched Nora go down the path. You deserve a little romance, my dear.

33

Sam had spent the weeks of Nora's absence trying not to think of their last meeting. He succeeded for the most part, for he was caught up in both estate and political responsibilities. He saw Miranda and Jeremy frequently, and from time to time inquired about Nora. But Miranda had heard nothing from her mother. On the one hand, the mails were slow, and Nora might not have written at all, thinking that she might be home before her letters would. On the other hand, Sam worried that something might have happened to her. What if she had decided to stay in Northumberland? What if she had met someone there? Sam would get caught up in his worry for her, and then find himself getting furious all over again. If she had only let me send her in my chaise, he would think.

One morning, some three weeks after Nora had left, he paid an early call on Miranda and Jeremy and found both of them getting ready to ride to Hampstead. Miranda had received a short note from her mother the day before, saying she was at home. "At last," said Miranda. "I cannot wait to see her," she told Sam as she pulled on her gloves. "You do understand if we do not stay for your visit, Sam?"

"Of course," answered the viscount. He could not admit to the great feeling of relief and anticipation he felt at the news of Nora's return.

"Do you want to come with us?" Jeremy asked.

"Oh, no. I think Miranda should see her mother first. I will be seeing Nora soon, I am sure."

Sam waited a week, but did not see Nora at Lavinia's musicale or during any morning calls he made to the young couple. On his third disappointing visit, he heard that Nora had sent a note excusing her absence. "She seems to have caught a bad cold,"

Miranda told Lavinia. "I do hope it does not turn into anything worse. I cannot get out there until tomorrow."

"Perhaps I might ride out there this morning," Sam said, trying not to sound too much like an eager twenty-year-old.

"Oh, would you, Sam? I would be so relieved."

Nora had not felt quite so ill in years. After Miranda's and Jeremy's visit and her tale of her journey home, the two young people had left. Later in the day, Nora had quite suddenly become nauseated, and after retching up all her luncheon, had taken to her bed with chills and fever. The nausea, thank goodness, did not last, but the fever and its accompanying weakness had reduced her to tears more than once. When Joanna's maid knocked at the door to deliver some homemade pear conserve, Nora was able to totter down and ask her to wait while she scribbled notes, one for Joanna, asking her to send Tilly again in the morning, and one to Miranda, explaining her absence from Lavinia's.

The next morning when she awoke, she was at last without a fever and lay there grateful for her recovery. The last week had been a kaleidoscope of sleep and fitful dreams, day and night blending into one. For the first time her head was clear, and she was at home in Hampstead, rather than wandering, crazed, from Northumberland to Edinburgh.

She fell back into her first dreamless sleep, and awakened again just before noon. She was not hungry, but she was thirsty and the pitcher next to her bed was empty. She pulled on her old wrapper and managed to get halfway down the stairs before collapsing on the landing, afraid she was going to faint, unable to go further even when she heard someone at the door.

That was where Sam found her, clinging to the banister and trying to stand, in order to get down and let him in. He had called and knocked and finally decided he'd better just walk in, in case she was in need of help or unconscious, for, he realized, they really had no idea how much worse her cold might have gotten.

There she was, pale as death, great circles under her eyes, hair a mare's nest, trying to get herself downstairs. When she saw him, she sat down and leaned her head against the railing, saying weakly: "Oh you did let yourself in. I am afraid I just couldn't make it down by myself."

Sam came up the stairs and sat down next to her. He felt her forehead and was relieved to find it cool.

"Oh, the fever is finally gone," she whispered. "And I am feeling so much better. In fact, I was coming down anyway to get some barley water, when I felt faint and decided to rest awhile. Then I heard you, but I am weak as a kitten," she said half-apologetically.

"Let me carry you back to bed, Nora."

"Oh, please, no . . ."

"Now, don't tell me you can do it yourself, woman."

Nora was too weak to respond to his remark. "No, it is only I have spent all week in bed. I need a change of scene. Could you help me to the parlor sofa, Sam?"

Sam put his arms under her knees and said gruffly, "Put your arms around my neck, Nora," and he scooped her off the stairs and deposited her on the sofa. "Have you got some sort of coverlet? It is too cold for you to be in here."

"There is an afghan on my bed. Oh, dear, it is in such disorder up there . . ." Her voice trailed off.

"No matter," said the viscount, and was back in a minute, with the old multicolored afghan she had crocheted years ago when Miranda was little. He tucked it around her, and only with the greatest effort kept himself from holding her to him.

"Let me get a fire going in here for you."

"Thank you, Sam." Nora leaned back, watching him start a lovely little fire in the hearth. She closed her eyes against the bright flames, not quite strong enough to look directly at them, and felt him sit down next to her.

"Are you all right, Nora?" he asked, and she felt his hand gently push the hair back from her face. She did not trust herself to look at him.

"Yes. May I ask you for one more thing, Sam?"

She thought he might have said "anything," but it was hard enough to get her request out. She felt she was crumbling inside as she said, "Could you get me a drink from the kitchen? Barley water for now." She grimaced.

A simple request, but it took everything out of her to ask. When he returned, however, she had pulled herself up a little and tried to comb her hair with her fingers.

He handed her the cup, and saw her hands shaking as she reached for it.

"Let me," he said quietly, and helped her guide the cup to her lips.

"I have been so thirsty," she whispered.

"Who has been taking care of you?"

"Oh, Joanna sent Tilly over a few times to see how I was."

"And you, no doubt, sent her away? How did you get water . . . ?"

"Tilly would get me some, and I was able to make it down the stairs a few times and brought up as much as I could."

"Did no one else come by?" Sam asked, appalled by how alone she had been.

"Oh, no," she replied after a few swallows of water. "With Tilly coming, I was fine."

She raised the cup to her lips by herself, and the cup shook, spilling barley water on both of them.

"Oh, I am sorry, Sam," Nora said, concerned for his breeches and trying to wipe them with the end of the afghan.

"It is nothing, Nora," he said quickly, and then saw tears pouring down her cheeks.

"I am very sorry," she sobbed. "It is just that I feel so weak. I am so sorry you found me like this."

Sam shifted so he was sitting next to her, and pulled her head onto his shoulder. He stroked her hair and she sobbed even harder.

"Nora, Nora, what is it, my dear?"

"I don't know," she answered, feeling humiliated, but unable to stop herself from crying.

Sam made soothing noises as though she were a child, and eventually the shuddering stopped. He moved a little, and Nora clutched at him convulsively. "Don't leave me alone for a while, Sam. I am sure Tilly will stop in today, but if you could stay until she got here?"

"I won't leave you alone, Nora," he replied. He wanted her to look at him, but she kept her face buried in his waistcoat.

"I won't leave you, my dear," he said, "but I do want to make sure you have enough wood for the fire. I will be right back."

Nora let him slide her head back on the sofa pillows, not willing to look him in the face after such weakness. She heard him go out for the fuel, but had fallen into another convalescent nap by the time he returned.

When Tilly arrived half an hour later, Sam sent her away. "I will stay the afternoon," he said, "but I would like you to return this evening. Mrs. Dillon should not be alone tonight, and it would not be proper for me to stay."

Tilly agreed to arrange it with Joanna, thinking that neither was it quite proper for him to be there alone during the day. But Nora was a widow, and the viscount almost a relation, after all.

Sam looked in at Nora, but she was still asleep. He slipped off his coat and rolled up his sleeves and went into the kitchen, where he boiled water and washed the few dishes in the sink.

He found a small loaf, still fairly fresh, and some butter in the pantry. Some tea and toast should be all right for now, he thought.

When Nora at last awoke, she found herself looking at a Sam with breeches spattered by barley water and dishwater, and sporting a dish-towel apron, bearing a tray of tea and bread, with a toasting fork balanced on the edge. She could not help smiling at the sight, and his own legs felt weak when he saw her smile. At least she didn't yet hate him for seeing her so helpless.

He pulled a stool near the fire, and sat there toasting bread. His cheeks were burnished by the heat by the time he offered her a slice of toast.

This time, her hands were steadier, and she managed to drink and eat by herself. "I am feeling so much better. I apologize for my weakness this morning."

"Will you stop apologizing for a natural weakness?" Sam asked with mock gruffness.

"All right." Nora smiled. "If you will forget you ever saw me like this. But you must have better things to do with your day than to tend an invalid. Where is Tilly?"

"I sent her home until tonight. She agreed to come back and stay with you."

Nora was too weak to argue or even resent Sam's high-handedness. She did not want to be alone, and he could not stay, of course. In fact, it was most improper for him to be seeing her like this, not to mention embarrassing. She pulled her wrapper tighter around her.

"Are you cold?" he asked immediately. "I could get you another blanket."

"No, no, I am fine. I was just wondering what Tilly must think." Nora blushed.

"Well, as she said, I am almost a relative." Sam smiled.

Nora smiled back, but wondered why such a simple statement of fact, which should relieve her embarrassment, made her, instead, feel lonely. Of course, Sam had been so understanding because he was concerned about Miranda's mother, not Nora Dillon. She had more than likely succeeded in killing off any tenderer feelings when she refused his help for her journey, and most certainly now, she was not a figure to inspire romantic feelings.

She drifted off again shortly after her tea, opening her eyes every half-hour or so, to see Sam sitting by the fire, reading what appeared to be one of her own books. She thought she heard noises at the door at one point, and the next time she awoke, there was Tilly smiling down at her, offering to help her up to bed.

"Where is Sam . . . the viscount?"

"He had an engagement back in town this evening, Mrs. Dillon. He asked me to stay the night."

"Yes, he told me, Tilly. And I appreciate it. I managed all right when I had the fever, so I don't know why I don't want to be alone now, but I don't, and am glad you are here."

Nora leaned on Tilly's arm and the banister and slid into fresh-smelling sheets, since Tilly had changed the bed.

"There is some fresh water next to your bed, ma'am, and a bell should you need me."

Nora smiled gratefully and slid under the covers. Despite all her rest during the day, she was asleep immediately.

34

When Miranda arrived the next morning, she found her mother sitting in the armchair by the parlor fire, drinking a cup of tea. Nora rose as she saw her daughter, and started to walk over to her before Miranda had a chance to stop her.

"Oh, Mama, you look so pale. And to think you were here all alone."

Nora was better but still weak, and after her welcoming hug said, "I truly am much better, but I do need to sit down immediately," and went back to her chair. Once she was seated, she was able to reassure her daughter that no, she did not need to be back in bed, and yes, she truly was better. No fever for over twenty-four hours. "But I imagine I don't look it," continued Nora, grimacing at the thought of her appearance. "My hair hasn't been washed in days, and I know I have black rings under my eyes."

Miranda sat down opposite her mother and nodded her agreement.

"Wait, you are supposed to protest," Nora laughed, "and tell me I don't look like an old hag."

"You don't look like an old hag, Mama." Miranda smiled. "But neither do you look well. Are you sure you don't need a doctor?"

"I am certain. Truly, I am weak, but that is natural after such a fever. But it was only that—nothing more serious. Now, enough of the invalid. How have you been this past week? It is good to see you."

"We have all been well and we missed you at the musicale. I've missed you," Miranda said, moving closer. "Your trip was so sudden, and I have been so busy. I feel I have neglected you."

"Miranda, my dear, you have not neglected me," Nora said,

pulling her daughter to her. "You are Jeremy's wife first and my daughter second. And that is as it should be."

"I'm not sure I like being a countess if it takes me away from you, Mama. There are times when I tire of boring parties and having to be polite to people I dislike. There are times when I miss our old life."

Nora smiled in sympathy as Miranda buried her face in her mother's shoulder. She had no intention of clinging to her daughter, but she had to admit she was glad Miranda felt the change in their relationship.

"There, there, you are tired and upset by both my illness and my trip. I miss your company more than you could know, but you love Jeremy, and so his countess you must be."

"I know, Mama, I know." Miranda sat up and wiped her eyes with her sleeve. Nora was amused to see the Countess of Alverstone staining her fashionable sarcenet walking dress with tears.

"Listen, I am home now, and we shall all be together for the holidays. And despite the fact that Lavinia will no doubt have great plans for entertaining, I am sure we will be able to relax as we did last summer. And in the spring, we will have family to visit with, when your grandfather comes to London for the Season."

"I am glad that you went home, Mama. But all I can think of is how different it would have been for us if you had received his letter years ago."

"Do you wish they had been different?"

Miranda thought for a moment, remembering the years with little or no money, the cheap lodgings, the times when her mother was cross from worrying about finances, the writing which finally supported them, but which took her attention away. She thought of the homes that her mother had created for them, the friends they had made in the village. And Jeremy. She would never have met Jeremy had their lives been different.

"No," she answered wonderingly. "There have been hard times, but we were together. And there have been good times, too. And there is Jeremy," she concluded simply.

Nora hugged her in relief. "That is the way I felt too, Miranda. Although I am happy to have found myself forgiven after all these years."

"It will be strange to have family. What will people say? Jeremy knows, but to everyone else I am Lieutenant Dillon's daughter."

"I think they will accept your half-truths. That my family opposed my marriage, but the estrangement has been finally and happily ended. Society will love the romance of it. And being the granddaughter of a marquess will only add to your consequence."

"You are probably right." Miranda laughed. "Now, what can I do for you?"

"I believe my appetite is returning," Nora replied, "and there is nothing in the pantry. Could you shop for me, and perhaps make me some soup? Although you are not dressed for shopping or cooking, my lady!"

Miranda grinned. "I still have my old merino wool here, Mama. Let me change, and I'll be off."

Nora sank back on the sofa, feeling like her old life had been returned to her. Only for a short time, she reminded herself, but she would enjoy her daughter while she was here.

Miranda stayed for three days, until she was sure her mother was recovered. Both Joanna and Jeremy paid short visits, but otherwise there was just the two of them. Miranda read aloud in the evenings, and got Nora to bed early. By the third morning, Nora came to the breakfast table, dressed for the first time in many days.

"I feel human again," she said as she felt a surge of appetite at the sight of fresh muffins and the smell of bacon.

"You look much better," exclaimed Miranda, "but you are still pale."

"I know; I looked in my glass this morning. But at least my legs no longer feel like blancmange. I am ready for a walk on the Heath."

"No, you're not," Miranda said firmly.

Nora was amused by the mothering tone in her daughter's voice.

"Well," she pleaded, deliberately mimicking a small child, "may I at least take a walk around the garden?" She looked over at her daughter quizzically, and they both laughed.

"Do you think you should?"

"Truly, a little fresh air will be welcome after being shut up for so long."

And so, when Jeremy arrived to reclaim his wife, he found the two women, warmly wrapped, strolling arm in arm in the yard. Miranda looked gloriously healthy, and Nora's paleness had at last given way to a becoming touch of pink.

"Sam sends his apologies for not visiting, and these," said Jeremy, and he pulled a basket of fruit and a bouquet of roses from the viscount's greenhouses out of the coach.

Nora blushed an even deeper pink as they all admired the flowers. Aside from his outburst before she left for Northumberland, Sam had never acted as anything but a friend. And his help during her illness had been nothing more than one would expect from an almost-relative. The fruit would have been a quite acceptable gift, but the flowers? Her fingers trembled as she took the bouquet of nearly full-blown roses from Jeremy and pulled out a small card: "The late-blooming roses of autumn have always been my favorite. I hope you are recovered. Marcus Samuel Vane, Viscount Acland."

After they walked back to the cottage and unpacked the fruit and admired the roses, Miranda changed from her old gown and reappeared as the fashionable lady.

"Good-bye, my dears, and thank you," Nora said, as she waved them off. "I will be fine alone tonight and I will see you soon."

As she returned to the now-empty cottage, she felt her eyes fill up. She would miss Miranda all over again, after this last visit. But I will have to get used to this, she scolded herself. And the sight of the roses on the table lifted her spirits. Had Sam meant anything more than a simple statement of preference in his note? She felt herself flush at the thought that he might have been speaking metaphorically, and the warmth of those seconds of desire caused her to raise her hand to her forehead automatically to check her temperature. Stop being ridiculous, Nora, she scolded herself, and broke the spell by fetching one of Sam's oranges from the kitchen and digging her fingernails into the peel, slowly eating it, section by section.

35

Sam deliberately kept himself away from Nora for almost two weeks. He did not follow up his gift with a visit, as she expected him to, and so she sent him a rather formal thank-you. He made his excuses to Lavinia for the small gathering she had planned because he knew that Nora would undoubtedly attend. He needed some time before seeing Nora, or he would forget that her moments of weakness had been just an illness-induced vulnerability which probably had nothing to do with her feelings for him. She had let him in, the wall of independence had crumbled, but would she regret it and rebuild it? And more to the point, could he keep himself from touching her the next time they met?

Sam could not have chosen a better way to increase Nora's interest. Ever since her visit home and her illness, some part of her, long closed off, was now coming back to life, and she found herself wondering about his feelings toward her. Had he really said he wished for more than friendship on his visit before she left for Northumberland? She had been so anxious about her journey that she could hardly trust her memory.

When Nora arrived at Lavinia's gathering and heard that Sam had excused himself, she was confirmed in her worst suspicions: he had acted only out of friendship, and was staying away so as not to lead her on. She was even more sure after dinner, when she overheard two ladies, full of *ton* news, and seemingly expert in predicting *affaires du coeur,* linking the viscount again with Lady Maria. "It does appear she will be his next *chère amie,*" said one. "I must say," replied the other, "that he has good taste in widows, though he does hold himself back from the Marriage Mart."

Nora moved away, hot with shame at her own idiocy, and then cold with despair. The viscount was clearly not attracted to her, much less in love with her. And at that moment she realized she was in love with him. How this had happened, and when her physical response had combined with her growing liking for him, she could not have said. But he was clearly not for her. He was obviously not interested in marriage, whatever his reason. He thought her still committed to her dead husband, and in any case, he would not be interested in a woman like herself. She had met this Lady Maria, and although she was mature, she was still a few years younger than Nora. And hasn't a care in the world, thought Nora resentfully, to produce one crow's foot. She walked over to join Miranda and the Duchess of Sutton, who were quietly conversing by the fire. By the time the men rejoined them, Nora felt recovered.

"I hear that you have been ill," said a voice behind her. It was Simon.

"Yes, but nothing serious, your grace."

"And your journey home? Was it all you expected it to be?"

"Would you like to take a turn about the conservatory?" Nora replied. "I would like to tell you more about it."

"So . . . did you go home?" Simon asked, as they walked.

"I did, Simon, and I am very glad. My father had thought me dead, for his letter was returned. He had forgiven me years ago."

"And you? Had you forgiven him? And yourself?"

Nora stopped and looked at him wonderingly. "It was easy to forgive my father. I understand his remarriage better, now that I am older. And I understand my young self better too. But how did yet another person realize before I did that I had been blaming myself all these years? My father and Joanna have said the same thing to me."

"It is not often that anyone can act against society's expectations without feeling some sort of guilt. And society's expectations for women are very strict. You were passionate and followed your heart. I don't know a better situation than that to create shame in a woman."

"You should be a novelist, Simon," teased Nora, "with your insight into a woman's heart."

"And have you forgiven yourself for running off with Breen?" Simon replied, refusing to be distracted by her attempts at lightness.

"Yes, I believe I have. Anyway, Miranda and I will need your help in the spring."

"Anything."

"My father and stepmother will be in town for the Season, and I need all my friends to confirm my story that I made a marriage that alienated me from my family, but that a reconciliation has finally taken place. I want no hint of scandal touching Miranda."

"There will be, no doubt, some excited gossip, but I think you can bring it off. And of course I will back you up. Have you told anyone else about your family?"

"Not yet. I suppose I will have to over the holidays."

"Lavinia will be a great help with the gossips. And, of course, Sam." Simon felt Nora's arm tremble slightly when he mentioned the viscount's name.

"Yes, you are right. I will tell them when we visit Alverstone."

"Come, we'd better get back to the others, or they will start gossiping about the Duke of Sutton and the most wicked Mrs. Dillon," teased the duke, and they rejoined Miranda and Judith for a comfortable discussion of Sophy's latest achievements.

36

Tempted as he was to visit Heathside, Sam decided that it would be safer to see Nora in public. When he received an invitation to a literary evening at Lady Hollingford's to which both Nora and Joanna had been invited, he decided to agree to Lavinia's request that he escort her. "For you know Miranda and Jeremy are staying home. You won't mind if we leave early?" she asked. "You know how bored I get at these gatherings. All these intelligent conversations about books I haven't read, and the bluestockings looking down their noses at me."

Sam laughed. "Lady Hollingford is hardly a bluestocking. She is having this little soiree to prove to her archrival, the Duchess of Devonshire, that she too can host a stimulating evening. I am quite sure that there will be other ladies there, equally bored. And Nora could hardly put anyone to sleep."

"That is true, Sam, but she will be in her element."

"Well, I will come to your rescue," Sam agreed. "Be ready at half-eight."

The next evening he found himself discarding cravats like any young man on the town for his first Season. As his valet smoothed his coat over his shoulders, the viscount surveyed himself in his glass and groaned at his image. He had never worried about his appearance before, but now, as he looked at his long, lean frame, he was dissatisfied. After all, he did not fill his coat to perfection, nor were his thighs noticeably muscular. The muscles were there, to be sure, but not outlined as on the heroes in Nora's books. Did she create her heroes for her audience or for herself? he wondered. And how had Dillon's breeches fit him?

He noticed Henryson's face in the glass and laughed at his

valet's puzzled expression. Sam rarely spent this much time dressing, and he and his valet knew that he looked as elegant as a tall, rangy type like himself could look.

"Come, we must cheer up. You have done your usual good job at turning me out."

Henryson's face brightened as he handed the viscount his hat and gloves.

"No one need wait up for me, John."

"Thank you, my lord."

By the time Sam stopped at Lavinia's and waited for her to finish dressing, he knew the evening was well under way. Indeed, they were two of the last guests to arrive, and as he surveyed the room, he saw Nora animatedly conversing with an editor from the *Gentleman's Magazine* and one of the bluestocking ladies Lavinia so feared. He made sure to settle Lavinia with the women he knew would be there, the women who attended these evenings to be fashionable, not to enjoy themselves. After working his way around the room, he finally reached Nora's corner, and was gratified to see her eyes widen in surprise and, he hoped, pleasure.

"Please go on with your conversation," he said.

It seemed, however, that they had exhausted their topic, Miss Grey was thirsty, and Mr. Woodcock quite willing to escort her in to the refreshment table.

"I hear you are quite recovered, Nora," Sam said rather stiffly. He had not intended to be alone with her.

"Yes, I have not been ill like that for many years. I suppose I never had the luxury, with Miranda to care for." She laughed. "I was most grateful for your help, Sam, and for the flowers," she said hesitantly, with her eyes on the carpet.

"Please. It was nothing," he protested, and they both stood silent for a moment, until Nora, unable, for the life of her, to be bright or witty, blurted out: "I hope you have been well. I have not seen you at Lavinia's these past weeks." Oh, why ever did I say that? she agonized. Why should I have missed him, after all?

So, my absence did pique her interest a little, Sam thought. "I have been quite well, thank you." Another silence fell and Sam watched Nora's blushes fade, leaving her a pale rose. She lifted her eyes to Sam's face, only to be put to the blush again by the intent look upon his face as he gazed down at her. They were both intensely aware of one another. He marveled at how the candlelight heightened the auburn lights in her hair, and was amazed he had never noticed the length of her eyelashes. She was idly wondering if his valet polished his boots with champagne, as she made herself focus on their shine rather than the scent of clean shirt and Caribbean lime which threatened to undo her.

They might have stood like two statues for longer had not Joanna made her way over to them and brought them back to a more expanded, if not as pleasant, awareness. Joanna had brought one of the young and promising dramatists who tended to plague her at these parties, and the four of them were soon involved in animated conversation about the latest play at Drury Lane. A few others soon joined them, and for the rest of the evening Nora was never available for any private conversation. Sam resigned himself and did his duty by Lavinia. He was determined to see Nora soon, however, and before he left, he found her at the refreshment table and bade her good-bye, adding as he turned away, "I hope to call on you in a few days, Mrs. Dillon."

37

Nora spent the next morning tormenting herself. Surely she had imagined what had seemed to be a mutual feeling of attraction. And even if the feeling was mutual, it probably meant nothing. Sam was evidently in the habit of attaching widows. He was certainly not in the habit of marrying them. And why was she even thinking of marriage? He was a confirmed bachelor with no desire for a wife at this late stage in his life. And surely she was not looking for a husband?

"Surely," she laughed to herself, "I'd better get my mind on something else!"

She attempted to write, but was suffering from a surfeit of physical energy, and decided instead to clean and rearrange the cottage. Miranda had taken most of her things with her, and her room, while it would ever be her room, might be used as an extension of Nora's "library-study." So she threw herself into two days of dusting and moving books. And sneezing. Her nose ran and her eyes watered as she dusted.

"A few days" had meant more than two to Nora, so she was surprised and almost angry when Sam arrived on the afternoon of her second day of cleaning. Drat him, she thought. He always finds me a mess: covered with dirt or dust or unkempt and ill.

As soon as they walked inside the house, she began sneezing. After three "God blesses" from the viscount, she put up her hand. "Don't bother," she said as she turned to him, her eyes streaming. "It is only the dust. Thank goodness I am just about finished."

Sam looked at her red nose and swollen eyes and was caught between amusement and concern.

"Are you sure you should be doing this so soon after your illness? Won't all this sneezing be an occasion for a relapse?"

"Truly, I feel fine," Nora protested. "And I am very pleased with my work. Come and see how much more room I have in my study."

Sam approved of the new arrangements and asked her if she had stored her books.

"Oh, no, I put in a few shelves in Miranda's old room."

"So you are getting used to her absence, then?"

"Oh, I'll never be completely used to it. But I feel more comfortable with her absence since I returned home."

"And how was your trip north? I have never really heard about it."

"You have hardly had the chance," Nora replied—rather evasively, Sam thought.

"Well, let us remedy that," Sam said. "Why don't you take a rest from your labors, and we'll go for a walk. It is an unseasonably warm day, so we should take advantage of it."

It was, indeed, a beautiful day, one of those isolated days before the full onset of winter, which teases with its memories of summer. Nora was quick to wash and change. She carried her old wool cloak, in case the sun were to play tricks with them.

She almost regretted it, for both of them were wet with perspiration after only fifteen minutes. Sam stripped off his coat, and folding it inside her cloak, constructed a makeshift knapsack, which he hung from his waist by the cloak-strings. Nora exclaimed in admiration, and asked where he had ever learned to do such a thing.

"I have been on many a long hike where one is overdressed for the first few hours and then regrets leaving cloaks behind. I've learned to make do."

"I am always in awe when I think of your travels to such remote parts of the world. I cannot conceive of hiking in mountains. I think of myself as fairly sturdy, but I am content with the small hills of the Heath, and with discovering the birds and plants here. While I have been admiring primroses, you have been discovering orchids and seeing leopards!"

"But you have raised a daughter. Now, that is foreign territory for me," Sam replied seriously. "Although I have been involved with Jeremy for the past few years, I have never carried the full responsibilities of a parent."

"Did you never wish to be married, Sam?" Nora asked quietly, surprising herself by how naturally the question came out.

"Years ago, I was passionately in love, or so I thought, with Lavinia. She chose the right man, however long it took me to realize that." Sam laughed. "I started traveling then, to get over my heartache. And I guess I mistrusted my feelings after I returned home and saw that Lavinia would never have been right for me. I did not want to marry only to produce children. And so I have done as many men: contented myself with my *chères amies*. Although I think I have been lucky to have at least found affection in my liaisons. And they have always ended by mutual agreement."

They had walked quite a distance, and Sam said, "Let us sit for a while in the sun. It will likely be our last chance until the spring." He spread out Nora's cloak and they both sat, knees clasped, facing the sun.

The walk had relaxed both of them, so they sat in comfortable silence. The sun's warmth had its way with Nora, who was tired from her work of the past two days, and Sam felt her head sink down onto his shoulder. He whispered her name, but she was clearly sound asleep, and he eased her down so her head was resting on his chest, and sat there with his arm around her.

The clouds Nora had predicted were beginning to roll in, and as she became chilled, she awoke, slowly becoming aware that her head was pillowed on Sam's chest and he was stroking her hair. She could have stayed there forever, but without thinking, stretched reflexively and turned toward him. Her mouth was open in an automatic yawn, but closed as she saw the look on his face. He traced her cheek with his finger, and then, cupping his hand under her chin, lifted her head up as he bent down to kiss her.

Nora was still half-asleep, and relaxed into his strong hands, letting herself be kissed into oblivion. Or into blessed awareness. She was disappearing into the pleasure of the kiss, and then, every cell in her body was awake and aware of him. She moaned as he explored her mouth with his tongue. The sun and his kisses had melted her. There was no wall between them, and she began to nibble at his lips and his earlobes. She had not realized how hungry she had been all these years, until this moment, when it seemed that nourishment was hers for the taking.

They slipped down on the cloak and her body acted on its own, having remembered everything she had forgotten.

Sam was kissing her neck and her ears as he reached under her dress. His fingers found her almost immediately and he smiled at how moist and warm she was. Her pleasure became his as he stroked her gently and then more forcefully, bringing her up and up and up before she came down into his arms, shuddering convulsively. He held her close and rocked her as she buried her face in his shirt.

She finally lifted her face to his and he leaned down to seal the moment with one last kiss before he pulled her up to sit beside him, his arm over her shoulders.

There was nothing to say, thought Nora, as the chill began to penetrate her dress. He must think her . . . well, what could he think of her after that? And she still had not told him anything.

"Nora," he said softly, "we should be getting back. Let me help you up."

They both spent a few minutes, backs to each other, smoothing clothes and hair, unable to look one another in the face. Sam placed the cloak over her shoulders after shaking off the dried grass and leaves. He shrugged himself into his coat, and they set off for the cottage, not having said a word.

Nora's silence worried Sam. Was she angry with him? She had certainly been willing, but he had not intended this kind of afternoon at all. He had hoped to get her talking about North-umberland, had hoped to probe her feelings for her late husband, and perhaps, just perhaps, touch on his feelings for her. Instead, he had talked of his own *affaires,* and taken advan . . . No, in truth, that would be a ridiculous statement. They had both been drawn to each other so strongly that all barriers had disappeared. But did she think, after this, that he just wanted her as another mistress? Well, he *did* most certainly want her, but he also loved her.

38

When they reached the cottage, Nora immediately hurried into the kitchen to make tea, leaving Sam alone in the parlor, where he stood at the window, wondering how he could begin. When she returned with the tray and started clattering the cups and plates, he turned to face her.

"Nora, we must talk."

"I know," she said, immediately quiet and sinking back into the armchair.

Sam walked over and sat down opposite her.

"I don't want you to think that what happened on the Heath was merely casual."

"I was hoping it was not the way you approached all your widows," Nora said, only half-humorously.

"There have not been that many, Nora." He smiled. "I have been, in my own way, rather monogamous, and my *affaires* have lasted longer than some men's my age. Do you feel ashamed of your own response? I did not mean for this to happen so soon, but it was a joy to give you pleasure."

"I don't know what I feel," Nora admitted.

"Nora, I know you have continued to love your husband, and perhaps you feel like you betrayed him. And perhaps you doubt me. But I hope I do not sound the great egoist when I say I believe there is something between us that might help you stop mourning your past."

"Oh, no, you're wrong, my lord," Nora said, choking on something between a laugh and a sob.

Sam started to protest.

"Not wrong about what is between us. Wrong about my husband. You see, I never had a husband to mourn."

"What do you mean? What about Lieutenant Dillon?"

"There was no Lieutenant Dillon."

"But Miranda's father . . . ?"

"Was one Dillon Breen. I ran off with him when I was seventeen."

"But you are a widow? I mean, he is *dead*?"

"Oh, yes, that part is true. He died in a tavern brawl before we could get married. I took what money I had saved and came south after Miranda was born. I settled here in Hampstead and supported us by working as a barmaid until I started writing. Miranda is illegitimate. And I am . . . well, whatever you wish to call me."

Nora's eyes were on Sam's face, but he found he could not look at her. His eyes fell, and he watched her fingers turning and turning what he had thought was a wedding ring worn in memory of her beloved lieutenant.

He went from shock to fury in an instant. Here he had been pitying her, thinking he had to woo her away from her dead hero, and there was no hero, only a drunken paramour. She had deceived them all. Lavinia had been right from the beginning, and "Mrs. Dillon" had got an earl for a son-in-law after all.

"How could you let Jeremy marry Miranda? Your—"

Nora's hand caught his cheek before he could get a word out.

"Don't you dare say that word. My daughter is worth ten of you. Get out of my house, you bastard. Oh, yes, I will use the word when it fits."

The slap had been enough to bring Sam back to himself, and he stood there appalled at the word that had risen to his lips. Miranda was everything he could have hoped for Jeremy. She was indeed innocent of her birth. But he could not understand Nora's deception. He saw her standing there, shaking with outrage, and knew he loved her, no matter how she had lied. He could not marry her after this, because she had destroyed his trust. But he loved her, despite it all.

"Nora, I—"

"Get out, my lord, or I will not answer for myself. And I wish you better luck in finding your next mistress."

There was nothing to say, and Sam left immediately. Nora stood there until she heard his horse's hoofbeats fade away. Only then did she cry. She hated herself for it, but she had hoped, even in those last few minutes, that Sam would not let her send him away without demanding more of an explanation, that he would at last understand, and love her enough so that the past did not matter. I am still a fool, she thought, only older this time. She left the tea where it was and went to bed, where she curled in a wretched ball and cried herself to sleep.

As Sam rode back to London, he was more and more surprised and appalled by his immediate reaction. He prided himself on being a tolerant man. He knew, after all these months, that Nora was not truly a scheming mother. And he loved Miranda as much as he did Jeremy. Why had he been so outraged? Why had that word come unbidden to his lips? The only explanation he could find was that he was hurt and angry at Nora's lack of trust in him, and more than that, her deception of Jeremy. He felt Nora had, in some way, made a fool of him. Here he had been approaching her slowly, not wanting to rush her because of her feelings for her dead husband, only to find out there was no husband at all.

What had kept her single, then? he wondered. It was admirable she had managed to support herself and her child on her own, but surely she had received at least one offer? And after her response on the Heath, he could not believe it was for lack of passion.

When he arrived home, he tore off his coat and cravat and settled into his library with a decanter of brandy. He intended to get thoroughly and mind-numbingly drunk.

He was halfway there when the Duke of Sutton was announced.

"Show him in," said the viscount.

Simon's footman led him in and settled him in a chair. He waited until Simon and Sam exchanged greetings, then was dismissed almost immediately by the viscount, who suggested he take himself down to the kitchen and have the cook fix him some tea.

Simon, who had wanted to hear about Sam's progress with Nora, smelled the brandy on his friend's breath and knew something fairly serious must have disturbed the viscount, who was not a heavy drinker. He accepted a drink, and sipped it occasionally as he listened.

"I have been made a fool of," Sam was saying. He paused and swallowed more brandy. "Or I have made a fool of myself. I am not sure."

"Nora?"

"How did you know?"

"I can't think of anyone else in your life who could get you drinking like this," Simon replied with a smile. "Did you rush your fences?"

"No. Yes. No, not in the way you mean. That is to say, she seemed very open to my approach and I intended to propose to her. But I opened by mentioning that damned husband of hers." Simon jumped as Sam hurled his empty glass into the fireplace. "How is this for a bit of humor, Simon. There never *was* a husband. Here I am hoping to woo her away from her memories, and there are none. Or so I gather."

Simon sat quietly.

"You know what this means, Simon? It means Miranda is illegitimate. The Countess of Alverstone is a bastard." There was no anger in Sam's voice now, only a great weariness.

"Does that bother you so, Sam, now that you have come to know Miranda?"

"No. You know me well enough to know it would not, after the initial shock. No, what bothers me is the deception. To let Jeremy marry without giving him a choice; I cannot forgive her for that."

"But that was the ground of her objection all along, Sam," Simon said, puzzled that the viscount did not understand. "Miranda herself was ignorant of her own history until Nora told her why she couldn't let them marry. And Miranda told Jeremy, so he could make a free choice. It was Jeremy's decision, and I can't say I blame him, to keep it all private. Didn't Nora tell you any of this?"

Sam sat very still. "I never really gave her a chance. In fact, I grossly insulted her and Miranda. She only told me she had never been married and that her lover had died. But how did you know all of this, Simon?" Sam asked, realizing Simon knew more than he did.

"Nora told me all of it months ago. When she realized Miranda and Jeremy were truly in love with one another, she did not know what to do or whom to turn to. My first advice, by the way, was for her to do nothing. Forgive me, but it seemed best for everyone concerned. Then, we both decided she needed to tell Miranda and Jeremy, and let them choose. And so all those most directly affected knew.''

"And you knew all of this when I came to you before, and said nothing?''

"It was not my secret to tell, Sam,'' Simon replied. "I knew if Nora came to love you, she would tell you herself.''

"She certainly told me, but not because she loves me.''

"I wouldn't be so sure. It sounds like you gave her no chance.''

Sam relived his scene with Nora. "You are right. And now I have lost her through my unforgivable insults.''

From the tone of his voice, the duke could almost see the expression of despair on Sam's face. He knew his friend had reached that stage of drunkenness when all optimism turns into its opposite, when the comfort of alcohol inexplicably disappears and one is left even lower than when one started drinking.

"Sam,'' said Simon, standing up, "I must get back, or Judith will be wondering where I am. I came over without leaving word. Would you ring for James?''

The viscount looked up, hurt at his friend's desertion. "You are leaving already?''

"I must. And right now''—Simon smiled—''there is nothing I could say or do to make you feel better. It will look different in the morning. Well, not immediately,'' he said, laughing, ''but after a strong cup of coffee. Then you must go back and face Nora again. Apologize. Give her a chance to forgive you and tell you her story. I know from my own experience, my friend, that even the most angry words can be forgiven if they are between two lovers. And while I don't *know* it, I suspect that Nora is well on her way to loving you.''

James arrived and led the duke out, while Sam stood at the library door. Suddenly sleepy from all his drinking, he stumbled upstairs, had his valet pull off his boots, and fell into bed half-dressed.

The next morning he awoke late, with his head pounding. He had intended to ride out to Hampstead early, but decided to wait until the afternoon, when his head, he hoped, would be clearer. To get Nora to even admit him, he knew he would have to be his most persuasive.

While Sam was nursing his hangover, Nora was furiously walking the Heath. She had awakened with far more energy than the viscount, and needed the physical activity before sitting down to write. Her heels pounded down the path, and all her energy was concentrated upon a red-hot ball of anger in her belly. Had she been asked what she was angry at, she would have been hard-put to answer. At Sam's insult, of course. But not simply that. His lack of trust in her. He should have known I would not deceive Jeremy, she thought. And how could I have let myself respond to him like that? Her cheeks, already flushed with exertion, became warmer as she remembered what had happened on the Heath. I have learned nothing, she thought. I am still too easy won. And yet, she thought, the Sam I thought I knew wasn't really such an intolerant snob. Why did he get so angry and not give me time to explain? But then, of course, I didn't give him a chance anyway.

Her walk did calm her considerably, however, and by the time she had a light luncheon of bread and cheese and apples, she was ready to work. She was truly absorbed by the time Sam arrived, and did not hear him until she finally became conscious of loud knocking on the door. Thinking it was Joanna or Tilly, she hurried out, intending to turn her visitor away, knowing either would understand when she said she was working. When Nora saw the viscount, she was so surprised, she started to tremble and her instant resolution to turn him away was shaken when she saw the hesitant, humble look on his face.

"Nora, you have every reason to wish me at blazes, but I beg you to give me a chance to apologize."

Nora could think of nothing to say, and motioned him in with her hand.

"May we go into the parlor?"

They were standing in the hall, and Nora had made no move, nor uttered a word.

She turned and led him in, gesturing him to sit as she crossed to the fireplace and added wood to the fire.

Sam watched her stir the still-glowing embers and lay two

apple logs on the fire. They caught almost immediately, and Nora straightened up and turned reluctantly to him. Still standing in front of the hearth, she said:

"You had something to say to me?"

"I wanted to tell you how sorry I was for yesterday. I don't understand my reaction yet myself, except I know I was furious you hadn't trusted me with your story. I felt made a fool. Here I have been, keeping myself from courting you because I thought you still cared for a husband you never had. At any rate, I beg your pardon. I had no right to question you, and I am as fond of Miranda as I am of Jeremy."

Nora wanted very badly to hold on to her righteous anger. It was the only protection she had against him and her feelings. But his tone was so obviously sincere, and his explanation reasonable, that she found it difficult.

"I accept your apology, my lord. I too said things I regretted. And I can understand your anger at being deceived." Her tone was softening, and Sam felt hope stirring when she continued. "But I cannot understand how you thought I could have deceived Jeremy, or believed I was lying when I said I opposed the marriage. Jeremy decided it served no purpose to tell you or Lavinia. And there is no fear the truth will ever come out. Unless you find it necessary to tell it."

"No. Jeremy was the only one I was concerned about, and if he knows, I feel no need to tell Lavinia."

"Thank you, my lord."

"I wish you would stop calling me 'my lord,' Nora. And could you not sit down? I wish to hear all your story," he added in softer tones.

Nora sat herself on the edge of the armchair furthest away from the sofa.

"I don't know what purpose that would serve," she replied. "Why would you be interested, now that you know the essentials?"

Sam leaned forward and looked intently into her eyes. "Because I love you. And now I don't have to concern myself with your feelings for some mythical hero. I want nothing between us. There was nothing between us yesterday afternoon, after all."

Nora's eyes widened, and Sam cursed to himself. Hardly the most effective wooing, to burst out with a statement like that.

"I want to know you better, Nora," he said gently.

He did. He wanted to know her in more ways than one, and Nora felt her last bit of resistance give way. He wanted to listen to her, to know the best and worst of her, and she was as vulnerable to that desire as to his touch. And so she told her story from the beginning.

As she spoke, Sam knew if he thought he had loved her before, it was nothing to what he was feeling now. He saw the young girl Nora had been, deprived of her mother and deserted by her father.

"Honora Margaret Ashton," he said softly, almost to himself. Nora looked up, startled.

"You were the daughter of a marquess?" he asked wonderingly, thinking how different her life might have been.

She nodded.

"Come, sit by me, Nora." She was drawn to him as though she were being drawn home. She sat next to him, and he leaned back, his arm around her.

"Tell me more."

And so she told him, haltingly, of her passion for Breen. Of how her love had clouded her vision.

"And after he died, you came south? Why didn't you return home?"

"I thought my father had disinherited me. I have only just found out I never received his letter."

"So your journey home was to a family you thought might still not receive you."

"Yes, but I was welcomed. Just like the young girl in the old song."

"So my version was the true one," Sam said, humming the refrain.

"Ah, but it is all true, Sam. My love *was* too easy won. And I didn't realize it, but I have hated myself for years for my naiveté."

"And now?"

"I think I have at last forgiven myself."

"I don't see any need for forgiveness, my dearest. Loving

is not a sin, and even if it were, you have more than paid for it.''

Nora pulled herself out of the circle of his arm. "Sam, I want you to look at me. I do not regret any of it. Breen, Miranda, my life here. Although I have blamed myself for loving so blindly, I could not regret it, for it brought me Miranda.''

Sam kissed her on the forehead and drew her back into his arms, this time pulling her head down on his chest and punctuating his sentence with kisses on the top of her head.

"Nora, I think we both owe thanks to Breen. There must have been some good in him, or you would not have loved him. And had you stayed in Northumberland, you would have wedded some young lord, and I would never have met you.''

Nora lifted her head at the same time that Sam was leaning down to plant another kiss. He groaned as her forehead met his nose, and the moments of quiet, almost sleepy affection were interrupted by Nora's apologies, Sam's mocking complaints, and their laughter. Nora pulled back for one moment and watched him rubbing his nose. She lovingly counted each wrinkle on is face and reached up to touch his thick, springy hair. As she did, she felt a surge of desire that surprised her, and pulled his head down to hers and kissed him hungrily.

"Nora . . .'' Sam said, as they interrupted the kiss to take a breath.

"Don't talk, Sam,'' she replied, moving her hand under his shirt and delighting in the tendrils of hair on his chest.

"Will you marry me?'' he asked.

Nora didn't stop her wandering hands for an instant. "Yes, Sam, yes,'' she whispered. This time it was her hand that found him. Without needing to utter a word, they slipped off the sofa onto the rug, and Nora unbuttoned Sam's shirt and pants and ran her finger down the line of hair from breast to belly.

When they came back to themselves sometime later, Sam had to grin at the picture they presented. Nora was clothed only in her shift, and her dress and underthings were pillowing their heads. Sam's shirt was off, but his pants hobbled him at the ankles, for they had not wanted even a moment's delay to pull off his boots. The fire had died down, and Sam could feel himself getting chilled. He shook Nora awake, and almost started kissing her again when she said, "Wait, Sam, the fire's died down. Let me add another log."

"Let me, Nora."

"No, no, I can do it," she answered automatically, starting to get up.

"Nora, let me do it for you." Sam enunciated each word, slowly and in mock anger.

She leaned her head back and said, "All right, Sam."

Sam shuffled to the hearth, his boots tangled in his pants, and leaned over to drop the log. He was hardly the picture of the romantic protector, and Nora started to giggle at the sight of his long bare legs. She tried to stifle her laughter, but it was hopeless, and as Sam turned to look at her, and down at himself, they both fell into whoops.

When they at last caught their breath, he sat down and pulled her into his lap.

"Just say thank you," he whispered.

"Thank you, Sam," Nora replied.

Epilogue

1819

Although Prinny's behavior at the christening of his niece, Alexandra Victoria, was the foremost topic of gossip during the Season of 1819, for at least one week in June no one could talk of anything but the discovery that the young Countess of Alverstone was the granddaughter of a marquess.

At first there was only a mild ripple of interest in the fact that the Marquess of Doverdale was visiting London again after many years' absence. "Not, you understand," said one intrigued dowager to another, "that the Ashtons ever left Northumberland very often. They were a family who clearly preferred to rusticate." But then, when an unobtrusive notice was discovered in the *Post,* announcing the marriage of Honora Margaret Ashton to Marcus Samuel Vane, Viscount Acland, no one was without an opinion.

It seemed that the Marquess's daughter, none other than a person of no great consequence, Nora Dillon, had been reconciled with her family. The fact that she had also managed to bring to the altar one of London's most popular but confirmed bachelors caused the ripples to swell into waves which washed through every polite drawing room.

The Duke and Duchess of Sutton did their part to calm the waters, quietly confirming that, yes, Lady Honora Margaret had made an unequal match with Lieutenant Dillon, and owing to a misunderstanding, had assumed herself cut off. And wasn't it wonderful that she had, in the past year, both reconciled with her father and found a most suitable husband.

A week later, when the Viscountess Newton was discovered in an intimate situation with a captain of the Guards, the tide of gossip turned and the newlyweds enjoyed a quiet Season, devoted for the most part to furthering the relationships between the marquess and his granddaughter, and Lady Honora and her half-brother, Richard.

Lavinia, who, between the engagement and the quiet marriage, had had time to let go of her half-serious, half-habitual expectation that someday her old suitor would renew his suit, hosted a Richmond picnic to celebrate the newlyweds. As Sam watched his new wife drinking champagne from the fine crystal Lavinia's servants had carefully packed for the outing, he could not help remembering that first picnic on the Heath, and the shared bottle of lemonade. He moved closer to Nora, who, with a fine-tuned awareness of his physical presence, without thinking drew his hand around her waist and moved next to him.

"I will be glad when we can go home, Sam," she whispered as he leaned down to kiss her neck.

And although she had naturally taken up residence on St. James Street, "home" for that night would be the cottage, which they had kept as a refuge from the city; a place where master and mistress could stretch out in front of a cozy fire on the plush new Turkey carpet, which Sam insisted his old bones needed, having taken to himself so unconventional and shameless a wife.

Don't go to bed without Romance!

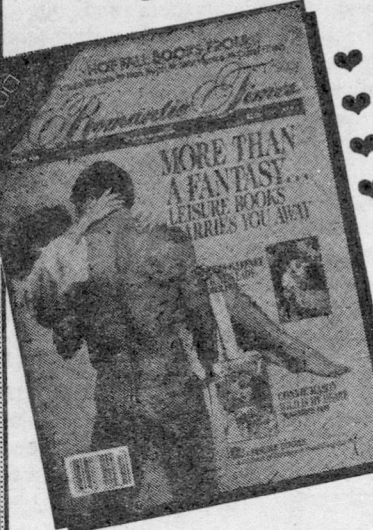

- ♥ Contemporaries
- ♥ Historicals
- ♥ Suspense
- ♥ Futuristic

- ✍ Book Reviews
- ✍ Ratings
- ✍ Forthcoming Titles
- ✍ Author Profiles

Read **Romantic Times**

your guide to the next two months' best books.
100 page bi-monthly magazine • 6 Issues $14.95

Send your order to: Romantic Times,
163 Joralemon St., Brooklyn Hts., NY 11201
I enclose $_____ in ❏ check ❏ money order

Card #_____ Exp. Date_____

Signature_____

Name_____

Address_____

City_____ State_____ Zip_____

Please allow at least 8 weeks for delivery.
Offer subject to change or withdrawal without notice.